A HERO WORTH SAVING

Liminal Books

Liminal Books is an imprint of Between the Lines Publishing. The Liminal Books name and logo are trademarks of Between the Lines Publishing.

Between the Lines Publishing
9 North River Road, Ste 248
Auburn ME 04210
btwnthelines.com

First Published: June 2023

ISBN: (Paperback) 978-1-958901-46-5

ISBN: (Ebook) 978-1-958901-47-2

Library of Congress Control Number: 2023936660

A
HERO WORTH
SAVING

K.T. Munson

For Nicky. You said make it steamy. You're welcome.

To all my family and friends who listened (a lot) and supported. Thank you.

Chapter 1

"You are going to marry the Hero of Mount Vere," her father said with a sneer. "Finally, you'll be of some use."

Odette stood quaking with fear at those words. She, the illegitimate daughter of the duke, who had been passed off as a real daughter for years, would finally be thrust into the world. Without a debut, or a chance to be courted, she would enter society already married. He'd hidden her alongside his two legitimate daughters, should the king ever demand fealty through marriage.

Today was that day.

"I heard he's a monster," Jestine said, a cackle in her voice.

"Perfect for our dear sister." Grace turned her nose up; Jestine's constant mimic.

Odette felt tears threaten at the biting words as her half-sisters baited her. She felt herself shrink, knowing the illegitimate son of a Duke who had been crowned hero and granted all the lands to the north as his fief, had killed dragons. Monstrosities that stood as tall as entire cottages had been bested by this mountain of a man.

"W-why…" her voice shook and her father slapped her.

"Spit it out, you daft girl." That same hard voice was all that greeted her from her place on the ground.

"Why me?" her voice sounded pathetic to her own ears. Her hand was clasped over her stinging cheek.

"He asked for my fairest daughter," Duke Wolverson said, disgust mingled with delight. "The one with the blonde hair. What a fool."

While her father enjoyed what he considered luck, Odette just reeled from the same question. Unlike her sisters who sported the ebony locks of the House of Wolverson, she had her mother's reddish-blonde waves. That still did not explain why the Hero of Mount Vere, one of the now richest men in all the lands, had wanted to marry her. He could have picked anyone, perhaps even royalty, but he'd picked *her*.

Perhaps it was because in his eyes she was as good or better than royalty. Although the king and his family ruled the nation, her father's family was older and richer. Her father was also the uncle of the current Empress. Power, prestige, and wealth were everything a marriage to one of the duke's daughters entailed. Their father had shrouded them in mystery, allowing them limited outages and acting like they were equal daughters in public. Even allowing them to attend tea parties, but never where men were present.

How had he learned of her? Or had he selected her at random from among her sisters?

"…it'll be too late by the time he realizes. Spurning my other daughters for you." She'd been so absorbed in her thoughts that she'd missed her father's musings. "He probably thinks he is getting revenge, but it is I who shall have the last laugh."

"When?" Odette asked, knowing full well she might be hit again.

"In three days he'll arrive from the capital and collect his wooden spoon." He roughly grabbed her arm, gripping it so tightly she was sure it would bruise, as he forced her to stand. "You shall play your part and keep your lips sealed or your mother and siblings will pay the price."

Odette cried out despite herself as she thought of her ailing mother and younger half siblings. They counted on her to survive. "May I see them once more? Before I go?"

"Nonsense. That bastard will soon collect you and shall be your only family. Forget them."

"But you will continue to provide for them?" Again, she sounded pitiful.

"So long as you keep your secret." Her father shook her, baring his teeth like a wild animal. "You are my daughter and that is all your foolish future husband need know." The sinister twinkle in his eye made her stomach turn over. "You say otherwise, and your pathetic family will be out on the street."

Odette nodded. "Yes, Sire."

He caught her chin and pinched her jaw painfully. "Now be a good girl and be the submissive wife I've trained you to be."

Chapter 2

~ Past ~

Odette sat beside her sick father's bed. A horrid cough wracked his body while she wiped the sweat from his brow. As she finished, she turned to do the same with her mother. The maid had abandoned them, leaving her alone to care for her parents. A cloth was draped across her nose and mouth like the Wisewoman had instructed, she'd done everything to keep her younger brother and sister away.

"Ettie," her mother whispered. Her face was drawn and thin. It was as though skin had been pressed around her bones where there was so little left of muscle or fat.

"Try not to speak." Odette tried not to cry, but she was barely ten.

Suddenly, a cry came from the next room. Her sister, not yet one, howled and mirrored how Odette felt inside. Standing, she was stopped by a surprisingly strong grip on her wrist.

"Ettie," her mother whispered. "I must tell you, and you must listen."

"But Melody is crying," Odette replied, torn between the urgency in her mother's tone and her sister's wails.

"There isn't time. I can feel myself fading." Tears streamed down Odette's face at these words, no longer held back in the face of her mother's naked honesty. "Your father will protect you."

Odette glanced doubtfully at her very still father whose breathing was labored and shallow. "Papa is just as sick as you."

"Go to the drawer," her mother said, her voice strained. "There, the top small one in my vanity. Find the medallion."

Confused, Odette went to the vanity and pulled out the only item in the drawer. It was wrapped carefully in an old handkerchief. Her mother waved her over as she sat back down on the stool. For some reason she felt a change, something whispering like a gentle hum.

"What is it?"

"Open it." Her mother's voice sounded so strange; it was practically lifeless.

Slowly she unwrapped it, and upon the medallion were three bears. The eyes had green gems that caught the low candlelight and seemed to stare at her. Instead of excitement, she felt a mixture of anticipation and foreboding. What would this strange necklace bring?

Her mother coughed and Odette helped her sit up, rubbing her back. Her left hand shoved the necklace into her pocket. After she'd drank the water Odette offered, her mother settled back, the same grim expression on her face, shadowed by death. The thought made Odette feel ill as Melody's wails intensified.

"Your father," she whispered. "It is your father's. The House of Wolverson. Go to him. Go!" Her finger pointed to the door. "Take the children and go."

-Present-

Odette couldn't stop shaking. Her fingers trembled as she saw the massive entourage of soldiers and courtiers arrive. She tried to see her husband-to-be through the crystal glass, but his back was turned. His clothing was black, and his armor glistened despite the cloudy day. Within the hour they would meet for the first time and tomorrow afternoon she would be wed. The idea left a nervous feeling in her stomach.

Thoughtlessly she gnawed at her thumbnail. Remembering herself when the door opened, she whirled around as the maid entered with tea. Her heart was in her throat, unsure how to face this man. The clock ticked, as the honored guest entered Wolf Castle.

The clock chimed on the hour, two for tea. It was time and yet she was alone. She sat down and then stood, paced the room before sitting again. Minutes crawled by before there was a knock on the door.

The head butler entered; his pale moustache hid his thin, disapproving lips. "Lord Jareth Chadwick of Vallerdale, Hero of Mount Vere and Protector of the Realm."

Odette stood; her nervousness intensive as she was expecting a wholly intimidating man to enter. She averted her gaze before curtsying low, showing him deep respect. She kept her eyes downcast as she spoke, "I welcome you to Wolf Castle, my lord. I am Odette Wolverson."

"You may go." His voice was commanding as he dismissed the servant, and Odette's eyes darted up in surprise.

He was a head taller than her and gave off a powerful aura, yet he wasn't as hulking as she'd expected. Furthermore, she couldn't tell if his size was truly his, or mostly just his armor. There was an intensity to him that made her stomach clench. *What if he hit her?* Fear wrapped its cold hand around her heart.

After a moment's pause, he addressed her. "Please sit."

She did as he said and immediately began pouring the tea. Her hands shook slightly as she filled both cups, mixing them in proportions as she would drink it. When it was done, she set the teacup down in front of him, looking at him through her lashes.

"Milk?" he asked, and she jumped slightly.

"Forgive me, I mixed it with warm milk as I enjoy it. I shall make another that meets your tastes." Odette chastised herself for how thoughtless she'd been. Of course, he'd want his tea a different way. "Please tell me what you'd like."

"I've never had it with warm milk," he replied, simply. She looked up at him in surprise and he added, "Finally, I get to see the green of your eyes. I had thought the rumors of all Wolverson's having green eyes a fanciful tale."

"No, my lord." She took the cup and saucer into her hands. "It is quite true."

"I can see that for myself." His eyes were sharp, almost amused as he took a sip. His eyebrows rose as he glanced into the cup.

"Does it please you, my lord?" Odette asked, hopeful that they might have something in common.

He nodded. "It is surprisingly comforting. Much more suited before bed I should think."

The mere mention of a bed made her face burn. She averted her eyes and an awkward silence fell. There was a formidable presence that emanated from the man across from her. The urge to hold something of his and feel what he left there, made her fingers itch. What emotions would she feel on the cup's handle? She was but a Mystic, the lowest of the three levels of magic users, but she could sense the emotions he'd leave.

"Did you have a pleasant journey?" As droll at it was, she'd take any topic over this infernal silence.

"Tolerable."

The same quiet settled in and Odette felt her stomach twist in knots. She watched him finish the tea and set the cup down. What exactly did he want? Finding courage she didn't know she had, as her nervousness grew into impatience, she posed a question. "The Duke told me you requested to speak with me alone upon your arrival. Was there something you wished to discuss?" Odette asked with more pluck than she felt.

Lord Chadwick was a difficult man to read. His expressions remained bland, almost cold, and his posture rigid. His gaze direct and unwavering. Even though he wasn't the barbarian she'd imagined him to be, he intimated her to the point of fear. Despite that she was dying to know the answer to all her questions as they were bubbling up inside of her like a pot of boiling water.

"Are you amiable to this marriage?" If she had not heard it herself, she would never have guessed that was his question. He had demanded her as a gift for his conquests and been given her hand in marriage as requested. What right did she have to refuse? Plus, her father would never allow otherwise.

She tried to pick her words carefully. "My father accepted the king's request."

His face darkened at her words. *Was her response to his displeasure?*

"I didn't ask what your father thought, I wanted to know if *you* accepted this marriage." She flinched at the harshness of his tone.

Odette studied his face, trying to discern why he would care. His skin was tanner than most nobles and his corded hair was cut short. His clothing was of fine fabrics, but it was simply adorned. He was handsome though his severe expression marred that impression slightly. Did he think she could ever dream of answering him seriously? It wasn't like she could say "no" and anything would change.

Cautiously, she answered. "I do." Then realizing she'd whispered it she sat up and cleared her throat before saying, "I accept."

He abruptly stood, and she struggled to catch up to his sudden movement. Before she could stand, he knelt in front of her, taking her hand and pressing it to his forehead in reverence she didn't feel she deserved. Shock mingled with confusion at the feeling of his gloves on her hands. She felt the steady use and the power behind them, but they shared no more secrets of the man before her.

"I promise myself to you, Lady Odette," Lord Chadwick said before kissing her knuckles.

Instead of objects, she wished that she could feel his emotions directly from his touch. She hadn't worn gloves due to the informal nature of their tea time, so the press of his warm lips to her skin caused a blush to slither up her neck and into her cheeks. How could one man's hand be so overpowering?

She was struck dumb by his act and just stared wide-eyed at the display. What was she to say? Then a thought struck her. "Until tomorrow."

He nodded, stood abruptly, and left. Her hand was still hovering in the air for a while after he was gone. Glancing at his abandoned teacup, she nearly knocked it off the table as she lunged for it, certain that the maid would be there any second.

She found one emotion she expected and one she did not. The worry was to be expected, but the excitement… He was excited to marry her? Or was he excited about the tea? Setting it back down, she hurried to sit back on the couch as the maid entered. Standing, she went to the window, still mulling over what that emotion could mean. Few objects kept emotions for long after a person left. She could feel complex emotions left behind, but usually just the strongest stood out.

In spite of everything, she wanted to believe this noble man may be more of a salvation than she thought.

Chapter 3

A priest from the holy temple stood before them, reciting their vows. Odette wondered if Lord Chadwick noticed the church was sparsely filled for what should have been an auspicious occasion. It was beautifully adorned and Odette knew effort had been put into making it appear as though she and her dress were of the finest quality. Her father had to keep up appearances, after all.

Mindlessly, she recited her marriage rites, listening as Lord Jareth Chadwick did the same a moment later. Their arms were bound in a cord that they would wear until they arrived at the wedding bed. She felt lightheaded at the thought of what would happen later to her. She had been told it was natural and that the pain she felt was proof of her maidenhood. That did little to comfort or prepare her.

Her lips felt numb and her tongue heavy, but she was able to finish reciting the necessary words. None of it stayed with her as Lord Chadwick walked them back down the aisle and to the banquet hall. She sat and food was served. She ate only what required one hand as the feel of his hand against her made her stomach clench and she refused to ask for his help to cut any meat. She was afraid to look at him, worried what she might find.

Her father had made it abundantly clear that her future husband had taken the dowry in full. The sum surprised her, thinking it was far too generous. She'd never expected anything would come from him, but then, there were appearances to keep up.

Heat emanated from Lord Chadwick as though fire burned within him. She felt cold by comparison, chilled to the bone. Sleep deprived and sick with worry, she ate little and drank more than she should have. Her maid had encouraged her to drink, as it might make the night easier.

Then suddenly everyone was clapping, and she was being pulled to her feet. A promenade followed them to the door of their wedding room. Every step was a labor as she was sure he had to half drag her down the hall. Suddenly, they were alone, and the world tilted. Her ears rung from the sudden silence as her husband walked them towards the fire.

Husband. That was who this man was.

Odette looked up at him, liquid courage coursing through her veins. She'd never drank so much in her life, and now she wondered why she never had. It made her feel invincible despite what was coming. He lifted their hands and began to unwind the cord.

He'd said little to nothing to her all evening, so when he spoke, "Are you cold?" she jumped.

"What?" she whispered before stuttering out "N-No."

"You're trembling." Had she imagined the gentleness of his voice?

Odette swallowed the bile rising up her throat at the realization that she wasn't invincible, her brain had just temporarily forgotten to be afraid. Apparently, her body had not. She only managed to shake her head in response.

"I know I asked you yesterday, but I could leave now and not consummate the marriage. By law, it would be annulled."

Was he going to leave? She shook her head and that made her dizzy as she whispered, "No. You can't."

"I would take the blame." Lord Chadwick's eyes shone with such assurance she almost believed him. "Say I could not perform my husbandly duties."

"Why would you do that?" The words were out of her mouth before she thought the question through. He would be the laughingstock of everyone if he did as he proposed.

She saw a sheepishness in his expression she hadn't expected. He scratched the back of his head. "I asked King Enry to grant me the right to court you. He instead demanded Duke Wolverson offer your hand in marriage. I had hoped we'd be able to court normally."

Odette was dumbfounded. Everything about him said he was telling the truth. It left her completely stupefied. She wanted to ask the question "why me?" but held back. She didn't want the answer in that moment. Instead, she thought of another way to accept this marriage peacefully.

"Since we could not," she said carefully, "can I instead ask for a promise?"

His eyebrows lifted at her words. "If I am able to fulfill it."

"Will you treat me with the respect owed to the daughter of a Duke and the wife of a Lord?" She did not want to be beaten or mistreated ever again.

She stood tall, and somewhat defiant as she spoke her demands. Regardless of his confusion, her new husband nodded. "Yes. I promise to treat you with every respect. I shall honor my vows made before God."

All of the bravado went out of her, and she slumped in relief. "Then I wish to proceed."

"You are sure? Once we begin, I will not be able to stop or take it back."

Odette didn't quite know what she was beginning but nodded. Whatever came, she could endure as she had always done. Yet when he touched her cheek, it was gentle; his fingers rough and calloused but his caress the opposite. She had expected him to set himself upon her like an animal, mounting her to brand her as his, as she had seen horses do as a child.

"Odette," Lord Jareth whispered, "look at me."

What she saw in his gaze took her breath away. She saw affection and desire. He wanted her in a way that made heat pool in her nether region. She gasped at the feeling as he pressed his mouth against hers, his tongue penetrating between her lips, and tasting her.

Taking his lead, she did the same, the alcohol rushing into her brain as she felt him pull at her clothing. Lord Jareth tasted like wine and something uniquely his. His passion fueled a new feeling within her, making her limbs float and her head light. She wrapped her arms around him as he tugged at her clothing.

Embarrassment mingled with the uncertainty of what would come next. Despite that, curiosity and the wonderful way he was making her feel kept her from pulling away. Part of her wondered if he'd change his mind later and discard her. Surely if he could convince the king to let him marry her, he could convince the king to let him have a divorce.

The feeling of his hot hand on her chest sent all thoughts away. He was pulling at her nipples and caressing her back. She turned her head and exclaimed in surprise as his teeth scraped her neck as he kissed the length of it.

"Be here with me," he whispered, before framing her face and kissing her on the mouth.

Her clothing fluttered as they fell back into the bed. Her limbs were not her own as they meddled with him. He was touching her, causing heat to spread through her like a raging fire. She was all feeling, completely out of control as he caressed her while he whispered her name. Lord Jareth was massaging her most sacred part; she could feel his ministrations as she forgot everything but the growing sensation. Panting, she moaned and felt herself reach some unknown peak before her body rocked wildly.

As she came down from whatever he had done to her, his voice cut through the chaos. "I'll be as gentle as I can."

Suddenly there was a sharp pressure and she immediately tried to guard against him. Her legs attempted to squeeze together as her hands pushed at his chest. "It hurts."

"Relax, breathe, Odette." His voice only made her stiffen more. This strange man was taking something from her.

"It hurts." She repeated.

A sob broke through as she felt herself stretch and a sharp pain laced up inside of her. It was worse than a beating because this was within her. She heard his voice in the pain, but not the words. He was kissing her, but she continued to cry as he moved deeper.

Through all other emotions she glimpsed his face in the candlelight and saw the twisting anguish on his face. "Forgive me."

When he moved again, she tried to twist away from him, feeling ill as the sharp pain became a dull ache. As exhaustion, pain, and the wine took its toll she heard him utter against her cheek. "It is done. You can rest now."

Chapter 4

-Past-

The carriage jostled down the road as Odette clung tight to her siblings. Her sister, Melody, was nestled against her while her brother, Caden, lay across her lap. She could feel the press of the medallion in her pocket as his weight pressed it into her thigh. A constant reminder that her entire life was a lie. Her father wasn't actually her father, and her siblings were only her half siblings. Yet holding them at that moment, the love she felt for them didn't feel like a lie.

It would take another day to arrive at the estate, crossing the northern boundary to enter the western one. Perhaps two, if they ran into any weather or issues. She might have taken her father's horse if it weren't for Caden and Melody. They couldn't have ridden with her, and honestly, she wasn't that proficient at horseback riding—not to ride long distances. Plus, she might get lost.

Odette should have been resting but feared falling asleep. They would be defenseless if something were to happen; it was better to stay awake, stay alert.

Notwithstanding these thoughts, she had to fight heavy eyelids and the dark carriage.

Next thing she knew, a particularly bad bump jostled her from sleep. She'd slumped back with Melody draped across her stomach. Caden had abandoned her lap at some point and was curled up against her side, sleeping soundly. The sun's light had penetrated the darkness but nothing else. It was dawn and she had slept more than she thought.

When she sighed, Melody roused. She immediately whimpered, pulled her thumb from her mouth, and began to cry. Odette lifted her up and patted her back, to let her know she was there. Melody settled down and began rooting around. Although it had been nearly a month since her mother had stopped breastfeeding due to illness, Melody had not yet adjusted.

Going into the bag, she pulled out the only pewter bottle with goat's milk. Melody greedily drew it to her mouth and began to drink as Caden sat up, rubbing his eyes.

"Ettie?" he asked before yawning. "Are we there yet?"

"Not yet."

She pulled a small apple from the bag and handed it to her brother. He smiled a toothy grin, leaned against her, and began to take small bites of the crab apple. She tried eating something as well, but her stomach was in knots. What would the future bring?

-Present-

Odette slowly opened her eyes, disoriented. Her head was pounding as she tried to orient herself. When she realized she was in a loose tunic and in a strange room, it all came flooding back. She'd been wed, then taken to bed. Instead of a sleeping husband, she found it empty beside her.

A knock came to the door. "Lady Odette, the priest is here to verify the marriage was blessed." It was one of her father's maids.

The knocking must have woken her. "One moment," she called back, scrambling out of bed to find her robe draped over the back of a chair. She practically fell at her wobbly legs and soreness between them. Her head's pounding took on a drum-like tempo as she massaged her temples. Libations were apparently not all fun—they had consequences.

"I am ready to receive you," Odette said, even though she felt the opposite.

The maid entered, followed by the clergy. The priest and two attendees entered, barely sparing her a glance before going to the bed. The older of the two monks held up a candle as the other one pulled back the bedding.

Shock laced through her at the rust-colored markings smeared on the bedding. She'd heard that maiden's bleed on their first night but expected it to be a few drops. This was more like a pool of blood. She suddenly felt lightheaded and practically collapsed into the chair.

"If you are done, I'd like to leave before exhausting Duke Wolverson's hospitality further." Her husband stood in the doorway, fully dressed and with a dark expression.

The priest declared, "This marriage is binding."

As they shuffled out, her husband nodded before saying something to the maid behind him. A young woman with dark clothing and pale skin stood in the doorway beside him.

"Odette, this is Kira. She will be your lady's maid from now on. She will help you dress and gather your things. We leave within the hour." Then he was gone, and she was left feeling hollow.

Is this how the rest of their marriage would go? He could barely look at her and spoke to her in such a formal way. With a heavy heart, she let herself be dressed. None of the clothes her father had ordered last minute mattered to her, but they were of fine quality. Her husband might find it odd if she left them behind, so it all went into traveling trunks along with the finest of the clothes she used to wear and a few personal items.

As her husband commanded, she was ready within the hour. She found him waiting by the carriage, his original entourage of knights on horseback. She held her head high as she left the place she'd lived but never called home. Gathering every shred of dignity, she approached Lord Jareth.

"Let me help you," he said, holding out a gloved hand. She took it, sensing lingering emotions of determination mingled with pain. She paused and met his gaze, watching his brows frow. "Is something wrong?"

Odette shook her head before settling into the carriage. Glancing out the window she saw her father's profile was in the study and she wished she was surprised he had not come to see her off. They would think it was to respect her new title and independence, but she knew what it really was. Her usefulness to him had run its course.

Her husband closing the door behind him brought her out of her dark thoughts. As he called for them to leave, she blinked at him in surprise. She hadn't expected him to join her in the carriage. They sat awkwardly in silence as they left the estate.

"How far is it to Vallerdale?" Although apprehensive, she'd been educated to run a household and looked forward to the challenge. She just hoped her husband didn't prove as terrible as her father. Though she suspected he wasn't, it was still too early to tell.

"We must go far north; by carriage it will take at least eight days." Jareth sounded almost annoyed.

Shifting in her seat she asked carefully, "Does it also take that long on horseback?"

He finally met her gaze, his eyes appraising her. "Do not worry about the delay. I will escort you the full distance."

She nodded and turned away, feeling like a burden. Thankfully her headache subsided, but she felt worn out. It didn't help that they rode most of the day without taking many breaks. Odette's legs were practically numb by the time they stopped that first night at an inn just inside the Western territory where her father held dominion.

Jareth stepped from the carriage first, stretched before reaching back to help her down. She hesitated, rising stiffly from her seat. Despite the wish to appear graceful, her steps were stilted as she struggled to just stay upright, her feet tingling. Her body was still recovering from her adventures the night before.

Suddenly, his hand was on her waist. He swore and she flinched. "I should have stopped more often."

That was not what she'd expected her husband to say as he steered her into the inn. The owner tried to speak with him, but another man stepped in as he whisked her into a room straight back. Although the rugs were worn and the furniture battered from overuse, the room itself was large and clean. He tossed his gloves onto a small side table, as he sat her on the bed, then knelt in front of her, and lifted her skirt.

Odette gasped and tried to push the fabrics back into place. "What are you doing?"

Jareth paused. "Your legs are sore; they need to be massaged." He pushed her skirt back up and she felt a warm hand on her leg through her stockings. She tried hard not to pull away, fighting every instinct. "They will feel better in a moment." He assured her.

True to his word, as he worked at her sore muscles, she did feel better. The pain and stiffness slowly reduced, and she was grateful to him. Upon realizing he was not angry with her, but upset that she was hurting, relief flooded through her, causing the tenseness she felt everywhere to ease.

"Thank you," she said after a few moments.

"Is it better?" he asked, finally looking at her and studying her face.

"Very much so."

His hand was still wrapped around her right foot as he smiled at her. "I am glad." When he withdrew and stood up, to her surprise she missed the warmth of his big hands. "I shall see to dinner."

With a sigh, she leaned back, staring at the ceiling before resting her eyes. Realizing dinner meant she needed to be at least halfway presentable, she fixed her skirts. Her eyes were drawn to the gloves. She touched them and this time she felt his concern mingled with the same earlier pain. Suspicious, she turned the gloves inside out before finding recent blood on the inside of the thumb.

Had he accidentally cut himself? Yet the earlier feeling of determination made her question if it was intentional. With another sigh, she stood and went before the old mirror. The image of her face was murky, her hair a mass of reddish-blonde hues.

A knock came to the door. "Mistress Chadwick?" Her newly appointed lady's maid had come.

Glancing back at the glove, she realized the quickest route to an answer was to ask him. She resigned herself to the evening and the fact that she may never know. "Come in."

Chapter 5

The knights and her husband were seated at the table when she entered. Jareth was talking with one of his knights, but they all paused to look at her. She'd had Kira prepare one of her finest dresses—a deep emerald color that complimented her hair and eyes. Her hair was drawn up in a pearl net.

"Good evening." She curtsied to her husband, trying to be every bit the noblewoman he'd expect.

He cleared his throat and stood. "Good evening, Odette." He came around the table to take her hand and then maneuvered her into the empty chair beside him. "You look lovely."

"Kind of you to notice, my lord." She wanted to make the right sort of impression. He didn't know what her past was or that she was anything other than the duke's daughter. If she was going to find a new life, she had to act the part—even if she wasn't as educated or refined as he thought. Once she was fully seated, she glanced around at the knights who were silently studying her. Giving them her most benevolent smile she added, "Please don't stop enjoying yourselves on my account." She lifted her glass to them before taking a sip of the wine. Unlike the establishment, which left much to be desired, the wine was superb.

"We'll have dinner shortly," Jareth told her before leaning forward. "Have a roll while you wait."

For a moment she was at a loss. How would she eat a roll without a servant to break it for her? She hesitated a moment and he chuckled before opening the steaming bread himself. She felt her cheeks warm as he set it on her plate.

"You shall have to bear with these rough conditions until we arrive in our northern home." Jareth's voice was pitched low. Despite the amusement in his tone, his eyes seemed sad.

"I shall adjust," Odette muttered.

He caught her left hand with his own. "Should you need anything," his tone and expression were completely serious, "you've only to ask."

She was overwhelmed by his kindness but managed to nod. Her eye caught the cut on his thumb. It was deep and narrow. Although it wasn't bleeding and there was no scab—it was a recent injury. Glancing down, she saw his left hand was resting on the chair's arm closest to her.

"My lord," she whispered, doing her best to fill her voice with concern. "You've injured your thumb." Her eyes met his, truly curious at how it came to be there. "When did this happen? It wasn't because of me, was it?"

He withdrew his hand. "I was clumsy. You needn't worry."

As he reached for his wine glass, he shifted his arm slightly so only his elbow was resting on the armrest as though to conceal the injury. Discreetly she leaned towards him, slipping her right hand across her body and under her armrest before she brushed her fingers against the polished wood of his. She felt his pain and determination again, but this time there was another emotion. Guilt.

Although not conclusive, she suspected he'd cut his thumb to add to the blood she'd seen in their wedding bed. The question was why? She folded her hands demurely in her lap as she waited for dinner. Picking off morsels of the roll to slip into her mouth, she contemplated what drove this man. It was not uncommon for brides to not bleed on their wedding nights. After her first cycle, her mother had explained it to her; that she must protect that part of her at all costs until her wedding night. Like her first blooming led to womanhood, her maidenhead's blood was proof of her purity. She knew she was pure, but why had he cut his thumb?

She started when a bowl of steaming soup was set in front of her. Odette glanced up at the older woman who barely acknowledged her as she set out the rest of the dishes before the knights. The woman refilled wine cups before leaving again.

The soup was so hot it took a while before she could consume it. Carefully she spooned the broth and let it sit in the air before sipping it. She delicately filled the spoon by moving it away from her, as proper and refined etiquette called for, but it was slow. Even when it was cool enough to consume quicker, she continued in the same fashion.

She stiffened when he whispered in her ear. "You needn't stand on formalities here." She glanced at him; he was a breath away from her nose. Their eyes met and she saw a tenderness there that was unexpected. Did he truly care for her? As she was, and not just as the duke's daughter?

Averting her gaze, she replied, "I am your wife. I must set an example that honors you."

His voice was husky. "There is nothing you could do to dishonor me. Not here." Her heart started to pound in her chest as he added, "Finish your meal, we should rest."

She nodded before turning back to her meal, eating in earnest. When they were done, he stood and offered an arm to her. "We will retire for the night. I shall see you all soon after dawn. We have much ground to cover."

"Yes, Commander," one of the younger knights replied eagerly.

"It's Lord now," one of the other men corrected him, whapping him on the shoulder. "We are no longer on expedition."

"Good night," Odette muttered as he led them away from the group.

A sudden realization and dread entered her body as they approached the room. Would he ask her to perform her wifely duties again? She was still sore from the night before. The idea of repeating that much pain—it sat heavy with her as they entered their shared room. When her lady's maid tried to join them, he sent her away.

Odette stood frozen in the middle of the room. The dress she wore required assistance to get out of. He took off his armor and set it on the ground. He wore a simple tunic underneath that made him look much slimmer than she'd first realized. She'd been too preoccupied with the coming demands of a marital chamber, to take assessment of her husband's physique. She was tall for a woman, but he towered over her. His shoulders were wide and his arms strong. She realized she'd married a warrior more than a nobleman.

When Jareth finished, he took a step towards her, and she instinctively took a step back. He paused, his eyebrows raised. She immediately realized her mistake.

"Forgive me. I am still not used to having a man in the room." She tried to cover up her fear and hesitation. Turning around, she offered her back. "Will you help me with the laces?"

He gave no reply, but a moment later, she felt him deftly unfastening the dress. When the fabric was loose enough, the bottom half opened and fell to the floor. She shrugged out of the top, reaching back for the corset's strings.

Suddenly she felt his fingers. "Let me help with this."

Unlike the dress, as these laces fell away his fingers grazed her skin. They were rough, yes, but they drifted across her skin like a butterfly wing. Even though her undergarments were loose enough, she felt his touch skim across her shoulder blades and spine. She was reminded of the night before and stiffened instinctively.

"My lord?" she asked, turning her head to the side.

"You're beautiful," he whispered, as though surprised by it himself.

No one had ever said that to her before. She was shocked to the point that she turned around more to see his face. His eye lids were heavy as he was looking where he'd been touching her. They flashed up at her sudden movement, but she saw the way he'd desired her. He blinked and took a step back.

"Please call me Jareth." He withdrew his hand and put more distance between them. "It will not do to have you referring to me formally all the time."

"Do you always break the rules?" Her hands were pressed tight against her chest to keep her corset in place and yet it wasn't out of fear.

He smirked at that. "Only when it suits me." Then his expression became serious. "We should rest. Change quickly."

Jareth abruptly left the room. She didn't know why that disappointed her so much, but it did. She knew he desired her and yet he restrained himself. Sighing, she did as he asked and quickly changed. The room was getting colder, so she tossed another log onto the dying embers. The flames rekindled as the bark caught, creating a bright orange glow.

Shivering, she returned to the bed and jumped into it. Once she was nestled in, she began to braid her long hair. Once secure, she settled back and tried to fall asleep. Perhaps it was because of the strange place or the day's excitement, but sleep was being elusive.

Glancing across the room at the candle she left lit, Odette wondered when Jareth would join her. Under the covers, her fingers folded across her stomach as she stared at the drapery above her head. Like the rest of the room, it was starting to tatter; moths had gotten to the fabric. Closing her eyes, she tried to imagine herself asleep. She wasn't sure how much time had ticked by when she heard the door open.

She kept her eyes closed and tried to keep her breathing even. Clothing rustled and then she heard him whisper, "Are you awake?"

Odette hesitated to reveal she wasn't asleep, but felt guilty about the deception, and she slowly opened her eyes. "Yes."

His hair was mussed; it made him look younger. He came around the bed and set a glass on the end table. "It's warm milk." He gestured to it almost awkwardly before trudging back around the bed.

Sitting up, she picked up the mug and drank. The heated milk was bland, rather than mixed with honey or something sweet like she preferred, but the gesture was incredibly thoughtful and warmed her even more than the drink. Should she try to sense his emotions on the mug? She focused entirely on the mug as he took off his pants and joined her in bed. Her cheeks felt warm as she decided against it.

"Thank you," Odette said. "This was very kind."

He nodded before rolling onto his side with his back to her. She diligently attempted to finish the milk so they might go to sleep. She nearly choked at how quickly she was swallowing it, but soon finished.

"Good night." Lying down she curled towards him, rather than away.

"Good night," Jareth replied before blowing out the candle and plunging them into darkness.

Chapter 6

-Past-

"I must see Duke Wolverson," Odette begged the guard who refused her entry. Her siblings were standing behind her, their eyes as wide as saucers. "Please permit me entry; we have traveled so far."

"Shove off." The guard pushed her away and she fell hard, scraping her hand. Tears filled her eyes as she bit her bottom lip.

"I must see him." She pulled the medallion from her pocket and shoved it towards him. "I was told to bring this to him."

The guard snatched it, ripping it from her fingers. She snagged the chain it was attached to as she screamed, "Give it back."

He shoved her away with her foot as her siblings began to wail behind her. She was having trouble breathing as the guard held it up to the light and declared, "Where did you steal this from, thief?"

"It was my mother's!" she cried, but her voice had lost any force as tears streamed down her cheeks; a waterfall of misery.

"Don't lie!" the guard replied, drawing the attention of another guard. "You'll have your hand cut clean off for your thieving."

"What is the meaning of this?" A woman's voice roared, stunning everyone into silence. An old woman, leaning heavily on a cane, stood by a carriage that had arrived unnoticed by Odette and the guard during their exchange.

Odette was stunned into silence because her features were so similar to her own. Her green eyes and nose were exactly like the old woman's. She'd never felt she looked like her mother except for her hair, and now she knew why.

"She's a thief," the guard said, but his early bravado was gone.

"What did she steal?" the woman asked, holding out a hand.

Odette suddenly found her voice. "I didn't steal it." Yet her voice shook as she wiped her running nose on her sleeve.

The woman took it and visibly paled. Her eyes pinned Odette to the ground before glancing at her siblings. She held out a hand abruptly. "Come here, child." Odette stood and approached her carefully. When she was within arm's reach, the woman snagged her chin and turned her face this way and that. She let out a heavy sigh before motioning towards the large house. "Come along; it seems you have a story to tell."

-Present-

Odette woke slowly to the sound of the door closing. Dim light came in through the break of the curtains, signaling it was nearly dawn. Reaching a hand out, she felt the cool, empty bed beside her and was instantly hit by a series of emotions she hadn't expected. Startled, she blinked, trying to decide if the jumble of feelings was his or if her half-asleep brain had mixed hers into it. Rubbing at her tired eyes with one hand, she glanced at the empty space. What had frustrated him so?

There was a knock on the door and a moment later Kira entered. The maid was carrying a pitcher and had a dress over her arm. Her red hair was braided over her shoulder and surprisingly long. It had been drawn back the day before and Odette had thought it short. There was a smattering of freckles across her cheeks that appeared all the more prominent with her pale complexion.

"Good morning, Mistress Chadwick."

"Good morning, Kira." Odette slipped from the bed and caught the surprised glance in her direction. Just because her family was horrible to the servants, didn't mean she needed to be. "When would my husband like to depart?"

"Within the hour." Kira's face set in a pensive frown.

"Then we don't have much time." Odette stood and lifted her arms. "We have just begun our journey and have a long way to go."

Kira seemed relieved by her words. "Yes, my lady."

It took nearly an hour to prepare and have a sampling of breakfast before she exited the room. Jareth and his knights were already packed. Her lady's maid joined the coachman as Jareth met her gaze.

He held a handout. "I am glad to see you so punctual this morning."

"I am sure after all this time away, you are in a hurry to return home." Odette took his hand before entering the carriage. Her body protested slightly when she sat down, already unhappy with that same position.

He joined her again. "I am. I have missed Vallerdale."

"I had heard the walls north of Vallerdale have stood for hundreds of years. Is that true?" She was genuinely interested in hearing about her new home.

"They have. The northern walls that protect the realm." Jareth's eyes shined and he had a pleased smile. "You will be impressed by them."

Odette simply nodded in reply. Before living with her father, the duke, she'd spent some time on the northern border. They would be passing mere miles from where she'd spent her first ten years of life, and yet she couldn't breathe a word. Even seeing the change of trees caused her to remember the flavor of the sweet peaches common in that area.

"Will the next stop have a market?" Odette asked, feeling nostalgic.

Jareth perked up. "Is there something you need?"

Odette was surprised at how eager he appeared. "I'm fond of the fruit that grows in this area. Particularly the peaches. I believe they are in season." For some reason she felt so strange making such a small request.

To her surprise, the corner of his mouth curled into a small smile. "I'm sure it can be arranged."

"Thank you."

Odette felt suddenly shy. Would it be better to remain silent or should she attempt to engage her husband in a discussion? She had so many questions, and yet as a noblewoman born for the singular purpose of marriage, all of them would be inappropriate. Then she remembered his earlier pride when discussing the northern wall, and she saw an opportunity.

"Do the northern walls run the full border?" Odette asked, although she already knew the answer.

"Yes." His answer was absentminded as he stared out the window, apparently lost in thought.

Sucking both her lips between her teeth she mustered up the courage to try again. "I'd read there is a whole team of engineers working on it year-round to maintain it."

"There is, and two mages." She wondered if he just assumed she knew that a Mage is of the middle class in terms of power. "It requires constant inspection and repair due to its age and size."

He still didn't look at her and Odette felt the sting of defeat. She'd hoped they could converse normally so she might ascertain her husband's character. So far, he was cold but kind to her. His way of handling matters brought mostly relief but also confusion. After a fair length of time, he rapped his knuckles on the side of the carriage.

She jumped at the sound as he called out, "Let's take a break."

When the carriage slowed, he practically jumped from it. Odette put a hand to her chest in surprise, feeling oddly rejected by how quickly he'd left her company. Perhaps she'd been more annoying than she'd intended to be? It put knots in her stomach.

Even though she didn't want to leave, her legs were sore. Kira was walking towards her when she exited the carriage. Glancing at the greenery,

Odette took a steadying breath and counted her blessings. It had been nearly a week since anyone had belittled or beat her. Being ignored hurt less than that.

"Would you like to take a turn about the clearing?" Kira smiled.

"That sounds nice," Odette confirmed.

The sun was cutting through the leaves as she breathed in the clean air. A sweetness from a bright-pink blossoming tree was mingled with the freshness of spring. Around its base was a carpet of petals and within a few days the tree would be hard to tell from those around it. They were common in the capital and the duke's residence, but it was typically too cold further north for them to grow. It may be the last time she saw one for a long time.

Without realizing it, she'd wandered up to it. Putting her hand on its trunk, she glanced up at the pale pink and breathed in their vanilla-almond scent. Her sister, Melody, had been fond of them. Reaching up she plucked one, bringing it closer to inhale its scent. Without its sisters, the single bloom wasn't as potent, but it was sweeter.

"Are you fond of the flowers, Mistress Chadwick?" Kira asked.

Since she couldn't share why she was fond of them, she only nodded. "They remind me of my childhood." Then she turned a keen eye on her lady's maid. "How long have you served Lord Jareth?"

"My father is the head butler for Master Chadwick." Her face lit up at those words. "I was living in the capital, finishing my schooling when he collected me to be of service to you."

She could hear the admiration in her voice. "Were you at schooling long?"

"Only while Master Chadwick was fighting the dragon." Kira seemed embarrassed.

Odette resumed their walk, wandering back towards the carriage, knowing their break was nearly over. "I'm glad to have you with me. Otherwise, I'd feel very alone."

Kira's cheeks became rosy. "Master Chadwick told me I was to serve you as though I was serving him. I promise to continue to serve you well."

"That is very kind of you, Kira." Odette touched her arm as they returned to the group.

"Are you ready to resume?" Jareth asked. Odette blinked in surprise as she spotted her husband atop a horse. Was he not going to join her? He must have sensed her confusion. "I'll be scouting up ahead to ensure we arrive before nightfall."

Odette nodded, fighting back the disappointment. "Then we should continue." She turned to her maid who was already preparing to climb up next to the coachman. "Kira, would you join me in the carriage? To read for me as we continue?"

Kira's surprise melded into excitement. "Certainly, Mistress Chadwick."

Jareth dismounted before coming up to help her into the carriage. She paused when he offered his hand. "I wanted to thank you for my lady's maid. Kira is proving to be quite adept."

When he seemed uncertain how to respond, she took his hand and entered the carriage. A moment later Kira joined her. Handing a book over, she settled back as Kira started to read. It was focused on trade distributions of fabrics and the economic impact of materials that were difficult to transport but were very effective at combatting different temperatures. She'd started it after one of her lessons a month previous and was nearly done. Hopefully it would either lull her to sleep or keep her busy enough to make time pass quickly.

Chapter 7

The carriage jostling hard to one side startled Odette awake. Her body was stiff and she had a crick in her neck. Stretching, she yawned, seeing that afternoon had progressed into early evening. It was not quite dinner time, but she was already feeling hungry. Kira was rubbing her eyes; apparently, she had also dozed off. They'd made it through the last of the previous book on fabrics and moved on to a book of poetry.

"Where are we?" Odette asked, stifling a yawn. "Are we to town yet?"

"I'll ask." Kira pushed a curtain back and said to one of the knights, "Todric, are we nearly to Hindsberg?"

"We're taking a scenic route," was the reply; the man sounded gruff at the prospect. "We will rendezvous with Lord Jareth soon."

Kira fixed the curtain. "It seems like we took another route from the main road."

Odette became nervous. Why would Jareth have them take an even longer way? Traveling by carriage had already added days to his return. It made no sense and she had to fight the urge to bite her bottom lip since she wasn't alone. Did something prevent them from taking the other route?

"Is Master Chadwick known to make impulsive decisions?"

Kira's eyes grew wide. "Oh no, my lady, he has always been very disciplined."

Odette worried her hands in her lap, trying to ease the growing tension. "I see."

"I'm sure if he had us take this route, he had a good reason." Kira tried to reassure her.

What was probably the passing of mere minutes, felt like hours. The road was rough and they were knocked around in the carriage to the point that Odette began to feel nauseous. She was relieved when one of the knights called an all stop. Holding her stomach, she gratefully took the coachman's hand when it was offered.

She took some deep breaths as one of the knights approached. "Lord Jareth is this way."

Without waiting for an answer, he began to walk towards the woods. Nervously she followed, still feeling a little queasy. It was still relatively light, but the cloud cover and the dense vegetation made it seem darker than it was. The forest ended and gave way to neatly lined trees. At the end of them was Jareth, standing very stiff as though at attention. What was going on?

"Do you need anything else, my lord?" the knight asked as Odette set her skirts down, no longer having to raise them to walk through the forest.

"You are dismissed. See to your next task," Jareth ordered, but his entire attention was on her. The knight bowed and left her alone with her husband. Jareth held out his hand. "Come with me."

She hesitated a moment before holding her hand out and walking towards him. The moment he clasped his hand around hers, he marched them through the trees. She almost fell at his breakneck pace; she barely had time to look around. Glancing up, she could see funny green fruits on the branches. Then she saw a splash of color—peaches!

Jareth stopped at the end of the row and picked something up from the ground. She tried to peer around him, jerking back when he suddenly straightened. He thrust the basket at her. "Pick as many as you want."

"What?" She was confused for a moment as she leaned away from him.

"Peaches. We have permission to pick as many peaches as you'd like. We'll eat dinner when you have picked what you want," Jareth commanded.

Odette turned around, completely shocked, and looked at the trees again, this time seeing more ripe peaches. It was early in the season but there were a few she could easily reach. She put a hand to her mouth, feeling suddenly overwhelmed with emotion. She felt tears threaten and tried to blink them back. She'd asked for peaches and he'd found her an orchard to stop at. No one had ever done anything like this for her.

"What's wrong?" Jareth sounded concerned. "Should I have a servant pick them instead?"

She shook her head and cleared her throat. "I'll do it."

With a lightness in her step she hadn't felt before, and happiness coursing through her, she ran to her first peach. It came off easily and she placed it in her basket. Like a child, she rushed from tree to tree, picking the one or two ripe peaches its lush branches held. She felt a giggle well in her chest as her cheeks hurt from how hard she was smiling, yet she couldn't stop.

Finally, she decided it was time to return when the basket became so heavy she could hardly carry it. When she turned around to find Jareth was leaning against a tree. She'd been so absorbed she hadn't even realized he'd followed her.

"I've never seen you smile like that," Jareth said, sounding pleased.

"Thank you," she said as she approached him. She didn't feel like it was enough, but felt it needed to be said again. "Thank you. This was so wonderful; I cannot describe how much so."

An emotion she didn't recognize passed over his face. Glancing down at her hands, she wished she wouldn't have worn gloves. Perhaps she could have felt something on the basket or something else he'd touched. The whisper of something against her cheek made her raise her head. His gaze was intense as his fingers brushed along her jaw. They stayed like that, frozen, as seconds stretched out to a minute. Was he going to kiss her?

Clearing his throat, he reached down to take the basket. "It looks heavy."

Startled from the hypnosis, she nodded vigorously while handing it over. "Very. Thank you."

"Mmhmm." He strode out ahead. "Are you hungry?"

At those words, her stomach gave a resounding response in favor of. "Yes, I am."

"I hope bread, cheese, and salted meats are enough."

"I am sure it will be."

Jareth led them out of the maze and back to the basket of food. He dumped all her peaches into a sack before tying it to the saddle. While he was busy with that, she knelt down to begin laying out their meal. Not only did she find what he described, but two jelly jars and some sort of peach dessert.

"Where did you get this all?" Odette asked as he joined her.

"The landowner's wife," Jareth replied, sitting beside her. "Though it would be more accurate to call her a widow."

He'd sat surprisingly close, and she was suddenly very aware of his presence. "It seems she packed a banquet."

Jareth nodded but wasn't looking at her. Instead, he was staring out over the orchard. "She was very kind when I asked to make use of her property."

Odette began to slather the peach jelly and raspberry jam onto the cheeses and bread, arranging the food so that each could be enjoyed. She found a small jar of olives in the bottom of the basket, along with a small serving spoon and added them to what she had already laid out. Although she tried to eat slowly, everything tasted so wonderful that she found herself sampling everything in every combination—even putting preserves on the sausages.

"She's an angel," Odette whispered when she'd eaten her fill. The dessert had been some sort of peach bread.

Jareth chuckled. "I'm sure she'll appreciate hearing that."

"I'll be able to meet her?" Odette asked, surprised.

"Yes. She has offered her home to us. I saw no reason to decline." Then he seemed to contemplate his words. "Unless you would prefer to stay at an inn."

"Not if I can have more of her cooking," Odette replied and then stiffened when she realized what she'd said.

To her delight, he laughed aloud, a genuine smile breaking his lips. "Agreed." Jareth stood, knocking the grass off his pants and coat. He reached down for her. "Ready to depart?"

Tongue-tied, Odette only managed to nod. His hand was warm and calloused; she was thankful she'd taken off her gloves when they were eating. He may confuse her at times, but this single act of kindness had completely altered her view of him. She stared into his eyes as she stood by him. He reached up and pushed some errant strands from her face.

"Are you cold?"

She shook her head slowly.

"Good." He let her hand go and gathered up their mostly empty food basket, before securing it to his horse. She was holding her gloves and she contemplated not wearing them. Resigning herself to proper etiquette, she slowly put them on as she walked towards him.

Before she could react, he turned around and took her by the waist. "Up we go." She was suddenly sidesaddle as he mounted up behind her. Due to the narrow saddle, she was pressed up against him. Gratitude at the heat coming of him mingled with embarrassment at their closeness. It was early spring and the day was warm, but night could drop considerably lower in temperature. She imagined it was worse further north. His closeness was doing odd things to her sense of reason, so she tried, with partial success, to focus on the weather as they wordlessly journeyed to the widow's house.

It was a simple two-story house. To the left and right of the main building were other structures. The whole layout looked like a horseshoe. As they approached, a servant came out to take the horse to the stables.

An older woman came to the main door, a lantern held high. Her neck was stretched out as she lifted the light up; already night had taken hold and cast darkness across this strange land. Yet most of Odette's unease was forgotten at the bright smile on the woman's face.

"Welcome!" she called, waving eagerly. "My lord, my lady, I'd thought you'd changed your minds."

"My wife spent quite some time picking the peaches." Jareth dismounted before helping Odette down as well.

When she was still in the circle of his arms, she put her hands on his chest. Still moved by his earlier action, she went onto her tiptoes and kissed his cheek. His eyebrows were raised when she settled back on her heels.

"Thank you again. I had a wonderful time," Odette told him before turning to their hostess who was holding the door open. "I am so pleased to meet the artist behind our lunch today."

"Artist," the old woman chuckled before calling over her shoulder, "Did you hear that Tildy? She said I'm an artist!"

Chuckling behind her hand, she passed through the door and into the house. Candles lit the worn but loved interior. It reminded her of her childhood home before it had been eroded with time.

"We prepared the west wing for you, my lady." She pointed to her left.

"Please, call me Odette. After all the trouble you went through to make us such a wonderful meal, it is the least I can do." She tried not to hug the delightful woman on the spot. "How should I address you?"

"My, you are such a fine lady. Let me get a look at you." She lifted the lantern as she took in Odette's face. She was thankful for the darker room as she blushed. "Pretty too. I knew you had to be to charm such an austere man." She cleared her throat as Jareth joined them. "You can call me Nonnie, everyone does."

"Thank you for opening your home to us, Nonnie." Odette followed her up the stairs, Jareth like her shadow.

"Happy to. We don't get many visitors of your caliber." Her way of brutal honesty was very comforting to Odette who tried not to giggle at their hostess's every comment. "I have missed all the fuss."

"Happy to oblige."

Nonnie cackled at that. "I like you, Odette. You remind me of a younger me. Ah! Here we are. Your room."

The fire was lit in the room and the sudden rush of comfortable warmth caused a yawn to slip through Odette's lips, which she tried to hide, unsuccessfully, behind the back of her hand. Jareth bid Nonnie goodnight and she rushed away, muttering about checking something before bed. When the door was closed, Odette suddenly realized she didn't have any of her clothes or necessities.

She nearly sank to her knees when she saw a pitcher, water, and clean washcloths. Shrugging out of her cloak, she set it on the chair, and removed her gloves, before pouring the water into the bowl. The water was bordering on cold, but she didn't care. Wiping off the grime of the day was divine. She groaned as it slid down her neck.

She heard rustling behind her and tried to not be overly conscious about the man in the room with her as she began to slowly undress. Unlike the night before, she'd had Kira secure her corset on the bottom so the strings could be undone herself. Once it was loose enough to take off over her head, she pulled herself free. The pinned skirt came next. She had only one layer of petticoat and it soon went the way of the first layer. She was in her shift at that point, which would be enough for her to sleep in. She just needed to take off her stockings and shoes.

"Would you like your nightgown?"

She froze at Jareth's voice, then turned slowly. "You brought one?"

Jareth nodded, holding out the lacy fabric. She didn't recognize it and assumed it was one of the ones her father had bought last minute. She crossed the room and took it from him. He kept her at arm's length and kept his gaze averted.

"That was very—" Her hand slid down to feel where he'd just touched the fabric. She was nearly knocked to the ground by the longing felt there "—thoughtful."

His head came around and the intensity in his gaze frightened her. Yet regardless of the initial fear, she also felt excited. Something warmed between her legs as she tried to remember what she should do next. Her arm went to her side as she was transfixed by his gaze. With a sigh, he turned around, as though he was going to leave her.

She reached for him, but then stopped short. "You're leaving?"

"I need to…take a walk." He glanced back.

"I don't want to be alone," Odette whispered.

His brow furrowed for a moment before his face became unreadable again. "I don't want to hurt you, again."

She slid her gaze to the floor. If her husband did not wish to touch her, who was she to refute him? Yet she wanted to. To her utter shock she realized she wanted her husband—wanted to feel close to him. The door closed as he exited, and she felt her knees give out. Sitting on the floor, Odette discovered she was starting to like her husband.

Chapter 8

-Past-

"This came from your mother?" The duke's mother asked, holding up the pendant.

Odette's two younger siblings were crowded against her as she faced this frightful woman who had invited them inside. The woman oozed elegance and refinement, causing Odette to feel painfully unkept and grimy by comparison. Yet she saw what she could be—the elder lady's features so like her own it was unnerving.

"Yes," Odette answered.

"Where is she now?" the older woman asked.

"She was sick last I saw her," Odette answered honestly as her brother started to cry next to her. Tears welled in her own eyes as she fought to remain strong.

The duke's mother rocketed into a standing position before screeching. "Lynn! Lynn, come quickly!" She marched towards the door and through it.

Melody erupted into tears at the sudden outburst, and a moment later Caden joined her. Odette tried to comfort them as they were suddenly left alone. It wasn't long before the older woman returned with a maid wearing a cloth across her face.

"Please don't hurt us," Odette begged, tears streaming down her cheeks.

"Silence," The duke's mother commanded, and all three were startled into compliance.

Lynn waved them forward. "Come along children, we're not going to hurt you, just rub you until every trace of the plague is off ye skin."

Sniffling, Odette carried Melody in her arms as Caden held onto her skirt. They were led through the house to the back, where there was a large tub outside that servants were pouring water into. Wide eyes and nervous stares put Odette on edge. Were they really that dirty?

"In ya go." Lynn pointed, before ducking back into the house.

Odette hesitated as she looked around for a place to change. When she didn't find one, she just kept standing there as Melody whimpered in her arms. Where exactly was she supposed to change?

"What are ye doing?" Lynn demanded, as she came back outside with a bar of soup in one hand and a bucket full of towels in the other.

Odette felt uncomfortably shy. "Where do I change?" The words a mere whisper.

"Right where ya stand, child." Lynn shook her head. "Hop to it."

Mortified, she set Melody down on the ground. Slowly she undressed her siblings. Melody had soiled her nappies and Lynn scowled at the offending odor. Odette peeled her clothing off, setting them in a nice pile before helping Caden in. He grumbled as a servant brought in a kettle and turned it over the tub. In spite of the small size, there was enough room in the lukewarm water for the three of them.

The moment Odette was seated, Lynn got to work. All three of them were scrubbed from head to toe until their skin was raw. Her hair was dripping as she stepped out of the chilled water. The evening air assaulted her as Lynn bundled all three of them up. Unsure of her fate, Odette followed her into the house with her siblings trailing behind her.

-Present-

Odette was content, like she was being embraced in the warmest of hugs. Snuggling in closer, she dreamed of Melody when she was young, and she used to sneak into Odette's bed. She caught a whiff of something muskier. Despite the allure of sleep, she blinked her eyes open. Freezing like a rabbit caught in a fox den, Odette stared into the face of her husband.

He appeared younger when he was asleep. The serious, almost solemn expression that constantly occupied his face made him appear much older than she suspected he was. Sometimes she even wondered if she might be the older one of the pair, even though his eyes seemed to have a lifetime of memories that Odette couldn't even imagine. Could she help bring some comfort and joy to this earnest knight? Might he one day care for her as her mother had cared for her husband?

That thought brought her back to reality—would she ever see her siblings again? Fighting back the rising emotions in her chest, Odette began to roll away. Before she could, a vice-like arm coiled around her waist, holding her in place. She let out a startled sound which was followed by Jareth's chuckle.

"Didn't mean to startle you." His voice was deeper in the morning, and it made her skin tingle. When she met his gaze, it was full of amusement. Despite herself, she smiled back at him.

"Did you sleep well?" The predictable words slipped out before she had a chance to actually think it through.

"Mmhmm," was his only response.

His hold on her hadn't let up. This time she chose her words carefully. "When must we rejoin everybody?"

To her surprise, he pulled her closer and she had to shift against his chest. He kissed the top of her head, like someone would a child. Except the closeness of him made her feel like anything but. The top few buttons of his shirt were open, and his masculine scent was doing strange things to her sensibilities.

"They will not leave without us," he said against the top of her head. "You can rest as long as you desire."

Odette found that was not all she desired. "I'm hungry, more than tired."

"Shall we go down for breakfast or shall we have it in our room?"

Her cheeks burned as she muttered her response. "I would like to spend more time with you."

"Hmm?" he asked.

Odette cleared her throat. "In our room." How could three words feel so intimate?

She felt his lips on the top of her head as he spoke. "As you wish."

Untangling himself from the sheets, he stood. She averted her gaze as he pulled on a pair of pants and snuggled deeper into the warmth of the spot he'd left. The door closed a moment later and she scurried out of the bed, quickly relieving herself in the chamber pot. Next, she hurried to fix her wild hair and drive the sleep from her face by pinching her cheeks to give them some color. Opening the curtains, she squinted at the daylight; dawn had broken and it was creeping into early morning.

Notwithstanding what Jareth said, she felt like they'd squandered most of the day. The estate, in the morning, was lovely, with a country ambiance. It was rustic and aged to be sure yet had this feeling of being cared for. The lawn was cut, and the hedges trimmed. The walkways were clear, and she watched a pair of servants chatting happily as they carried in the wash.

When the door closed behind her, she turned back. Jareth paused when he entered and something about the way he was looking at her made her chest tight. He looked like a dark knight with his black hair and cold eyes, yet the heat she felt from those eyes caused butterflies to form in her belly.

He continued to stare, and she touched her hair on instinct. "Is something wrong?"

"No," he replied. "Everything is fine."

She nodded. "Nonnie isn't too inconvenienced by our request?"

"Not at all." He closed the door and chuckled slightly. "She seemed quite thrilled at the opportunity to be called an artist again."

Odette laughed freely, feeling the tight coil in her stomach loosen at the thought of Nonnie's reaction the night before. Regardless of their short acquaintance, she found the older woman to be quite endearing. Perhaps they should have joined the rest of the household for breakfast.

"Do you need assistance getting dressed?" Jareth asked as he tucked his shirt into his trousers.

"What?" Odette's hands flew to her chest. Did he intend to help dress her, himself?

"Should I call a servant to help you dress?"

Relief flooded through her. Her heart could barely endure what had happened that morning, let alone being naked around him. "Yes, but I also need to wash before dressing."

He paused in buttoning up his shirt the rest of the way. "Wash. Right. I am used to bathing rarely when in service to the king. I should have known the daughter of a duke would need more." He ran a hand through his hair. "It seems I am already falling short on my promise."

Odette was so startled by his strong reaction that she just stood there mutely. Without confirmation, he left her. It wasn't long until a servant returned with another pitcher of hot water. She was at least a decade older than Odette with a smattering of freckles across her nose and cheeks.

"Good morning, Lady Chadwick." The maid curtsied. "I shall help you wash."

It was a small tub, but the water was warm and the maid thorough. She was nearly done toweling dry when there came a knock at the door. Odette nearly gasped when it opened but relaxed when she saw it was only Nonnie.

"Aren't you a sight to behold?" Nonnie's eyes twinkled as she presented the dress in her arms. "This good enough?"

The dress was dark blue with silver embroidery. At first glance it seemed simple but elegant, but when she slowly approached it, her fingers moved over the intricate embroidery.

"It's beautiful."

"It was my late sister's," Nonnie replied with a bittersweet smile. "You have her figure, so I think it will suit."

"Oh, I must not take something that is a family heirloom," Odette protested.

"I only had sons and they only had sons. It would warm my heart to see it worn again. I have not seen it for some time," Nonnie insisted, setting it down on the bed as though Odette had already consented to wearing it. She glanced at the maid. "Go get breakfast; I'll see to Lady Chadwick myself."

"I couldn't," Odette said politely.

"Is that what you really feel?" Nonnie asked, her eyes pinning Odette in place.

"No," Odette answered honestly. "I welcome your earnest company."

Nonnie patted her cheek affectionately. "There is my witty girl."

It did not take long for Odette to be dressed, while Nonnie told her stories of her sister and her family. Odette listened as Nonnie gathered her long hair into braids before securing them to the back of her head in a massive, braided bun. It was a simple but elegant hairstyle and was one of the best mornings she'd had in a long time.

As the maid was leaving with the last of the dirty water, Jareth entered carrying the tray of food. She jumped to her feet to help as he made his way towards the table. Instead of being helpful, she found herself fluttering around him like a wayward moth. Jareth sat across from her and began to eat.

Carefully, she did the same, taking a sip of tea, and finding that it was in need of sugar. At least milk had been added to cut the bitter taste. She shouldn't be so harsh—making tea had become a pastime of hers. She'd worked on perfecting it in her free time.

"Is it too bitter?" Jareth asked, his expression sheepish. "I remember the one we drank at your father's residence had milk in it. It seems it also had some sweetener?"

"It'll do fine." She tried to reassure him by taking another sip.

He watched her for a moment before turning back to his food. He was not at all what she expected him to be. Although Jareth seemed to be cold, he had a kind and caring side to him. She was coming to realize that her husband was a complex man. A puzzle she was going to have to piece together, her only aid being time.

"You shall have to make it for me once we are settled in Vallerdale," Jareth commented as he finished eating, wiping his mouth with his napkin.

To her surprise, his plate was clean. She immediately dug into the remaining food, eating to her fill but still leaving much on her plate. He eyed her remnants but said nothing. They sipped tea in silence as Odette tried to read his impassive expression. He seemed both tense and relaxed at the same time. Perhaps her efforts were in vain. He was a knight and an illegitimate child of one of the most noble families—he would have been schooled to conceal his emotions. Maybe even as much as she had.

He set down his teacup. "Is something wrong?"

She was just about to finish the cup but paused with it halfway to her lips. "Not that I am aware. Why?" The cup met the saucer with a clink as dread's bony fingers slid across her spine.

"You've been very quiet."

"I'm sorry." She realized she should have tried making polite conversation but had decided against it because she thought he wouldn't like it.

Jareth sighed and ran a hand through his hair. "You don't need to apologize. That wasn't my intent."

Was he getting frustrated with her? She wasn't sure what he wanted. "W-what would you like to discuss?"

His only response was to stare at her. She shifted uncomfortably in her seat before he finally responded, "I assumed you'd have questions."

"Oh." He wasn't wrong, but most of them were not appropriate for her to utter. So, she asked the one that had been brimming on the edge of her consciousness. "Will any of your family be at the castle?"

"You are my only family," he replied, and the intensity of his stare stole her breath. "My only family that will be in the castle."

She froze, completely overcome by his words. That was the last thing in the world she'd expected him to say. Then, like a bolt of lightning, she knew exactly what to respond with. "I will endeavor to deserve it."

A sense of connection passed between them, an understanding of sorts. He relaxed back in his seat seemingly pleased by her response. She did the same, warmed by the exchange. It seemed they were improving their communications. Perhaps there was hope for the pair of them yet.

"I am glad we came," Odette told him, grateful for all he had done.

To her surprise, he put his hand on the table and unfurled his fingers. She carefully set her hand inside, his thumb brushing across her knuckles. "So am I."

Perhaps more than hope, Odette thought as she met his earnest gaze.

His expression went immediately grim, but in a flash, it was gone. Had she imagined it? Yet she sensed what he was going to say next. She knew his legitimate brothers were in the west and very uninterested in their illegitimate brother. She had hoped there was someone else who had been there for him.

"You're my only family." Odette met his steady gaze, completely caught off guard by his words. "The only family that will be in the castle."

"I'll do everything I can to deserve such distinction." The idea of family had never meant so much as it did in that moment. Although she couldn't tell him about her mother and maternal siblings, she could treat him as she would them. He deserved at least that much.

Jareth searched her face for a moment before standing abruptly. He came around the table and she looked up at him, unsure of his intent. When he leaned forward she shifted back, then his lips touched her forehead. Her breath caught in her throat as his hands clasped her upper arms.

His face was very close to hers when he leaned back. "I look forward to it."

Chapter 9

Odette touched her forehead as the memory of that morning came back. They had rejoined the group and were headed north once more. Jareth continued on horseback while Kira had joined her in the carriage. She was reading a book that Odette had enjoyed dozens of times so that she could think without being distracted but still give Kira the feeling she was being helpful.

Odette wished she'd asked why Jareth had wanted to marry her when she had the chance. She knew it wasn't proper, but it really was the greatest mystery surrounding her current situation. She was not aware of any communication between them. It was unlikely they had met before. Yet he seemed to already be fond of her, like he knew her. It was a very odd sensation.

While riding on horseback to reach the rest of their group, she'd asked him simple questions like what his favorite season and his favorite pastime were—winter and horseback riding, respectively. He answered her questions patiently, seemingly amused by her innocent inquiries. With each question, he'd ask her to also share. The ride back to rejoin the rest of their party ended quicker than she expected. She had been disappointed he hadn't joined her in the carriage so they could continue their conversation but knew he had matters to attend to that he'd neglected yesterday. She'd learned he preferred darker colors, his favorite time of the year was the first snow of the season, and that he had two large dogs.

She didn't know why she felt the need to ask about these little things, but felt they were somehow important. Each question helped her discover the person her husband was. Each answer acted like a brushstroke, and when she was done, a portrait would form.

"Shall we eat?" Kira asked a while later, picking up a container.

"Is it already that time?" Odette's stomach hadn't made much room since breakfast. It wasn't that her father starved her, she'd just never had much of an appetite.

"It's past lunch, Lady Odette." Kira lifted a pocket watch, showing it was indeed well past the hour.

"Perhaps later," Odette said with a smile. "But please don't hold back on my account."

Kira didn't seem convinced, but after Odette urged her a second time, she ate. Odette tried to think of a clever way to ask about her husband's past without seeming overeager or intrusive. It took everything in her willpower not to bob her foot up and down or gnaw on her thumbnail—habits her father had tried to beat out of her to some success. She forced the gloomy thoughts away.

"Are you hungry after all?" Kira asked, her eyes wide with wonder.

"Why do you ask?" Odette was surprised by her question.

"Forgive me. I was trained to try and anticipate my future mistress's needs. Is there something you need from me?" Kira sounded genuinely interested, unlike at her father's house where she was barely tolerated by the servants. Here they didn't know how little regard her father had for her. Nor how much of a disappointment she was. With a sudden awareness, Odette realized she could remake her entire image. Here was her chance to start over.

"Can you tell me about Vallerdale Hall?" Odette finally asked. "I've never been there and I'm curious about the place I'll soon call home."

Kira's eyes lit up. "Of course! I should have thought to tell you about Vallerdale Hall. It is a wonderful place, although a bit cold in the winter. You'll never see as much snow as you do there. The air is clean and crisp, not like the capital. The castle is very long but not very deep because it sits parallel to the Great Wall. The main entrance has this amazing, colored glass that casts the entire room in a rainbow of color. I thought it normal as a child, but once I visited the capital, I realized that only the temples had so much colored glass."

"Do the windows depict particular scenes like the ones at the temple do?" Odette was enthralled by how enthusiastically her lady's maid spoke of Vallerdale Hall.

"They depict the deeds that raised Vallerdale and the house of Chadwick from the earth. It is said that the first Chadwick beat back the monster horde long enough that the Great Wall could be raised from the ground. You can see the story depicted in that great hall. It's beautiful. I cannot wait to see it once more." Her hands were clasped to her chest as she spoke.

There was one thing that Odette still didn't understand. "How did my husband come to be Lord Chadwick's heir?"

Kira blinked in surprise. "Lord Rupert Chadwick had no heirs, but offered to raise whoever proved they were worthy. Many families send sons and even daughters to compete. Yet it was Master Jareth who mastered every weapon and dominated every tournament." Kira put her hands on her cheeks. "He was only twelve years old when he joined, but in the five years that followed, he proved to be the best in all areas. We are truly blessed to have him as our master."

An odd pang in her chest sounded out—it felt like envy but that wasn't quite right. It wasn't that she was jealous of Kira. No, she realized it was because Kira's words made her feel like an outsider who didn't belong in his world. It didn't lessen her wonder at what her husband had accomplished, however, and she decided it was best to focus on that.

"I heard the king specifically selected him to defeat the Dragon of Mount Vere." Odette still could not imagine facing such a fearsome creature. When Kira hesitated, Odette reached over and put a hand on hers. "What is it?

"I don't know if I should say…" Kira's level of discomfort was palpable.

Odette had not expected such a response to what she thought was an innocent topic. "I promise you shall not get in trouble."

She bit the bottom of her lip for a moment. "When Master Rupert passed, the king wished to test the new Lord of Vallerdale. The Dragon of Mount Vere was his test."

"I see," Odette replied but only felt the sting of being ignorant. Her father had kept her and her sisters far from court life. He'd kept them isolated but focused their education on being competent wives—among other lessons that he'd inflicted upon her physically.

"Forgive me." Kira's voice was low. "I do not wish to seem disloyal. I am sure his majesty had good reason."

Odette patted Kira's hand before straightening. "Don't men always?" Her lady's maid's wide-eyed shock quickly devolved into giggles. "If you are amenable, can we agree that you can be honest with me without repercussion?"

"Like friends?" Kira asked hopefully, her eyes shining.

Odette felt her heart soar as hope surged. "Yes. Exactly. I have needed a friend for a very long time."

"You can count on me, my lady!"

Odette nodded, heartened by their exchange. "I believe I will have some lunch after all."

When they arrived in the next town, she had not seen her husband all day. Odette knew she should care more, and it did bother her slightly, but she was so exhausted that she had dinner brought to her room. She ate it quickly and barely lay down before sleep took her. In the morning, she found the blankets curled back but the bed was void of her husband. Pushing her wild hair out of her face, she felt a sense of rejection.

Was he avoiding her on purpose? she wondered as she stood and went to the window.

It was still early but already the streets were bustling. She saw the knights loading supplies as her husband directed them. Determined to at least speak with him, if only briefly, she began to dress herself. She couldn't get the corset quite tight enough, but the rest was in place. Her arms were tired as she began to loosely braid her thick hair. She secured it with a ribbon before smoothing down a few errant shorter hairs to her scalp.

Odette sat down to begin lacing her boots. She was nearly done when a knock sounded at the door. "Lady Chadwick." It was Kira.

Excited, she tied off the top and hurried to the door. Kira was openly surprised to see her mistress already dressed. "Good morning, Kira. Can you tighten my laces and then gather my belongings? I'd like to leave the moment my husband is ready."

"Certainly." Kira rushed in behind her and quickly fixed her sloppy laces. "I didn't expect you to be awake so early."

"I used to wake with the sun, but the constant traveling took more of a toll than I care to admit," Odette replied.

"All done," Kira said, appearing pleased.

Odette patted her hand. "I'll see you downstairs."

Flying from the room, she hurried to the main floor. The entry area had the scent of cooked eggs and baked bread, and her stomach demanded she stop but she ignored it. Instead, she opened the door and hurried out into the street. She recognized some of the knights as she approached but didn't see Jareth.

A knight with darker skin came towards her. "My Lady, is there something we can assist with?"

"I was looking for Lord Jareth." She didn't see his imposing presence among the smattering of knights.

"He departed moments ago," the knight told her, his expression concerned. "Is there something you need?"

She was surprised how quickly he wanted to help. "N-no." She cleared her throat. "I only wished to speak to him. Is there a reason he left early?" The knight hesitated, glancing at his comrades. She felt an outsider to a secret and that didn't sit well. "What is it?"

"A village to the north was attacked by a monster from beyond the wall. The Commander is going to try and track it, and confirm our route is safe."

"Monsters." The word sat heavy in the air. "Should I be concerned?"

"We'll keep you safe," he said proudly. "You have nothing to fear, Lady Chadwick."

She shook her head. "I meant should I be concerned for Jareth. I mean, Lord Jareth." The idea of him facing a monster from beyond the wall didn't sit well.

Stunned silence followed her statement. Then an older knight laughed out loud. "Tis the monster who should fear Lord Jareth."

The knights all agreed in unison, making Odette feel a little foolish, as was evident by the warmth she felt coming to her cheeks. "Well then, when shall we depart?" Her cheeks felt warm as she asked.

"Whenever you are ready, my lady. We have a rendezvous place with Lord Jareth." The imposing knight straightened his posture.

"I would like to leave post haste," Odette told him, then had a thought. "How should I address you, sir?"

He blinked at her. "My lady?"

"Your name. What is your name?" Odette realized that to be the one speaking with her, Jareth must have left him in charge of her care. If her husband trusted him, she should endeavor to become acquainted with him.

"Lex," he replied. "Everyone calls me Lex."

"Sir Lex, thank you for explaining the situation to me. Please prepare to depart immediately." Odette did her best to channel her grandmother, to be both elegant and firm as she had been taught.

When she approached the carriage, one of the knights lunged forward to open the door for her. She was startled when Sir Lex was suddenly at her side, holding out a gloved hand. He helped her into the carriage. Without her gloves, she caught the feeling of fatigue on the doorframe, but it wasn't from the knights, it was from Kira. It felt old, likely from the day before.

"I shall see that we leave shortly," Sir Lex said with a brief bow before closing the carriage door.

She heard Sir Lex begin issuing orders and smiled. He'd seemed caught off guard by her demeanor but had quickly adjusted. There must be a reason Jareth trusted him with his wife's life. He seemed very capable as she listened to him prepare their party for departure. It wasn't long until Kira joined her, with two steaming sweet breads, and they set out soon after.

Chapter 10

-Past-

They had been locked in the same room for nearly ten days. They'd been fed and cared for but only one maid came in and out. No one would tell her what was happening but at least they were together. Caden was stacking a pile of blocks on the floor while Melody watched, her eyes gleaming as she lunged forward, swatting at them. As the blocks toppled to the ground, her sister gave out a gleeful squeal.

Undaunted, Caden turned away slightly and began stacking another set as Melody crawled slowly into position. Like a young kitten hunting its first mouse, her sister positioned herself by the growing tower. When it reached a height that she deemed tall enough, she brought them crashing back down again with an eager swat.

Content despite their circumstances, Odette returned to the book she'd been reading. It was an adventure story about a boy who accidentally floated away from home in a little boat and was trying to get back again. She always read a few chapters ahead before reading it to her siblings at night, just to make sure nothing too scary happened that she'd have to reword as she spoke.

There was a jingling of keys outside her door and she expected it to be the maid with their food. Putting a finger in her book she leaned forward to pick up a bookmark when the housekeeper, Lynn, entered.

"The Dowager Duchess requests ya presence," Lynn informed them.

The book clattered on the ground as Odette shot to her feet. Sweat slid down Odette's back as her mouth became dry. Her time was up. She was going to find out what fate her grandmother had in store for her and her siblings.

"Coming." Odette picked up the book and set it on the dresser as she crossed the room.

"Ettie?" Caden asked as Melody sucked her thumb on the floor beside him.

"I'll be back." She sounded more certain than she felt.

"Ruri will watch the children," Lynn said, holding open the door. "Come along. We mustn't keep Lady Minerva waiting."

Odette's mind raced as she followed Lynn down the hall. She felt lightheaded and her hands were clammy as she suddenly found herself standing in a room with the duke's mother. There was tea on the table and a very disapproving stare from the hostess.

"Come and sit." Lady Minerva waved her to the couch positioned across from the one she sat on. "We have a few things to discuss."

As stiff as a tree trunk, she made her way across the room. By the time she took her seat, Lady Minerva had poured a cup and set it on her side of the table. She didn't even reach for it as she sat down, her hands poised in her lap as her stomach twisted in knots.

"I am Lady Minerva, mother to Duke Olier Wolverson. How should I address you?" Her emotionless face was impossible to read and her curt manner off-putting.

"Odette." The word felt like sand in her throat.

"Normally I would doubt such a claim as the one you are making, but you are every bit a Wolverson. Except for your hair, which I'll assume you inherited from your mother. I remember a girl my Oli was fond of when he was still in his youth. A young nobleman's daughter. I believe her hair was similar to yours." She took a sip of her tea. "Thus, it is not your claim that is a concern, but the shame it will bring to this family. Thankfully, I have thought of a solution."

How could she speak so calmly in a situation like this? As though Odette's entire fate wasn't in this woman's hands? Yet she felt like she was reading from a book, the air of elegance and refinement made the dowager duchess seem like a talking statue.

"What is your solution?" Odette asked, her voice shaking slightly.

Lady Minerva set her teacup down. "Tell me. Do you know what the role of a nobleman's daughter is?" Her stern expression did little to quell Odette's fear.

Confused, Odette only shook her head in response.

"Marriage. Unions that can bring honor and connections to the Wolverson family." Her eyes gleamed with pride as she spoke. "My union brought a trade route that doubled the family wealth. As Lord Wolverson, my son will do the same for his daughters. Do you understand what I am saying?"

Despite her nervousness, she did understand. "As the duke's daughter, I should serve this role?"

"Yes." She nodded. "I am heartened to see you have some sense."

"I thought the duke already had daughters," Odette pointed out. She'd heard the maids talk of Lady Minerva's granddaughters—the legitimate ones.

"He does, but one is already intended for Duke Nuvian's family. That leaves him only a single daughter for the entire kingdom. If he has an additional legitimate daughter wouldn't that be to the benefit of the Wolverson household?" She picked up and drank some tea as Odette felt like throwing up in the corner.

"And my siblings?"

"They have no Wolverson blood, but if you are good, I shall ensure their every comfort since they are children of a Count. Even if the Baccus family was near ruin, they are noble born. They will be raised by the servants, and you can visit them between lessons," Lady Minerva replied. "I will ensure they are given opportunities other children only dream of."

The sweet smell of tea wafted around her as Odette realized her fate could have been worse. She would not be cast out or killed. Instead, she would gain legitimacy and guarantee the safety of her siblings. There was little more that she could wish for. Except perhaps one thing.

"Can you see if my mother or my…sibling's father lives?" She had to know what fate befell them.

"I shall send word," Lady Minerva confirmed. "Now drink your tea before it gets cold. I'd like to assess your manners."

-Present-

Even with the looming threat of monsters, their morning progressed without any issue. Kira spent the morning talking about her family. Her father and mother were the primary caretakers while the Lord was away. They had served the Chadwick family for generations. Kira had two siblings; a brother who would be starting as an apprentice knight in the fall, and an older sister who was already married to a merchant in the capital. She had one nephew that she spent nearly an hour telling stories about. It reminded her of Caden when he was younger, though she didn't say anything about him.

"…then he carried the rock around like it was his friend for the rest of the day." Kira finished with a triumphant smile. "He still has it!"

"Woah!" the carriage driver called as they slowed to a stop.

"What is it?" Odette asked, pushing back the curtain.

Suddenly, Sir Lex appeared on horseback. "Forgive the sudden stop, my lady. We've reached the rendezvous point ahead of schedule. We'll wait for Lord Jareth to join us."

"Would it be possible to take a walk around?" Odette asked. She didn't want to slow down their expedition, but if they were waiting anyways, she didn't see a reason to waste an opportunity.

"Stay inside for now. We're scouting the area. Once we've confirmed it is safe, you can leave the carriage." When he finished his report, he bowed his head slightly.

"Thank you, Sir Lex." Odette felt relieved at the possibility of stretching her legs after hours of sitting. The knight barely waited for her reply before he was urging his horse forward.

"Should we prepare a picnic?" Kira asked, before rummaging in a basket. "I could prepare a small one while we wait, if her ladyship approves."

"That sounds lovely as it is nearly the lunch hour." Odette confirmed sitting up. "What are my options?"

Before Kira could respond, a mighty screech cut through the air like a whip. Her blood chilled as the carriage rocked. She couldn't see anything, but it seemed like everyone was shouting at once. The horses stomped the ground and whinnied. The coachman yelled something before the carriage lurched forward and she nearly fell out of her seat.

They were gaining speed as the carriage jostled them around like yokes in an egg. She felt ill as she tried to stop from smacking her head. Kira was screaming as a pair of screeches broke through the air. When Odette tried to see out of the curtain, she accidentally tore it. Gasping, she saw a flash of scales as something collided with the carriage.

Next thing she knew she was lying at the bottom of the carriage. With a groan she looked up, the opposite door was crunched into the compartment, hanging on by a single hinge. Whatever had attacked the carriage had tipped it over onto its side. That's when she noticed Kira was on her stomach, laying halfway through the doorway next to her, her arm was lying on the ground through the window of the slightly ajar door.

"Kira?" Odette reached over and touched her head. The girl didn't respond. Taking her handkerchief out, she held it to the girl's bloodied scalp. She tried shaking her awake as Odette's hands trembled from fear. "Wake up."

Kira groaned and opened her unfocused eyes. "What happened?"

"Something attacked the carriage," Odette whispered, suddenly afraid whatever had attacked them hadn't left.

Odette jumped out of her skin when a shadow fell across them. "Are you hurt, my lady?" One of the younger knights with short blond hair reached down for them.

"I'm fine, but Kira hit her head," Odette replied. "What attacked us?"

"Wyverns. There are still a few of them around," the knight replied. "We need to move away from here. They'll be drawn to the scent of their fallen brethren."

"You need to stand up," Odette said, helping Kira to her feet. The girl was a limp doll as Odette helped hoist her up to the knight. Once she was pulled free, Odette clasped onto his hand and was hauled out as well.

The back of her hand pressed against her nose and mouth as she caught sight of a dead monster. It had narrow wings and a body like a snake. Big powerful legs would have supported it like a frog. This one had been eviscerated and its guts lined the road. The smell of putrid meat made her gag. She refused to look at the other one that was further down the road, feeling queasy at the carnage.

Another knight was on the side of the carriage and helped her down. Kira was leaning heavily against a third knight who had a mace in his hand and was actively scanning the tops of the trees.

"We're too exposed here," the blond-haired knight said when he jumped down to join them. "We need to head towards the river. The running water will confuse them."

"We'll follow you, Jonas." The knight with a scar across his cheek that had helped her down immediately fell in behind him. "I'll keep close to the lady."

"See that you keep her safe, Mance," Sir Jonas ordered.

"She isn't fit to travel." The third knight said, indicating Kira. A glance passed between them, and Odette's heart hammered in her chest.

"We're not leaving her behind," Odette cut in, seeing the look on their faces. "She is my lady's maid, and therefore, my responsibility."

After another moment for two of changing glances, Sir Jonas said, "Follow me." And turned to lead them into the forest.

Relieved she didn't have to fight them, she quickly complied. Her side was sore, but besides that, she felt mostly unharmed as they entered the woods. The smell of damp leaves and overturned earth replaced the horrid odor of the slain creature. Her shoes were not suited for such terrain, and she had to lift her skirts up to keep from tripping. The already heavy fabric was further weighed down as the earlier rains worked their way up her hem.

When she slipped, Mance steadied her. "Be careful."

She was about to respond when she saw something coiled in the trees. Her fingers instinctively gripped his arm as she froze. Slits of yellow eyes watched them before it shook its massive head. She felt Mance shift as he very slowly drew his sword, his entire focus on the monster.

"It can sense movement. Whatever you do, don't move," Mance warned.

A screech cut the air like lightning, and she shivered in fear. Bile crawled up her throat as the creature unfurled its wings. If it were possible, this one seemed bigger than the last.

"Scatter!" Jonas yelled as the creature launched itself toward them.

Even if his instructions had been different, it wouldn't have mattered; Odette was rooted to the ground. Mance picked her up and slung her over his shoulder as he dashed out of the way. The creature collided with the tree just behind them. Leaves and sticks rained down on them as Mance fled and the creature roared.

Odette glanced up at the trees as she was jostled on his shoulder. Her ribs screamed against his unforgiving armor, but she couldn't relax. A sense of horror gripped her as the Wyvern quickly recovered and hissed in their direction. She immediately started slapping her hands against his back.

"It's coming!" she cried as it turned its attention to her.

Mance turned back to face it as they neared the river. Her thudding heartbeat melded with the sound of the rushing river as Mance threw them out of the path of the approaching Wyvern. Something slammed into them, sending them sprawling. The ground met her as she slid across the wet leaves and the rocks bit into her hands.

When she opened her eyes, the monster was wrapped around a tree and searching the area. She held still, remembering the knight's words. The creature moved its head around while scanning and sniffing the area.

Suddenly, a groan pierced the air and the Wyvern spun its head around. Heart in her throat, she lifted her head slightly and saw Mance rousing on the other side of the creature. He'd taken most of the impact and she could see a dent in his armor. When he started to move, the Wyvern zeroed in on him.

"Stop," she whispered, but he didn't seem to hear her. Tears slipped down her cheeks as she clenched her hand. Something was hard against her palm, drawing her attention.

The creature's shriek cut through the air as she threw a handful of rocks towards the river. They splashed into the running water, causing the monster to look towards the sound. Mance had gone still, his eyes locked with hers as an understanding passed between them. They needed to get to the safety of the river.

No longer content with using just its eyes and ears, the wyvern climbed down the tree, deeply inhaling the air to catch their scent. It would be on Mance in a moment, and she feared it was going to kill him!

"Stop!" Her scream caused the wyvern to raise its scaley head; milky white eyes focusing on her as she quaked in terror.

"Odette!" Jareth's alarmed voice cut through her panic, but he sounded too far away as the monster closed in.

Stumbling back, she instinctively lifted her arms to shield herself. The wyvern's mouth opened, its teeth bared, as it passed by Mance and sprang towards her. In a flash, Jareth appeared to the creature's left. It tried to shift away but was too late as Jareth's gleaming sword connected with its neck. Steel met flesh as her husband appeared every bit the hero he was proclaimed. That was the last thing she saw as she collapsed with relief. Somewhat dazed, the sound of Jareth's voice and the feel of his hands checking her for injuries brought her back to reality. She inhaled sharply as he touched her left side. "You've likely broken a rib."

"It hurts," she whispered glancing up at him. His face was contorted in anguish as though he were also injured. "Is it bad?"

Everything about him radiated intensity as he met her confused gaze. "I should have been here." He scooped her up into his arms.

Despite the pain in her side, she was comforted by the feeling of being in his arms. After seeing him defeat such a massive creature, she felt he could protect her from anything. Her eyes popped open at that thought.

"Where is Mance?" Odette asked, gripping his shoulder.

"Here, my lady." Mance was covered in mud, leaves, and blood, but in spite of how haggard he appeared, he was standing on his own and it brought her immediate comfort.

"I'm going to take her to the closest town for a healer," Jareth said. "Follow as quickly as you are able."

"Kira also needs a healer. Please help her," Odette muttered, suddenly feeling utterly exhausted. She was having a hard time focusing. She felt something strange on her skin, like rain prickling against every inch. She tried to inhale, but she wasn't able to. Jareth's arms were so tight around her, crushing her against his armor. Sounds and lights flashed around her. Even though she tried to focus, she could feel something taking hold.

"Hold on." It was Jareth. He was talking to her, saying her name, but it was so hard to focus.

Just when it was getting nearly impossible to breathe, she felt a comforting warmth enter her. Someone was healing her, likely from the temple. Her father was always calling a holy man to heal her whenever his cane went too far. Regardless of the unhappy memory, the pain subsiding caused her to relax and drift into sleep.

Chapter 11

-Past-

The stick rapped against her knuckles. "A lady does not slouch."

Despite the sting on her skin, she immediately fixed her posture. She was so tired from all her lessons that, apparently, she'd started slumping forward over her desk.

"Sorry, Countess," Odette said demurely. "It shall not happen again."

"See that it doesn't," Countess Hobbes said, her voice as tightly drawn as her hair was into a perfect bun.

"Now add these figures as quickly as possible."

Her hands still hurt as she picked up her chalk and began performing the computations written on the board onto her slate. She was nearly done when someone knocked on the door. The countess looked up in surprise. "Who is it?" Her voice was sharpish.

"Lynn." The maid said, opening the door and coming inside without hesitation. The countess emanated annoyance.

"What is it?" The countess at least tried to contain her annoyance at the interruption since she knew that there was no one Lady Minerva cherished more in that household than Lynn. The two women had been together since before the dowager duchess was married to the prior duke and they'd stayed together after. Even Odette had figured out the dynamic of the household after a few days.

"Are Miss Odette's lessons done?" Lynn asked courteously.

The countess looked to the clock which indicated she had only a few minutes left before Odette was free to go. Instead of answering, she walked across the small room and snatched the tablet from Odette's desk. She read the answers, which Odette were positive were correct, before glaring at her a moment.

"We're done for the day," Countess Hobbes said.

Odette stood up and curtsied. "Thank you, Countess Hobbes." Then she hurried to follow Lynn from the room.

Lynn led her to the front of the house where Lady Minerva was waiting. She had a cane in one hand and was dressed to go out wearing a fancy navy spencer. In spite of its simplicity, it was ornate and flattering.

"The duke will be visiting later this month, so we are going shopping for proper apparel." Her nose was tipped up slightly as she turned and left the residence. Lynn quickly helped Odette into a simple coat before following her grandmother outside and into the carriage.

The carriage ride was uncomfortably silent as they went to the tailor. When they arrived, she was ushered inside and dressed in all manner of clothing. Stays, bonnets, chemise, and petticoats joined a rather fancy pelisses coat. Not to mention every type of gown imaginable—for morning, walking, and balls. It was a whirl of color where no one asked her anything and her grandmother directed the staff at breakneck speeds.

By the time they were done, Odette was exhausted. She trudged towards their carriage when suddenly a hand grasped her arm. Shocked, she pulled back until she looked into the face of the hand's owner. The woman's cheeks were sunken in, and her skin stretched tight against her face, making her appear skeletal. Despite that, Odette threw her arms around her mother's waist, pressing her face against her mother's clothes.

Her mother cried. "Oh, my daughter," she whispered.

Odette clung to her as tears slid down her cheeks. "Mama."

"Odette?" Lady Minerva's voice cut through their reunion like the sharp edge of reality.

Odette raised her head and looked at the older woman, whose eyes were appraising her. Even with the knowledge that she should gather herself, her hands fisted in her mother's ragged clothing—she didn't want to let go for even a moment. Certain if she did, her mother would simply vanish again.

"Lady Minerva." Her mother straightened and faced her, moving Odette behind her as though to use her body as a shield. "I…"

"Before you speak," Lady Minerva said with unfailing dignity, "might we move into the carriage instead of discussing this in the street?"

Her mother wavered. When Lady Minerva strode by them into the carriage, they followed. Odette gripped her mother's hand as they joined her grandmother. Despite being reunited with her mother, Odette knew that life would never return to the time before she'd learned the truth.

-Present-

The ceiling had a wood carving of flowers. It matched the bedpost of the bed she was in. Disoriented, she glanced around, trying to get her bearings, when she saw a shape in the chair by her bed. Jareth's head was slumped forward, his eyes were closed, and he seemed to be sleeping. It was the first time since they'd met that she'd seen him not clean shaven. If she didn't know any better, she'd say he was exhausted.

Visions of the last day came back to her mind, and it felt like they had happened to someone else. She remembered his voice when she'd been in pain. The all-consuming fear followed by the relief when she'd seen him—her savior.

When she shifted to sit up, Jareth immediately roused. She blinked in surprise when his brows furrowed, and he hurried to her side. "How are you feeling?"

"I am well," Odette replied, and she meant it. She felt a little tired, but there was no pain. "How long have we been here?"

To her surprise, he touched her face and seemed to be searching for something. When he didn't find it, he let out a sigh of relief. Sitting heavily on the side of the bed, he took her hand in his. Its warmth was an immediate comfort to her as they gazed at each other. It delighted her to realize he might truly care for her—not just as a wife or the duke's daughter—but as a person.

She instinctively touched his cheek and saw him turn into her touch. "I truly am well now."

"You almost weren't." His gaze, like his voice, was firm. "My heart stopped when I saw the wyvern coming for you. You wouldn't have been there if it wasn't for me."

"You couldn't have known." Odette sat up completely, upset by how he burdened himself. "It could have happened any time and you saved me."

"I almost didn't. I should have been there." He appeared despondent as he met her gaze. Despite being able to read him, she shifted the hand he was holding so she brushed against the blanket he was touching. Her suspicions about his guilt and regret were confirmed.

"Then you mustn't leave my side for the rest of the journey," Odette said and felt content at her words. "Do you think you can do that?" He seemed confused by her words for a moment, but she could see already he felt honor bound to accept, so she raised a hand to stop him. "Let me explain. I understand you feel guilty for bringing me here. You told me as much on our first night, that this was all unintentional, but it doesn't change the outcome. We are here, married, and yet you are avoiding me." His face flushed in shame. "I don't blame you. Instead what you have done and what I know of you gives me hope. Hope that you and I might become more than husband and wife in name. That we might find friendship or even something more…but that cannot happen if you stay away."

He considered her words before responding. "You are not at all what I expected." He had this far off look in his eye as he said it.

"I never expected you at all. So perhaps that is a place to start," Odette said, brushing her thumb across his hand. "I am Odette Chadwick, once the eldest daughter of Duke Wolverson, and now your wife. I like to think that I take after my grandmother, who was clever and spoke her mind. I don't like to stay still for long and must have something to occupy my time. On normal days, I like to wake up with the sun. I have left everything I ever knew behind and ask only that my one ally take my hand and not abandon me out of guilt."

A smile spread across his face with each word. By the time she finished, his eyes held that same amused glint she'd seen in the drawing room of their first meeting. Then he leaned forward and kissed her; it was soft and sweet.

"Yes, I was feeling guilty," he said, smoothing some of her hair back. "How could I not after all that I'd done? You are correct in everything you said, except one. I didn't avoid you because I was guilty. I avoided you because if I stayed close to you, I'd want to touch you." He kissed her cheek as she tried to grasp his words. "Yet you seemed afraid of me, and I couldn't stand that look in your eye."

She met his gaze head on, refusing to falter. "I'm not afraid anymore."

His fingers slid into her hair as he pulled her forward. He gathered her against him like a prized possession, before his eager lips found hers. Every part of him felt like unforgiving corded rope, but not his lips. They were velvety soft as he opened his mouth and slid his tongue into hers to do battle with her own. Lightheaded, she clung to him as he kissed her with the passion of a starving man.

When she felt him move away, she found herself inhaling greedily for air. He kissed her cheeks and forehead—placing a smattering of kisses across every part of her face and even on her neck. She felt a giddy sense of excitement at the way he was almost worshiping her.

"I should stop," he said against her collarbone. "You should rest."

A moan slipped out as he nibbled across her collarbone. Their conversation left her yearning in a way she never had before. This desire to be joined to him, to be connected in a most intimate way. It slid over the top of her head like a hood, blinding her. His fingers caressed across her sensitive nubs through the fabric of her nightgown, but she wanted to feel him.

"Jareth." Her voice sounded alien at its airy nature. What was this man doing to her?

He groaned as he lay his forehead on her shoulder. "We really must stop. The healer said you needed rest."

She didn't feel tired, but to admit that was beyond even her sense of honesty. Just the feeling of his hot breath on her skin felt like too much. She felt like an animal, craving its mate. How many times had she witnessed the mating of a stallion and a mare? She understood quite well the principles required to complete the act.

"You must be hungry." Jareth finally sat up. "I'll see what I can find."

When he went to stand, she caught his sleeve. "How is Kira?"

"Her wound was superficial," Jareth assured her. "Head wounds have a tendency to bleed profusely."

"Were any of the knights killed?" She was almost too afraid to ask.

Jareth raised an eyebrow. "My knights? Not at all. Though Mance was nearly done in by that female wyvern. They can be quite deadly." He tilted his head. "He told me you protected him. Is that true?"

Dread filled her at the sudden question. "Should I not have?"

He hid behind an emotionless mask. "Why did you?"

"He protected me. I couldn't leave him to be killed because of me." Odette averted her gaze as though she'd done something wrong.

His fingers slid under her chin to turn her face back towards him. "That is his job. Though you were as brave as any knight, I would ask that you not put yourself at risk like that again."

She felt both complimented and cowed at the same time. "I will try my best."

He leaned forward and kissed her forehead. "Rest; I'll see about finding some food so you can regain your strength."

She lay back and pulled up the blanket to her nose as her cheeks burned. Where had that wonton behavior come from? Not to mention what he'd said to her. She giggled like a child and wiggled in delight. Despite her earlier vigor, she did feel drained. With a heart full of joy, she drifted off.

Chapter 12

It was night when she awoke; she could tell instantly because of the silvery color of the moonlight and dimly lit room. She shifted in the bed, but she was alone. The covers were turned back and there was a place where he had been, but Jareth was not there. Disheartened and hungry, she slid from the bed. The chill of the room made her shiver as she looked around. A tray with a covering sat on the table by the dying fire. After relieving herself, she quickly added another log before wrapping it in an old blanket that had been on the back of a chair.

The food was stew and there was even bread that had butter congealed on it. Despite it being as cold as the room, it was quite good. The meat was tender and the sauce flavorful.

She finished eating as the newly started fire warmed her legs. She nibbled on the bread, but the state of the butter made her put it back mostly uneaten. Snuggling into the blanket, she felt content, though she wished she wasn't alone.

Minutes ticked by as she considered returning to the bed but found the comfort of the fire too great. She'd slept so long that her body resisted rest now.

Even with a full belly, she didn't feel the pull of sleep. Instead, she only wished to speak more to her husband.

Perhaps she should seek him out? As the thought crossed her mind, the door opened. The light from the candle being carried revealed the very person she'd been thinking of as he closed the door. She abruptly stood, the blanket slipping off her shoulders as he turned to her. Their eyes met across the shadowed room, and he stopped.

"Is something wrong?" he asked.

When he drew close, she put her hand on his chest and went up on her tippy toes. She planted a chaste kiss on his lips before settling back. He blinked at her in surprise, and she didn't blame him. She saw he'd shaved while she'd slept and knew that his earlier state had been due to his worry over her.

"Thank you for taking care of me."

He set the candle on the table before turning back to her. His hand smoothed down her hair before cupping on the back of her head. Slowly he moved forward, scanning her face. She wanted him to kiss her and opened her mouth in anticipation. He met her lips with his own and she surged against him.

Jareth crushed her body against his, his powerful arms holding her close. She didn't need to handle anything he had touched to know he desired her. Their passionate kiss left her breathless as she felt him pull back.

"Are you sure this is what you want?" Jareth asked, that same gaze looking but not finding.

She gazed into his eyes and saw true concern. "I..."

He rested his forehead against hers. "Not as my wife, not as a duty, but as Odette."

"I don't know." She felt suddenly hopeless. "I'm sorry."

"Don't say that." He said, his voice almost a whisper. "May I kiss you?"

"Yes," she said with a giggle. "For the very reason that you ask me such a question."

The next kiss felt all consuming. Thoughts and feelings mingled within her as all reason left her. She reveled in his taste, lost in the feeling of him. His fingers brushed against her skin, leaving sensitive little trails.

"Relax," he said, leaning forward to kiss her thoroughly. "Close your eyes and just let yourself feel. This is completely natural between a husband and wife. I promise we shall remain dressed."

Odette felt the looming fear of his manhood joining with her womanhood fall away. Her breathing increased as he leaned forward to nibble across her jaw to her ear and neck. His teeth and lips sent sparks of pleasure through her body. Her fingers wove into his hair as she moaned, and her knees felt weak.

"Jareth," she sighed, breathless, confused by what her body was doing.

As Jareth wrapped his arms around her waist to lift her up, pain laced through her side. She jerked back and braced her arms against his shoulders as she gasped. He quickly moved her to the chair and knelt in front of her.

"Did I hold you too hard?" Jareth asked, trying to assess her pain.

Already the ache was subsiding. "I think it's where I was hurt earlier."

He cursed loudly. "I should have known better. You are still healing."

Without hesitation, he lifted her out of the chair like a princess. Odette inhaled sharply as she clung to him. He quickly moved her to the bed to sliding her between the covers. For a moment she thought he would leave, but he lay down next to her. She glanced at him as he put an arm behind his head. Raising up she gazed down at him, taking in how handsome he was.

"What is it?" he asked, caressing the side of her face.

"Thank you for being so...considerate." The word didn't do justice to what he was, so she bent down and kissed his cheek.

He chuckled as she eased back. "You never cease to amaze me." Jareth gently gathered her against him. "You truly are beautiful, Odette."

Her fingers rested on his heart as she felt a sudden unspoken connection to her husband. "Thank you for choosing me."

He eased back and they gazed into each other's eyes. His thumb brushed across her cheekbone. Her very being reached out for him as she framed his face with her hands. Then he kissed her forehead and tucked her against his side.

"It is I who am lucky to have you," he said.

She nuzzled against him, comforted in the scent of leather and man. "How are you so wonderful?"

He tucked her head under his chin as he pulled the blankets up around them. "I've had practice."

Chapter 13

Lady Minerva waited for the carriage to start moving before speaking. "I remember you now."

"I could never forget you," her mother said. Odette blinked in surprise—it was the first time her mother's voice had such venom. "Or what you did."

Her grandmother crossed her hands elegantly on her lap. "You may not believe me, but I am the only reason you are alive."

"You are right. I don't believe you." Despite her frailness, her mother's voice was firm.

"Then you are smarter than you were back then. When you decided to try and convince my husband that the union he'd denied must proceed because you were with child, he was going to have you killed." Odette's stomach was in knots as her mother gasped at the admission. "I couldn't imagine any grandchild of mine dying, even an illegitimate one. I told my son to break your heart so that you might live. Then I gave you the financial means to leave our domain." Her grandmother's voice turned almost gentle as she spoke. "You knew how ruthless the former duke was. You must know I speak the truth."

Her mother's earlier anger seemed to go out of her, with each word spoken, until she hung like a discarded empty flour sack. Odette could barely believe her ears. Her grandfather had been a truly horrible man. Yet the one truth she focused on was the fact that her father hadn't willingly left her mother. Perhaps her father might accept her. She was brimming with hope.

"I wouldn't have put it past him," her mother conceded. "Is that why you helped my children?"

"I didn't help your children. I helped Odette because she is our blood," Lady Minerva corrected her, her voice impartial. "Which is why I have a proposition for you." She shifted in her seat with her head held high. "The inquiries I sent, at Odette's request, revealed your husband died. You were missing and had not been seen for at least a week. I had promised to provide for Odette and to let her siblings be raised by the servants.

Instead, you may take your children home. They are healthy and cared for. Your household should be able to bear the burden of two young children. However, the expense of seeing all three of them to adulthood will likely be too great. Therefore, Odette will remain here. Arrangements are being made to transition her into a legitimate daughter, who was sickly and stayed with me until she outgrew her illness." Her grandmother fixed her other with a meaningful gaze. "Consider what would be best for your daughter before you answer."

"Unlike nobility, who prefer to order their children around like soldiers, we commoners speak to our children," her mother said before turning to take Odette's hands. "I leave the choice to you, Odette."

Odette glanced between them. "Is what she said true? Would you have difficulties providing for us all?"

"That isn't your concern. The question is, do you wish to stay with your father's family or return with me and your siblings?" her mother asked, smoothing her hair back. "You've grown so much since I last saw you."

Odette wanted to go home. She wanted to ride horses and missed her pony, Jewel, horribly. If she went home, it would be like the last few months hadn't happened. Yet a part of her thought of how her family would suffer. In six years, she'd be of a marriageable age. If she married well, she could take care of her family for the rest of her life. Part of her knew that wouldn't be an option if she left with her mother.

"What do you want me to do?" Odette asked, torn and confused.

Her mother glanced at Lady Minerva. The older woman's brow creased before her cane struck the top of the carriage and she called to the driver. "Let me out here." Due to the chaos of the street, it took the coachman a moment to get them stopped. "I'll have the carriage circle the block and come back to get me. Make your decision before it returns." Then she stepped out onto the sidewalk and commanded the carriage circle the block because she was feeling nauseous and wanted some fresh air.

Odette watched as her grandmother stood like a statue in the streaming crowd, her eyes hard and her bearing regal. If she stayed that is what she might become.

Suddenly, her mother pulled her into a fierce hug. Instantly, tears sprung to Odette's eyes as she sobbed against her mother. The realization that until that moment she believed her mother dead, finally caught hold.

"I am so proud of you." Her mother's words were barely audible.

"Mama." Odette sobbed, feeling like the nightmare was finally over.

Her mother smoothed her hair back, touching her cheeks and wiping away her tears. "I need you to be stronger than you have ever been. Can you do that for me?"

Odette nodded as she sniffled. "Yes, mama."

"Lady Minerva and the duke's family can provide you so much more than I can. I would have you stay with them; it would put my heart at ease." Her mother's voice shook. "No matter what happens, you hold your head high and you show them. Show them that you are my daughter with everything you do, and I will be there with you." She touched a hand to Odette's chest. "I am in your heart as much as you are in mine. No matter where I am."

"Will we ever see each other again?" Odette felt like she was saying farewell permanently.

Her mother kissed the side of her head. "I have to believe we will."

"How can I leave you?" Odette sobbed.

They cried together, whispering how much they cared and were going to miss each other. Odette had never felt so loved and torn apart at the same time. Once they circled the block, Lady Minerva didn't hesitate to rejoin them.

"Your decision?" Her grandmother was addressing her.

Taking a deep breath, Odette wiped away her tears and held her head high. "I'm staying."

"So be it," Lady Minerva said with the barest of smiles.

"Your grandmother was always a great lady. She will teach you how to survive in this world," Odette's mother said. Hugging her daughter close, she turned to face Lady Minerva. "May I write to her?"

"Yes, but you will do so as her nanny; it will allow you to write to each other. If she does well in her studies, I shall allow her to visit once a year until she comes of age." Her grandmother waved to the carriage door. "I shall make arrangements for your children to be delivered to you, but you must leave now."

With one final parting hug, her mother stepped out of the carriage. Odette reached out of the door towards her, but her grandmother caught her wrist. "You must act like a lady of this house."

Odette spared a final glance at her mother's fading figure. "Yes, Grandmother."

-Present-

Odette felt a blush creep up her cheeks as she sat in the prayer room for morning mass. The day before, she'd thought they were staying at an inn. Perhaps even another noble's home, which was not abnormal. Instead, they were sitting in one of the most prominent temples in the northern domain. She did not even want to think about what they had done the night before in the house of the Gods. They were married, so she felt it would be forgiven, but that did little to alleviate her shame.

It didn't help that her husband had stifled a laugh when she'd come face to face with the head priest. Her shock and realization of where they were, as she thought about what they'd done, had Odette ready to abandon him and run out of there in an instant. Instead, she elbowed him when the priest turned to lead them to the dining hall. That had only caused him to laugh harder. She was happy at least one of them was having fun.

"We pray to the Gods for their divine guidance. In their name we pray." The priest concluded, raising his hands up to the sky before calling an end to the morning mass.

Jareth offered her a hand, but she hesitated. "Still angry?" he asked, but he didn't sound at all worried.

"Considering it," Odette said, but after a moment couldn't suppress the smile. She found it was increasingly fun to be around him.

His hand was warm, and when they stood, he didn't let it go. His fingers intertwined with hers in such a way that she felt another rush of heat on her cheeks. She had never experienced even a dash of romance in her life. Everything this man did was new and different.

"Where are we going?" Odette asked, breathless from excitement as he pulled her through the stone halls.

"You'll see," was Jareth's only response.

They went through the courtyard and over a small bridge. Brightly colored fish swam leisurely in the pond as they entered a vibrant garden. He went to the back wall where he opened his arms and threw her a triumphant look.

"Have as many as you want."

She blinked in surprise, and stepping closer, she caught sight of the rows of golden berries and gasped. Tears sprung into her eyes as she covered her mouth.

"What's wrong?" he asked, rushing forward. "Do you not like them?"

At his genuine concern, she threw her arms around his waist and buried her face in his chest. He felt smaller than he looked, this imposing man who kept showing her endless kindness. He patted her back, almost awkwardly until she let go.

"I love them. How did you know?" Odette asked.

He paused, and she could see his gears working. "They are a delicacy. I don't know anyone who doesn't like them."

"Thank you. Besides peaches, golden raspberries are my favorite," Odette said, laughing as she rushed forward.

She ate two and was savoring a third when she felt him approach. They were honey sweet and their flavor blander than its red counterpart, with only a touch of tartness. It was something about their subtleties that made them her favorite. Kneeling, she began picking a small handful before twisting around and holding her hand out.

"Would you like one?" She reached as high as she could without standing.

She'd expected him to take it from her; instead, he bent over and took it right out of her fingers with his mouth. She just stared at him slack jawed at his scandalous behavior. What if someone saw them?

"Can I have another?" he asked with that mischievous twinkle in his eyes.

Unwilling to fall for his tricks, she smiled and held up both hands with the pile she'd picked. "Take as many as you want."

Apparently, her ploy did not sufficiently deter him because he bent right over and ate a few. She blinked as he smirked at her. For just a moment she considered throwing the remaining ones at him, but she heard someone's footsteps approaching.

"Lord Chadwick?" A young scribe approached them.

"What is it?" Jareth didn't sound pleased to be interrupted.

To hide her smile, she returned to picking raspberries, as many as she could hold. Knowing her hands weren't that big, she picked them slowly, only taking the ones that were in perfect condition.

"The members of your household have arrived," the scribe said. "They are ready to collect you if you are ready to continue."

"Our items are packed. Please retrieve them from our rooms so we can depart," Jareth ordered. The scribe was quick to comply and hurried off to see to his duties.

Kira! Odette immediately thought of her dear lady's maid. She enthusiastically tried to stand while clenching the berries but quickly realized that it wasn't that easy with her skirts. She tried twice before realizing trying to get up from kneeling required both hands. Should she set the raspberries down? The walkway was dirty and the berries almost pristine. While she was trying to figure out the best course of action, large hands took hold of her waist and hoisted her up. One moment she was on the ground and the next she was standing. Glancing at Jareth, her cheeks colored when she recognized the most logical thing to do was ask for help. Why hadn't that occurred to her as an option?

"Thank you," Odette said.

"Happy to help." He produced a handkerchief from his pocket and held it out for her. It was pretty and pristinely white, so she hesitated. "Come on now." He gestured as she set the berries in the cloth. It was much easier to carry than what she'd been doing.

"Thank you." She felt like she was suddenly only capable of using two words.

He offered his arm. "Shall we?"

Clutching the bundle of golden berries, she put her arm through his offered one and they walked. It was only then that Odette realized how familiar Jareth was with this place.

"I never asked. Have you been here before?" Odette was genuinely curious if he'd visited as a boy.

His steps suddenly slowed. "You could say that." His voice was light, but she caught an undercurrent, as though her inquiry had troubled him. "Did you enjoy your time here?"

"Yes. Everyone was very kind." Odette was relieved he'd changed the subject.

"I hope you feel the same way about Vallerdale Hall." That same pride in his home shone through.

"I can't wait to see it," Odette said, and she meant it.

They walked down a long hallway with pillars that did little to shield the beautiful garden. After going down a set of steps, they turned right and entered the main building. It was a maze of architecture, and at times Jareth would point to a particularly unique crowning or piece of art. He didn't elaborate, mostly just saying their name or calling out what it was supposed to depict. She was so distracted by his explanations that she was surprised to find they had suddenly arrived at another courtyard.

"My Lady!" Kira flung her arms around Odette and cried heartily. Jareth left her side wordlessly, a content smile on his face.

"I'm so happy you are well," Odette said, hugging her back.

"Me? It was hardly anything, but you were nearly killed." Kira kept going between moving her to arm's length to talk to her and then hugging her close. The silliness of it made Odette giggle.

"Really everything is well," Odette said, waving her hand.

"What is this?" Kira asked, cupping the bottom of the bulging handkerchief.

"Raspberries! For us to have on our journey."

Kira deftly slid the package out of Odette's hand. "I'll get them loaded up right away."

"Are you ready to depart?" Jareth asked, already on horseback.

Odette nodded, noticing for the first time they were securing the items they'd had at the temple onto the carriage. "Yes, my lord."

She strode towards the carriage behind Kira when suddenly a group of knights lined the pathway to the carriage. They stood at attention with Sir Lex and Sir Mance, closest to the carriage. She glanced at Jareth, expecting an explanation for their sudden behavior, but he just smiled at her. Was that pride in his expression?

Kira was grinning broadly as Odette tried not to trip, she was so nervous. When she reached the door, Sir Mance opened it and Sir Lex held up a hand. She took it, thanking him, as she ducked into the carriage. Once seated, the knights hurried to mount their own steads.

"What was that?" Odette was not familiar with such a custom.

"The knights were honoring you." Kira's voice was at least two octaves higher than normal, and she was vibrating with excitement. "It is an old custom in the North. They will continue to show you their loyalty through actions."

"Yes, but why are they doing it?" Odette asked, slightly embarrassed as Jareth called all knights into formation.

"You risked your life for a knight and thus have become one of them." Kira's eyes twinkled at the words.

"Kira," Jareth's voice cut their conversation short. "You may spend time with my wife while I secure our accommodations, but tomorrow, on the final leg, you must relinquish your seat to me."

Excitement that her husband was joining her again filled her heart. Kira nodded excitedly, her gaze sliding between the two of them. "Yes, sire. Gladly, sire."

With one final glance back at the towering temple of stone and mortar, they returned to the road and their journey. In spite of, or perhaps because of the excitement, Odette was ready to arrive at her new home. She would not admit it, but the journey had been a drain both physically and emotionally. She only hoped that the worst of it was behind her.

Chapter 14

-Past-

Odette stared at her toes as though they might know a way out of her current situation. Her grandmother was standing by the door as her father stared down his nose at her. She didn't know what she expected from the duke, but it wasn't this frigid man. He was looking at her like she was dressed in rags and begging for money. The only thing she'd really wanted was affection, but she could tell immediately that was never going to happen. Her heart held out hope, but her head already knew. She'd had a father and he'd died. It didn't matter if he wasn't blood related, he'd been her father in everything that mattered, and when he'd died, the only person who she'd ever call papa, was gone.

"Does she have the Wolverson eyes?" His voice was as cold as his countenance.

She lifted her eyes at that, resolved to not let his words affect her. He must have seen her defiance because his eyes narrowed. With the hallmark black hair and green eyes of the Wolverson blood, the duke's physical appearance was as imposing as his title. She was surprised to find that he was handsome, or at least he would have been if it wasn't for his perpetual scowl. Although she should have been afraid, she was only disappointed. Even Lady Minerva had accepted her into the family in her own stern way. This was the opposite; this was outright rejection.

"Yes." Lady Minerva said, watching her closely.

"It doesn't seem as though she is refined enough to join me yet. She'll remain with you until she can demonstrate civility and dignity as is expected of one in her position," the duke said, roughly cupping her chin in his hand. "She isn't unsightly in her looks. At least in that her mother did well."

She felt anger and frustration swirl with the tears that formed because she had no outlet. He let go of her and she let her chin fall forward to her chest. She didn't want him to see her crying.

"I shall keep her here until she can pass your test. It is important that you begin to spread rumors of her recovery and life with me here. We must make them believe it is real or this will all be for naught." Lady Minerva didn't mince words.

"You always liked your schemes, Mother. Even the risky ones. This one could devastate us if it fails. Let us hope this isn't a mistake." The duke didn't even bid them farewell; he simply exited the room.

Hot tears clung to her lashes before plopping in the carpet. To her surprise, she felt a hand on her shoulder. Glancing up, she saw a look of concern on Lady Minerva's face. It was not something she was used to seeing.

"You must never let them see you cry. If you cry, do so alone behind closed doors. If they see your weakness, they have won," Lady Minerva said with all the command of a queen. "Focus not on the emotions, but on the wall you'll build to hold them in. Would you like me to teach you this?"

She sniffled before nodding. "Yes, please."

"Then wipe your tears, child." Lady Minerva patted her shoulder. "Your father showed you as much regard as you can expect. There is much you must learn and there is much you must master in the coming year."

"I shall do all that I can," Odette replied. Her heart was heavy, but she was determined. The sacrifice she and her mother had made had to be worth something.

Lady Minerva nodded as she led them out of the room. "The first thing you must do is turn every disadvantage others see in you, into an opportunity."

-Present-

They arrived at a fine manor in the evening. There were knights stationed along the way, holding lanterns to light their path. Most were men but occasionally, she'd spy a woman. Was this the famous training academy she'd heard about? If it was, this place was just a few hours from Vallerdale Hall by horse. Unlike in the other domains within the kingdom, the knights were not all from prominent families. Here skill dictated accomplishments, not birth. It stuck with her because she always felt inferior due to the circumstances of her origins.

"Is this the famed knight's academy?" Odette asked as they approached.

"Yes." Kira replied. "The grounds consist of multiple buildings such as the main hall, barracks, training grounds, and armory. My brother is attending here." Kira slid closer to the window. "We weren't going to stop here originally, just pass through. Now I hopefully get to see more of him!"

That was something Odette marveled at—Kira always seemed to be so fully of energy. It seemed to radiate off her. Which is why the earlier exhaustion she'd sensed was so out of place. Though even Kira seemed spent after a long day in the carriage—the likely cause. Sometimes Odette swore she even saw a faint pale orange glow around her from her overabundance of vigor. She would have to tell Jareth again how thankful she was for Kira's companionship.

The front façade of the main hall held a multitude of windows. As they came to a stop in front of the main entrance, it seemed that light shown through every one, giving it a warm and welcoming feel, despite the hour.

Jareth met her at the carriage and helped her step down. He seemed happy to see her and even bowed ceremonially over her hand. To her surprise, she noticed all the knights they'd passed had trailed in behind the carriage and were like large fireflies as they waited behind the procession.

"I welcome you to the training grounds of my knights." Jareth spoke loudly so those around him could hear.

"The lady has demonstrated the bravery of a knight when saving one of our own," Sir Lex called out. "She is to be shown the respect as Lady Chadwick, but also as one of us."

Odette felt herself blush and was thankful for the dark to help conceal her embarrassment. It seemed she could not change the way her cheeks turned rosy at the drop of a hat, no matter what her grandmother had her try.

The knights began to chant and it took hearing it a few times for her to make out the words. "Nos pro vobis." After a brief search of her memory on the history of the north and its ancient language, she could not recall what it meant. She would have to ask Jareth about it later.

Jareth escorted her inside; he walked proudly, like a victorious man. Her heart thudded in her chest from the excitement as her smile spread so large her cheeks started to hurt. Everyone was treating them like royalty. It was such a contrast to what she was used to; for a moment she forgot everything else and just enjoyed herself.

They entered a massive dining hall where a feast was being served by younger boys and a few girls. Unlike many of the others she had seen, they were dressed in simple clothing. As she was seated, she watched them, quickly assessing they were the lowest on the hierarchy of this place.

As the knights took their seats, Jareth stayed standing, holding up a goblet. She promptly picked up her cup as well, surprised by the remanent feelings she sensed of annoyance and duty, before raising it. Apparently, whoever had touched her cup last had left an impression.

"To victory and few quiet years at home!" Jareth called, raising his cup. "Nos pro libertate morimur."

"Here, here!" Many called and drank after he did.

She did as well, but realized it was wine and stopped. She did not want to repeat their first night as husband and wife. With all these sayings in the ancient tongue, she thought none of them would make sense, but she recognized one word. Libertate was liberty.

"Tell us the story of the monster of Mount Vere." A boy called out.

To her surprise it was young Jonas who stood. "Deep in Mount Vere, the treasure waited but also the monster who came and stole our sheep and attacked our exploring ships. On the King's orders, we marched for our country. For two years we quested deeper and deeper into the dark lands. We fought all manner of beast, some with wings and some that swam. Each fell to our blades and our Commander's strength." Everyone was enraptured by this story, many ignoring the steaming food that was set on the table as he spoke. "When we found the dragon of Mount Vere. It rained upon our men torrents of fire and brimstone. Our steel was no match for its flames."

"What would you like to eat?" Jareth whispered, leaning close.

"What?" Odette had been so focused on the story she hadn't expected him to speak to her.

"You should eat instead of listening to these ridiculous tall tales," Jareth said, dishing a glob of mashed potato onto her plate.

Thoughtlessly, she covered his mouth with both hands. "It is not a ridiculous story. It is your story." She gasped and immediately withdrew her hands and shoved them into her lap when she realized what she'd done.

His eyes twinkled with amusement as he leaned closer to her. "You sound so defensive." His voice was practically a purr.

"I will defend you," she muttered since his face was so close. "Even against yourself."

He pecked her lips, before he smiled broadly. "You may listen all you wish but eat as well."

Every inch of her was burning, from the crown of her head to the tip of her toes. It was only then that she realized Jonas wasn't speaking and every eye was on them. Curiosity, awe, and even amusement colored the room with a variety of expressions, many craning their neck to see more. Jareth seemed unperturbed as he piled more food onto her plate. It was as though the man was in a completely different room from her.

"Tell the story of our brave lady!" Sir Lex called.

That caught everyone's attention as Odette considered sliding under the table. Was there to be no end to her mortification? She hated being the center of attention and yet she couldn't seem to escape it as of late. She did her best to remain unmoving but knew she must be as red as a beet.

"There we were on the road, when a flock of wyverns attacked. They set upon our party and overturned the carriage. A trio of knights fled into the forest only to come across the most deadly of wyverns. A female!" A few of the younger apprentices gasped. "Our lady may have hailed from a home of nobles, but within her beats a heart as brave as any knight. When our mighty Mance was knocked out protecting her from the wyvern, did our lady flee?"

"No!" The crowd cried back. She blinked at them in surprise. How could they possibly know?

"No, she called out and faced the lethal wyvern like the queen of the monsters herself. Were it not for our noble lady and her noble deed, our Mance would surely have perished."

She felt like that was an exaggeration. Knights were not that easy to kill.

That's when she noticed how still Jareth had become. His earlier swagger was gone and in its place was a tenseness. His eyes were watching Jonas, but his gaze was unfocused as though his mind was elsewhere. Despite the uneasiness it caused, she reached out and covered his hand with her own. His gaze shifted, focusing on her, and she watched him visibly try to relax. He was attempting to conceal his quiet fury. She let her fingers brush across the tablecloth where his hand was resting. She tried not to react as she felt his gut-wrenching remorse mingled with a strong desire to protect.

"Eat before the food gets cold," Odette said coyly before turning to consume her meal. In spite of her earlier embarrassment, she suspected they had more in common than she originally thought.

Chapter 15

Odette was disappointed when she woke alone the next morning. As Kira dressed her, they were brought tea and she enjoyed a simple breakfast, along with one of the peaches she'd picked. The window revealed a busy courtyard but little else. Apparently, her husband intended to leave in a few hours but had made no demands on her time due to his busy schedule.

Part of her knew she should stay in her room, but another part of her yearned to explore. Perhaps it had been hasty of her to excuse Kira for a few hours. Without an escort, she really should remain in the room. She tried reading, she tried sewing, and she even tried drawing a little. She was distressed to discover that not even an hour had passed. What was it that married women did to occupy their time? Her days until then had been about how to please a husband and run a household, not how to fill her time.

Then a thought occurred to her. The reason she'd always needed an escort was because she was unwed. That was no longer the case now, meaning she should have some liberties that her unmarried self would never have dreamed of. After ten minutes of deliberation, she could no longer stay still. Under the pretext of a walk, which was not uncommon for great ladies, she left the room.

The hallway was empty, so she decided to go left and take the stairs down to the main hall. Once there, she saw a few servants, but no one paid her any mind as they were busy going about their duties. Thrilled by her newfound freedom, she began to wander the corridors, looking at works of art and admiring the masterful architecture.

Eventually, a rhythmic clanging drew her attention, which led her to a doorway at the end of the building, and she stepped onto the threshold. Out in the sun were dozens of people in similar apparel practicing their swordsmanship. Jareth was standing not far from her, but his back was turned as he watched two young apprentices spar. To his left was Sir Lex and to his right was an older man Odette didn't know. The apprentices couldn't have been more than eleven years old.

Sir Mance and Jonas were watching as two instructors had their pupils move through a series of movements while wielding wooden swords. The area was dusty and loud, but Odette didn't move away. It was unlike anything she'd ever seen.

When a dark-haired boy was able to disarm a blond-haired boy, the towheaded boy retaliated by barreling into him. The two boys were wrestling, and Sir Lex was laughing heartily at them. The older man didn't look at all amused. Jareth and the old man were speaking as older apprentices pulled the two boys apart.

"Off to the infirmary with you," Sir Lex ordered, thumbing over his shoulder in her general direction.

Suddenly realizing she was blocking the doorway, she had to decide to take a step in or out as the dark-haired boy's drooping form moved in her direction. She was about to take a step back when the boy lifted his head. Their eyes met and she froze—his were almost violet like her brother, Caden. Then she noticed the blood on his nose.

A sudden impulse overcame her as she reached into her pocket and retrieved a handkerchief. It was red with a simple black embroidered flower. She stepped out into the courtyard and held it out to him.

"Your nose is bleeding." She felt rather lame as she realized what she was doing. When he didn't move, she took a step closer, took hold of his hand, and pressed the handkerchief into it. "You need to press it against your nose." She pointed to try and drive the point home. His movements were slow and his expression one of bafflement as he did as she said. Satisfied, she ruffled his hair. "There you go. You'll be better in no time."

"Off you go, Kilian," Jareth's voice reminded her she'd exposed herself.

Uncertain how he would react, Odette slowly turned to him. He seemed amused more than anything and she felt relief flood through her. Of course, he wouldn't get angry at her. When was she going to start trusting him?

"Forgive the interruption," she said with a curtsey. "I was trying to familiarize myself with the grounds."

Jareth glanced around. "By yourself?"

"Should I not have?" Odette asked, losing her nerve.

He moved closer to her and held out a hand. "Not when I can escort you."

She was about to put her hand into his when a voice cut in. "Is this her?" The old man stepped closer to them, his expression hard.

Jareth reached up to grip her hand before tucking it into his arm as he turned to face the older man. "This is Odette, my wife. Odette, this old, onery man is Ault: master instructor."

After a lifetime of disapproving stares, she recognized his right away. The tension was thick as Odette felt the words flow out of her without thought. "Were you also my husband's instructor?"

His gaze appraised her. "I was."

"Tell me, Instructor Ault. What kind of student was my husband?" Odette met his gaze head on. She was no longer the unloved child, but the cherished wife.

The three of them seemed stunned by her words. Sir Lex's laughter burst out of him as he turned away, hunched over. She liked how his white teeth stood out when he smiled because his skin was so dark. It made his smile seem so much bigger.

Jareth's stiffness went out of him when he assessed Ault's shocked expression.

"Whoo-wee lassie." The crinkles around the old man's eyes grew more pronounced at his sudden smile. "I see now why our young lord was charmed by you. Duke's daughter or not."

"You haven't answered my question," she pointed out.

"Perhaps that is for the best," Jareth cut in. He patted her hand. "We will have to leave after lunch; would you like to see more of the grounds?"

He began to maneuver her away, as laughter followed them. When they reached the doorway, he held her hand out and had her go first. Even as they entered the hallway, he kept their hands together, including when he brought it back to his arm.

"What would you like to see first?" Jareth asked, glancing around. "There is a small library and an armory."

After a moment's consideration, she had a thought. "What is your favorite place?"

He paused and glanced at her, his eyebrows raised. A slow smile spread across his face as he nodded. "I hope you don't mind climbing stairs." Then he whisked her through the building's hallways at blurring speeds.

When they reached the tower, she was a little out of breath. "What is up there?"

"You'll have to wait and see," Jareth seemed as excited as a child. "Come on."

She tried to keep up, but after a dozen or so steps she lagged behind. Trying to take her time as her chest heaved, Jareth asked at least twice if she needed help. Her pride wouldn't let her give in and she eventually reached the top. Sagging against the wall, it took her a moment to notice Jareth. He was standing by an open window, leaning out of it as the wind pressed his hair back. His eyes were closed as he took a deep breath.

Then she heard a soft cooing and glanced around. Little white birds were napping in a variety of little homes. Their necks were pulled against their bodies or tucked back towards their wings. Despite the fresh air, there was a soft scent of animal smell. Yet she couldn't smell excrement, like in a stable or farm.

"A rookery?" she asked.

"I used to escape up here as a boy. Old Chadwick used to assign the cleaning-up to me. I suspect because he knew I liked it; thus, he gave me an excuse." It was the first time she'd seen that expression on him—unreserved affection.

"Were you close?" Odette moved closer but paused when the wind was cold against her face and neck.

His eyes were downcast. "He was as close to a father as I knew."

Though she could not say it, she understood his loss. Before she knew of the duke, her step-father, Count Baccus, had been a true father to her. He'd taught her how to ride, and many of her happiest memories included him. It seemed that Jareth understood that blood did not make a father.

"Can you tell me about him?" Odette linked her arm with his in the face of the cold.

He shifted to face her and situated her between his legs as he leaned back, effectively shielding her from the cold. "He was very stern and exacting. He pushed every boy who wanted to be his heir to their breaking point. Yet, there was something indescribable about having him recognize all your efforts. I lived for that man's praise; that nod of approval after a victory."

She was surprised how Jareth described him. The former Lord Chadwick seemed as unfeeling as her actual father. Not at all like Count Baccus who had loved her and showered her with affection and opportunities, even when they'd had little food on their table. When they'd all had to work in the stables from sunup to sundown, she'd always felt loved. Yet what Jareth described was so different.

"How did you become his heir?"

"We were taken to the tournament in the capital. A hunting tournament with jousting and an archery contest." He seemed to be lost in thought a moment before continuing. "I'd won the jousting contest and was on the top of the world. Lex and I were tracking a massive bear together. We'd decided to combine our efforts since Lex was likely to win the archery contest."

"What happened?" she asked, putting her hands on his chest.

"We underestimated the bear's strength. There was a reason it had been hunted but never captured. There were markers around its territory, but I was certain we could bring back its head. I had something no one else had. I…" he paused, his gaze focusing on her. "Our horses ran. We brought it down, but in the process, Lex was badly injured. I left the bear and brought him back."

"You lost?"

"The rule is we had to present the prize before midnight. I wouldn't leave Lex's side, even when he insisted. It had been my arrogance that had hurt my friend. He was the only one I had back then." Jareth shook his head. "I thought Rupert…Lord Chadwick…would be angry." He sighed, tipping his head back with a chuckle. "I thought after that he'd kick me out and I'd have to go back to my blood relatives."

"Was he proud you chose your friend over victory?" It seemed like a perfectly Jareth thing to do.

Suddenly his hand slid into hers and held it tight. "Yes. I don't even remember most of it, but apparently my reaction had a profound impact on the other boys competing to be heir. They went and found the place with the fallen bear and brought it back. Lex and I were crowned Kings of the Hunt, but all I remember was feeling like an imposter.

"The next day Lex couldn't compete because he was still healing. So, I took his place, declaring it was in his honor and all points should go to him. I won. That put Lex and I in direct contest. Right there on the stage I turned to Rupert and told him that Lex deserved to win, that I would step down." There was a half-smile on his face that made him appear impossibly handsome. "Lex refused. So did many of the other boys, including Jonas. It was then, when I was sixteen, that Rupert named me his heir." He chuckled. "It felt unreal."

"Did he ever tell you why?" Odette asked, holding tight to his hand.

"Yes, but it was two years later. He said it was because I chose friendship and to do the right thing over power." Something passed over his face, an emotion she couldn't place. "That in the moment when I should have forced everyone to accept me as their leader, I opted to do the opposite."

"It is not adversity that tests a man, but power," she quoted. It had been a long time since she'd read the book about the warrior who became king.

Jareth straightened and finished the quote. "For it proves that the man who does not desire power for himself is the one that should have it." She could tell he was pleased. "Raham."

"A wise man," Odette replied.

"Raham was a very wise and honest man. I have studied many of his teachings." His eyes were bright with an adolescent eagerness that was instantly endearing. To think this man had ever felt cold to her.

Odette leaned towards him. "I meant Rupert."

Jareth immediately nodded his head. "He'd like that." Then his gaze turned playful. "Do you mean he was wise for *why* he chose me or *that* he chose me?"

"Both." Odette felt a shift in the air. "It is apparent to me that you are more than deserving."

His arms went around her, drawing her close. Odette closed her eyes a moment before his lips touched hers. It was a soft kiss, not demanding but instead, utterly sweet…like a softly spoken thank you. It was so gentle, it was as though she'd imagined the fiery kisses of the night before.

"Your words fill me with such pride. It makes me question once more if I am deserving of you." His fingers caressed her cheek. When she turned her head, wind slid across her neck, making her shiver. Or perhaps that was that the anticipation of his touch? "It is cold; we should go back inside. We must depart soon."

As Odette followed him down the stairs, her hand tucked in his impossibly warm one, she said, "I can hardly wait to see your home."

He glanced back at her. "It is *our* home. Whatever you need, whatever you want, you have only to ask."

Odette steeled herself as she blurted out, "Dinner."

Jareth paused. "Dinner?"

"Every night. I want to have dinner together." *Like a family*, she thought, but the last went unsaid.

"That is all?" Jareth smiled as though her words amused him. "On nights when I am there, I shall dine with you."

They continued down the steps. "On the nights you are there?" She didn't like the way that sounded. "Do you anticipate being gone?"

They faced each other when they reached the bottom. "I have currently been gone for more than two years. I must see to matters under my jurisdiction. Take care of any monsters that slipped through. Inspect the wall. Settle matters that have languished in my absence."

"Can I help?" Odette asked as he tucked her hand under his arm.

His movements slowed. "The castle will likely need repairs and updating. It has been some time since Vallerdale Hall has seen a mistress. Not since Rupert's mother."

That didn't seem like much, but perhaps other opportunities would present themselves. Her father may not have thought much of her, but her grandmother had seen to her education. She would not embarrass herself, at least. For the time being, her days would not be as boring as she feared.

"I shall do all that I can," Odette said, feeling cheerful about arriving and assessing the state of the castle.

Jareth began walking. "When we arrive, I'll speak to Jay, the head steward. He'll present you with the finances set aside for castle repair. He will also present your allowance. Should it be lacking, simply let me know." He lifted her hand and kissed the back of it, eliciting an immediate blush. "A promise is a promise."

How could he always muddle all her thoughts? One moment she'd been contemplating how best to go about determining what most needed her attention and now she was fixated on him. Her thoughts turned to their future and what it might hold. Although he'd never spoken the words, she could tell he held her in high regard. Perhaps one day love might form between them. If Odette were being honest, she knew it likely already had. At least on her side.

"I am grateful for your dedication to upholding our agreement," Odette said, trying not to dwell on her initial thought that led to that agreement. "It puts my heart at ease."

They walked in amiable silence until they reached their room. Once more he kissed her hand, and she felt her emotions swell. His thumb brushed across her knuckles, as though he didn't want to let go. She shared his sentiment.

"May I kiss you?" His voice was pitched low as he moved closer, still holding her hand.

"You didn't ask earlier," she pointed out, feeling breathless.

His smile was coy. "True, but I am now."

Odette put her free hand on his shoulder and went on her toes. His lips were soft as she boldly kissed him. His hand went around her waist as she tipped her head, and this time his lips met hers with eager passion.

When she rested back on her heels she felt so daring. "Now we are even. I didn't ask either." She turned to enter the room, struggling not to react to his shocked expression. As the door closed, she heard his peals of laughter, which made a bubble of indescribable happiness burst in her chest. Yes, she was certainly well on her way to forming a deep attachment to her husband.

Chapter 16

-Past-

Odette picked up the needle and again felt the contentment on it. The teacup whispered of anger, already fading. The block held the sadness her brother felt when Lady Minerva had told them that their mother had recovered enough and sent for them. At first, she thought she'd imagined these things, but with each new emotion she felt that wasn't hers, she knew this was an ability. As shocking as it was, she was a Mystic. Only the older bloodlines typically produced people with abilities, and it was said the abilities were unpredictable. During the last two weeks, it had become more and more apparent, as she touched objects other people had just handled, that she also had an ability.

Shaking off the distraction, she picked up the dolls she'd sown and embroidered as practice, taking them to the parlor. It hadn't taken long for Odette to realize stitchwork was Lady Minerva's favorite pastime. On most evenings they'd had tea by the fireplace and worked on their stitching. Due to her sibling's departures, Lady Minerva had granted her half a day of free time.

Once the dolls were properly hidden to ensure they would be surprise gifts for her siblings, she made her way to the servant's quarters where her siblings were being housed. Dawn had hardly broken so she found Melody asleep, having been fed in the early hours and returned to sleep. The little room was basically the size of her walk-in closet, but the bed and crib were in fine condition. It may be small, but Odette could tell the maids had taken proper care of her siblings. Caden was not asleep but was instead curled up on the only chair, tears on his cheeks, his eyes puffy and red. Her heart immediately clenched at the sight of him.

"Caden? What is it?" Odette knelt in front of him.

"Why aren't you coming with us?" he wailed.

Odette glanced at the crib, but her sister hadn't even moved despite his outburst. She was thankful Melody was a heavy sleeper. Taking Caden's little hands in her own, she tried her hardest to be brave.

"Mama has you and Melody, but Grandmother doesn't have anyone. I'd like to stay with her." The last word caught in her throat, and she had to clear it. "Is that all right?"

His expression became thoughtful. This entire journey had forced Caden to grow so much in the last few months. It was impossible not to notice the change in the way he spoke and the way he looked at the world.

"Will I see you again?"

"I'll come visit as soon as I can, but I'll write all the time and mother will read the letters to you." Odette held fast to his hands. "Now I need you to be brave. The bravest you've ever been. Can you do that?"

Caden nodded, wiping his nose across his arm. "Yeah."

"Good, because Melody is going to need you to be the best, bravest, big brother." Odette pulled him into a hug.

He wrapped his arms around her and rested his head on her shoulder. "I love you, Ettie."

Odette couldn't stop the rush of her own tears and tried to blink them back. "I love you too. Forever and always."

"Always and foreva." Caden clung desperately to her.

"Ettie?" Melody called, drawing their attention.

She was standing up in the crib, gripping the side. Her dark blond hair was like her father's. With a sudden rush, she missed the only man she'd ever considered a father. Melody was rubbing her eyes and her pink cheeks made her look so young.

"That's my big girl!" Odette said, picking up Melody and twirling her around. "I'm so happy you are finally awake. We have a few hours before the carriage arrives. Lady Minerva has agreed to let us have a tea party with sweets and cakes."

"Yum!" Melody exclaimed.

Caden didn't appear as convinced. He put on a brave face though and she ruffled his hair. It didn't take her long to change and dress Melody. Lynn was already waiting in the parlor. She was wiping tears from her eyes on her apron.

"Lynn?" Odette was surprised by her show of emotion.

"Oh, Miss Odette." Lynn sniffled and tried to smile to hide the tears. "Ya're early."

Caden ran over to Lynn and threw himself against her legs, holding onto her skirts. Lynn laughed before reaching down to pick him up. Bouncing him in her arms, she kissed his cheeks.

"Ya sure are the sweetest, darling," Lynn said, patting his head. "I am going to miss you mightily."

Lynn had apparently been spoiling them. Odette was moved by her words and had a sudden thought. "Would you care to join us?"

Lynn blinked in surprise. "Me? Oh no, I couldn't."

"Peas?" was Caden's version of "please."

"Yes, join us for tea," Odette insisted.

Melody clapped her hands. "Tea, tea!"

"It wouldn't hurt for a few minutes." Lynn seemed quite pleased as she sat down on the loveseat. "It'll be such a lovely memory of you darlings."

Lynn patted each of the children's heads as they crowded around the shorter table situated between the two couches. Odette sat across from them, focusing on pouring the tea into the cups and pretending with Melody's bottle. They sipped tea and pretended to be princesses and princes.

"What is this?" Lady Minerva stood in the doorway.

They'd all moved to the floor and were draped in scarves Lynn had unearthed from somewhere. Wide eyes glanced at each other and their newest addition. Odette stammered, trying to think of something to defuse the situation as Lynn struggled to stand and slipped the fancy hat off her head.

"Forgive me, Mistress." Lynn bowed her head as she made her way towards the doorway.

Lady Minerva put her cane down sharply, blocking Lynn's path. "I asked for an explanation."

"We're having tea, like a prince and princesses." Odette felt her cheeks burn from embarrassment.

To Odette's surprise, her grandmother smiled. "You have tea without inviting the queen?" There was stunned silence after her announcement.

"Tea!" Melody blurted as she waved her bottle around.

The room filled with laughter as Lady Minerva took a seat. Until that moment, Odette didn't think her grandmother had interacted with her siblings. She had assumed Lady Minerva didn't like children, but as she interacted with Melody, and eventually Caden, that didn't seem to be the case.

An hour later, Lynn returned with the children's coats. The carriage had come and Odette helped them put their coats on and went to the door. The entire world felt off kilter and so dark. They each had a little pile of luggage that contained a few articles of clothing and presents from the household. She mutely watched as the carriage was prepared.

"Ettie?" Melody was staring at her with big round eyes.

Caden was openly crying and doing a poor job of trying to hide it. That's when she remembered the dolls she'd made. Rushing back into the room, she picked them up. Once back before her siblings, she knelt in front of them.

"For each of you," she said as she handed one doll to each child. "When you miss me, just look at the dolls and know I'm thinking of you." She kissed each of their heads. "I love you both." Tears threatened once again as she took one last look at them. Hugging them close, she stood and faced the maid and pair of guards that Lady Minerva had hired to escort them. "Please take care of them."

As the children were picked up, they began to call out to her. "Ettie?" She had explained to them that they'd be leaving without her, but they were so young.

"Stay together!" she called as they were placed in the carriage. She stood in the courtyard long after they were gone.

A firm hand touched her shoulder, drawing her out of her daze. "They've gone."

Odette turned into her grandmother's chest and held tight. She felt a hand on her back, comforting her as she started to sob. Now she truly was alone, the world she'd always known was behind her and the uncertainty of her future was in front of her. So many negative emotions swirled within her, except for one. The determination that all of this would be worthwhile.

-Present-

Vallerdale Hall was situated high on a hill framed by a steep mountain in the distance and overlooked the city below. Its dark gray stone matched the wall that surrounded it. Further in the distance, rising above the forest that existed beyond the castle's defensive walls, was the Shield of the North. It was almost inconceivable to imagine how such an imposing piece of construction was made, especially since it was made of such a heavy stone—granite.

"What is that darker stone?" Odette asked, pointing to the castle's upper battlement.

"Slate," Jareth answered.

It would be impossible not to be impressed, and slightly intimidated, by the building off in the distance, and she could only see the top half, as the outer wall was blocking the rest of it. I

"When will we be there?" Odette asked, straining to see more as they approached the outskirts of the city.

"Thirty minutes at most," Jareth replied.

Suddenly she could hear a mighty roar in the distance. "What is that?" Odette thought monsters were attacking again.

He chuckled. "Halt."

The carriage slowed as Odette tried to understand what the growing racket was. Jareth exited first but turned back to help her from the carriage. When she stepped out, they were just beyond the city's gates. Inside were hundreds of people cheering.

"Up you go," Jareth said.

"Wait, why up here?" Odette asked, confused.

His hands encircled her waist, and she was suddenly on a horse. A moment later, Jareth joined her as she stared around in wonder. As he urged their horse forward, she was shocked at how happy the people were to have their lord returning. "The Hero of Mount Vere" or "The Dragon Slayer" were the most common thing she heard, in addition to "my lord" and "Lord Chadwick." She couldn't believe her eyes—a place who loved their lord. Her father had never received such fanfare when he returned. Even when he went to the capital for over a year, there was only a solemn ensemble of unenthusiastic compliance; this was true celebration. Some seemed curious about her, but most were more interested in their returning knights and lord.

She turned around abruptly to question its regular occurrence. "Is this…?" The words died as she realized how close he was.

Glancing up, their noses were practically touching. "Yes?" Jareth asked, his words barely audible over the noise.

Odette swallowed. What had she been about to ask? This close, he was every bit the hero atop his faithful stead. The sunlight lit up his entire face, and although his expression was controlled, she could tell with sudden clarity that he was happy. It made him seem to glow in a soft yellow light. For a moment she was transfixed.

"Odette?" Jareth's arm that was holding her in place tightened. "What is it?"

"They're all here for you," Odette whispered, in awe of him.

A voice boomed over the crowd. "Who be that with you, Lord Chadwick?"

A man stood on a cart, he was short, and his auburn hair was braided. His hands were on his hips as the crowd quieted around him. Odette couldn't see him clearly because her back was turned to him and only caught a glance of him over her shoulder.

"Don't be causing trouble, Mac," Sir Lex said, but Jareth spoke louder.

"My wife."

The attention had been one thing when it was on the knights; but once more it swiveled to her. She shifted closer to Jareth, as though to shield herself from their prying eyes. The crowd was a buzz with sudden excitement about who this mysterious Lady Chadwick was. Apparently, they'd traveled faster than the news of their wedding. Mac jumped down and joined them in the street. He stood a respectful distance away as he walked beside them.

"I had heard rumors you'd snagged a bride," Mac said, wagging his finger at Jareth. "Was it this lassie's beautiful face that melted your frozen heart?"

Odette bristled at his effrontery and disrespect of her husband. She immediately sat up straight and met Mac's inquisitive gaze head-on. No one would disrespect her husband.

"Better a cold heart than a loudmouth." Her voice was only loud enough for Jareth and Mac to hear.

Mac's eyebrows shot up, but his jolly laughter returned as he hit his fist on his chest when a ragged cough took hold. She forced herself to keep the haughty expression on her face, but inside she was suddenly very aware of what she'd done. Her grandmother had warned her that her sharp tongue may one day get her into trouble.

"You like them fiery, it seems," Mac called, slowing his footsteps as they reached the end of the city's road.

"How else do you think she melted my heart?" Jareth asked, his voice containing that same tone of amusement.

Odette turned her head to meet his gaze. She heard the crowd chanting for them to kiss as they reached the gate. He leaned forward and she expected him to comply with their request, and so she closed her eyes. Instead of her lips, she felt him kiss her forehead. Her eyes shot open as Jareth urged the horse forward and she was jostled against his armor. Although she appreciated him keeping to decorum, Odette couldn't deny the disappointment. She'd wanted him to kiss her and declare to everyone that he'd married her because he loved her. If he'd done that, she might have convinced herself it was true.

Chapter 17

-Past-

After her siblings had left, Odette spent more time with Lady Minerva. She no longer embroidered just to try and get on her grandmother's good side as now; she almost enjoyed it. Although she wasn't very proficient, she often joined the dowager duchess by the fireplace to work on her stitching. It was one such evening, when they were by the fire, that Odette let her secret slip out. Winter had come and with it a horrible snowstorm. It was not uncommon for them to get snow, but they'd been buried in it that season.

Lady Minerva complained of typical aches and pains, so she'd spent much time in her chair with a wrapped hot water bottle on her hip. Odette would refresh the water from time to time with the hot water pot that was set next to their teapot.

Rubbing at her eyes, Odette set the iris she'd been stitching on her lap. Two of her fingers had bandages wrapped around them, and she was starting to get a headache as the fire was beginning to die down. Standing, she stretched and tossed some logs on the fire.

"More tea?" Odette asked.

"That would be nice." Lady Minerva didn't stop in her quick and precise movements.

Odette took hold of the teacup and immediately felt love. It shocked her how deeply her grandmother felt it—and it was for her. The teacup clattered on the saucer as she stared in shock.

"Do you really love me that much?" Odette asked. Although she knew her grandmother was fond of her, she'd never guessed it was to that level.

"What did you say?" Lady Minerva's eyes narrowed.

"I..." Odette realized her mistake too late. "That is..." No words came to mind as her stomach twisted in knots.

Lady Minerva looked at the teacup and then at her. "What made you say that? Be honest with me."

Odette felt the truth bubble out of her. "I felt it. On the cup."

"You can feel my emotions?" She set down her needlework and turned her full attention on her. "Can you do anything else?"

"I can feel everyone's emotions," Odette admitted. "But only on stuff."

"Have you told anyone else?" Her voice sounded urgent, almost angry.

"No." Odette felt tears threaten.

Lady Minerva let out a sigh. "Do you understand what you have?" Her words were direct, but she sounded sad.

Odette nodded. "I'm a Mystic."

"That is right." She waved her hand. "Go and lock the door."

Odette did as she was told. Her hands were shaking slightly when she threw the lock. When she tried to sit back down, Lady Minerva reached over and pulled her by the arm until she was standing directly in front of her.

"You may not know it, but your father is a Magician, and your grandfather was a Mage. It is a secret." Her voice was pitched low.

"I thought having powers was...good?" Odette wondered why her grandmother wasn't thrilled.

"It can be, but it is also a burden," Lady Minerva said, gravely. "I am going to tell you something, that you must never tell another soul." When Odette nodded, she continued. "Every few generations, a Wolverson is born with the ability to create wealth. Your father has the ability. It comes in different forms, but the ability to create gold and gems always has at least one level, typically the Mage or Magician level."

"Why is that bad?" Odette asked, when her grandmother paused.

"The wealth is made by blood, sweat, and tears." She must have seen the confusion on Odette's face because she added. "Rubies for blood, diamonds in tears, and opals in sweat. That is what comes out of your father."

"But that's amazing!" Odette exclaimed, excited.

Lady Minerva shook her head. "Imagine if everyone knew. What do you think they would do to my son?" Understanding hit Odette square in the chest as the older woman continued. "They would butcher him, cut him for his powers, until they bled him dry of every last ruby."

"That's horrible." Odette tried to swallow the thick lump in her throat.

"Unless you are blessed like a hero, it is best to keep your powers hidden. People fear what they do not comprehend." Lady Minerva shook her a little. "Do you understand?"

Odette bobbed her head, her chest tight with terror. "I'll never use them again."

"I didn't say that." Lady Minerva leaned back. "When it comes time to find you a match. I shall use this to our advantage. For prominent families looking for those with gifts such as yours, it shall be the ticket to win you a first born."

"Are you sure?"

Lady Minerva chuckled. "Do you think you are the only Mystic in this room?"

Odette gasped. "You?"

"Yes. How do you think I see so well at my age?" Her grandmother patted by the corner of her eye. "I can see in the dark."

"What else can you do?" Odette asked, eagerly.

"Nothing else. Sometimes we do not progress beyond Mystic. Yet I have a feeling you will," Lady Minerva said, patting her cheek. "Starting tonight, we shall begin training you to control your ability. Perhaps then one day you shall be a Magician like your father."

-Present-

The castle was old, but it was well maintained. It looked like a claw coming up from the ground. Unlike the city, which had buildings made of rock and wood, Vallerdale Hall was all stone. It had been made for functionality not beauty, and yet there were little additions that showed past owners had pride in its existence. Kira was right, the stained glass almost made the entrance charming.

Jareth dismounted first and then helped her down. "Welcome home, Lady Chadwick."

Before she could react to his words, he picked her up princess-style. She gasped but didn't fight it; it was a normal thing for newlyweds to do. He carried her up the stairs like she weighed nothing. His strength was a marvel to her as they entered the hall. It was sparsely adorned, but the stained glass made the room full of all manner of colors. Servants were standing in formation at the entrance with an older man standing at the front.

Jareth set her down and she straightened her skirts as the elder man stepped forward and bowed. "Welcome back, Lord and Lady Chadwick."

"Kenith." Jareth reached out and shook his hand, patting him on the shoulder. "I see you kept the place from falling apart."

"As always, I do my best," Kenith replied with a genuine smile.

"Daddy!" Kira cried, throwing her arms around her father.

"My goodness, you've grown, and here I thought you'd have learned some manners." Kenith shook his head, but his smile didn't diminish at all. "Forgive me, Lady Chadwick. My daughter has much to learn from a fine lady such as yourself." He seemed a little apprehensive as he addressed her.

"Nonsense," Odette said, hoping she might put him at ease. "Kira has been a fine lady's maid for me." Kira had been away at school for some time and had hinted how much she missed her family more than once.

Kira beamed at her words. "Thank you, my lady!"

"Shall I show the lady to her room?" Kenith asked.

Odette opened her mouth, but Jareth took hold of her hand and tucked it under his arm. "I'll show her."

"As you wish, my lord." Kenith and the other servants bowed.

"Kira, join me shortly, in time to dress for dinner," Odette called over her shoulder as Jareth led her away.

Kira curtsied. "I shall."

"You needn't stand on formalities here," Jareth assured her. "You can dress and wear what you wish."

"It is my first night. I'd like to change into dinner dress." Odette knew it was silly, but the familiar routine would be nice. Even if her father didn't give her new clothing, he always made sure she followed proper etiquette.

"How do you find Vallerdale Hall?" Jareth asked. He sounded off—almost apprehensive.

For a moment she hesitated, unsure how to answer since she'd seen so little of the place. "It is well cared for and I found the stained glass quite…charming."

"Do you…like it?"

"Of course." She was confused. "It is your home. Why would I not like it?"

He licked his lips. "I know it is not as grand as where you grew up." The rest went unsaid.

Odette realized, with sudden clarity, that he was nervous. Her opinion of Vallerdale Hall mattered a great deal to her husband. He was comparing Duke Wolverson's castle to this military fortress. Although she had to admit they were not on equal footing, Jareth's home was not without its merits.

"Like any new place, it will take me some time to settle in." She had moved many times in her life, even if he didn't know it, and her least favorite place had been the duke's principal residence. "I never liked my father's house. My grandmother had a smaller property that I spent my childhood in." That was not completely untrue. "It was not as grand, but she made it a home. I believe I can do the same here."

He visibly relaxed as they entered a decently adorned hallway. "You may decorate whatever you wish. Change what you do not like. Everything within Vallerdale is yours to alter; I don't care what you do with it."

Odette shook her head. "There must be something you like that you wish to stay the same."

"They are just objects," Jareth said firmly. "Your comfort is more important."

"What needs the most work?" Odette asked.

"The conservatory. It used to serve as the mistress's private gardens." He opened a door and led them through it as she contemplated his words. "This is your room. I had them pull furniture from storage. You may replace whatever you wish."

The room was set in soft purples and blues. Hydrangeas were embroidered on the curtains and much of the decorations matched. The flowers were even painted on the white furniture. She found it charming, although some of it was a little too lavish for her tastes.

"Jareth." She put her hand on his arm. "It is lovely."

His lips brushed across her temple. "Settle in; I'll see you at dinner."

He let her go and turned to leave when she called out, "Where is your room?"

Jareth halted, his hand reaching for the doorknob. He seemed embarrassed for a moment before he gestured to a door within her room. "They are adjoining rooms. Should you ever need anything, you have only to unlock your side." He cleared his throat. "I will never lock my side."

Chapter 18

Odette arrived at dinner, surprised to find Jareth sitting at one end of the long table and her place setting arranged on the other end. For a moment, she was reminded of the duke's dinners, where she'd been treated like an unwanted guest. It made her throat feel tight.

She stiffly took her seat on her side of the table. She'd dressed in a beautiful green and black gown that had draping fabrics and sheer sleeves, in hopes of catching his attention. Yet he'd hardly seemed to notice her as he kept his nose buried in the document he was reading. When the food was laid in front of her, she ate slowly, watching Jareth as he also consumed his meal while he continued to read. Why didn't he realize how unhappy she was?

Groaning internally, she realized she was waiting for him to save her. How foolish when she could simply manage her own happiness. Her grandmother would be disappointed in her dependance.

"Jareth?" Odette asked, gathering her courage.

He glanced up from the document. "Yes? Is something not to your liking?"

Odette shook her head. "May I dine beside you?"

His eyebrows shot up in surprise. "Is this not the proper way to dine?"

"Was it not you who said I needn't stand on formalities?" She stood and turned to a servant. "Please move my place setting next to Lord Jareth's."

"Yes, my lady," a younger servant said, bowing before her, and a fellow servant rushed to comply.

Jareth stood quickly to pull out her chair himself. She gratefully took the seat as the servants put everything back in its place in front of her. She expected her husband to pick his papers back up, but he was watching her eat instead.

"Do you want to ask me something?" Odette asked, smiling to let him know she wasn't upset.

"You continue to astound me," Jareth replied, his voice as direct as his gaze.

Laughter unexpectedly bubbled out of her. "That isn't a question."

To her surprise, Jareth reached out a hand, palm up. It was not normal to show such displays of affection, even though it was only in front of the staff, and for a moment Odette hesitated. He must have seen her hesitancy, because he shifted closer. Her fingers brushed his palm a moment before he brought her knuckles to his lips.

"Jareth," she whispered, trying to gently retract her hand, but he held it in place.

"Everyone is dismissed," Jareth said.

The servants were quick to comply, closing the doors behind them. Jareth kissed her hand one more time before letting it go. She placed it into her lap where her other hand was waiting. How could such a little thing make her heart clench so hard?

"Why did you have everyone leave?" Odette asked, thinking he was going to kiss her or something else that others shouldn't see.

"So we can talk freely," Jareth said with a smile, "and you can eat without having to stand on decorum."

He was right. Even though there was no longer a need to use proper etiquette, it was too deeply engrained for her not to. She'd been taught the way to eat as though she were living art. A picture of grace and refinement. The downside was it took so much time, each movement methodical, and the portions miniscule.

Odette took a large swallow of her wine as she realized how silly it all was. The food was delicious when she didn't have to focus on how she was eating it and could just enjoy it. The savory flavor of the steak was perfect, and she ate every bite. In the past she would have left food, to show she was dainty, but why waste?

When her plate was clean and her stomach full, she looked at her husband. He seemed content and comfortable, as he leaned back in his chair. His plate was also empty, and he cradled his glass of wine, his gaze fixed on her.

Odette stood suddenly, surprising them both. "Please walk with me?" She knew they would normally turn in for the night, but she didn't want to be parted from him yet.

Arm in arm, they left the room. "Where would you like to go?"

"The gardens; I haven't seen them yet," Odette said, hoping she sounded convincing.

Jareth stopped in the hallway, and her heart fell into her stomach. He slipped off his jacket and held it up for her. "Wear this. It is still chilly at night and that dress, although lovely, will hardly keep you warm."

"Thank you." She slipped his jacket on, instantly surrounded by his scent.

Moments later, when they stepped outside, Odette was thankful for it. Unlike further south, the northern evenings still had a noticeable bite to them. Instinctively, she shifted closer to Jareth, drawn to his warmth. It seemed to radiate off him, like his body was the sun.

"Too cold?" Jareth asked.

"Not with you here," she replied honestly and then realized what that implied. "I mean, you are very warm."

Jareth chuckled as he accepted her closeness. "I always have been. Your body adjusts to the cold after a time. Soon it will not bother you as much."

"How long did it take you?" Odette asked, trying and failing to brace herself against the cold wind that swept even Jareth's heat away. "To adjust I mean."

"A year; once I went through a full cycle." Jareth kept them close to the house.

Odette barely saw the gardens as she went through the cycle of his warm comfort, to the cold breeze pulling it away, then the return of warmth, only to have it taken away again. She knew the moment she shivered, or her teeth chattered, he'd march them right back inside and this evening would end. Perhaps she might not see him until their next dinner, a whole day away.

"How long do you think I'll take?" Odette asked, not believing only a year would be enough.

He shrugged his shoulders. "Oh, in your case, it'll take multiple years."

Gasping, her head swiveled up just in time to catch the twinkle in his eye. "Jareth!" His mischievous streak always caught her off-guard.

His arm went around her as he laughed heartily from his core. It was such a free laugh that she felt a zing of happiness. She joined him, feeling the tension from earlier melt away.

"Come on," he said, steering them back towards the door. "It is far too cold out here."

She nodded as they went back into the warmth of the castle. Her cheeks and nose burned from the sudden change in temperature, but it wasn't warm enough. When she shivered, Jareth marched them directly towards their rooms as he ordered servants to draw a bath.

When they reached her door, she paused. She thought back to their journey and how many times they'd shared a bed. Yet here, in their home, she was expected to be alone. Although she wasn't ready to perform her wifely duties, she found the idea of a cold, empty bed quite unappealing.

"If you hesitate like that, it may give me the wrong type of hope." Jareth's finger hooked under her chin, turning it up so he could plant a chaste kiss on her lips. "It should be very warm. I made sure the servants heated the room and your bed."

Odette opened her mouth but realized what she wanted to say wouldn't be fair to her husband. He was right; if she asked him to join her, it would be sending the wrong message. It would be better if she simply slept alone.

"It seems I will forever be thanking you for your kindness." Odette pecked his cheek. "I shall see you tomorrow."

Although his eyes were still warm, his face was suddenly composed. "Rest well."

Odette watched him go before sighing. She very much doubted she'd be getting any rest at all.

Chapter 19

-Past-

Odette was exceedingly nervous. For nearly two years she'd been living with her grandmother and today was the first day she'd meet her sisters. Already twelve years old, Odette was the eldest of all her siblings. Her father had given her two sisters from his legitimate marriage—Jestine was the closest to her in age at ten and Grace was eight. It made her wonder how much Melody had grown after all these years. She'd be the same age Caden was the last time she'd seen them.

Shaking her head, she schooled her emotions, just as her grandmother had taught her. The summer day was warm with a soft breeze, but the frosted glass roof above the veranda kept the worst of the sun at bay. Birds sang in the tops of trees and bees sampled sweet nectar from nearby flowers. They helped her find her center as she waited, impatiently, for the moment to come.

When she heard voices just inside the door, Odette stood and smoothed the front of her dress. Lady Minerva had reminded her, more than once, she only had one chance at a first impression. When it came to her sisters, she hoped it might be a good one. As far as society would be concerned, they would be the only siblings she'd have moving forward.

Two ebony crowned girls entered; their black locks seemed almost blue in the light. Their skin was pale and their dresses of the finest quality. Odette had been gifted a dress of equal quality, but theirs was covered in special adornments that displayed their family's vast wealth. When she saw their eyes, as green as her own, she was reassured they were in fact her sisters.

"Have fun, girls," Lady Minerva said, before taking her leave.

"Welcome to my garden party. I am Odette." Odette curtsied flawlessly. Her sisters followed suit.

"I am Jestine Wolverson," the eldest said, her countenance standoffish.

"Thank you for inviting us. I am Grace." The eight-year-old curtsied better than Odette had. It reminded her that two years could not make up for a lifetime of study.

"Please," Odette said, sweeping a hand, "take any seat you wish."

Although Jestine seemed almost annoyed, Grace happily took a seat. "Is this lemonade?" She pointed excitedly at a pitcher.

"Yes. With strawberries." Odette could still remember how decadent the honey-sweetened drink had been the first time she'd tried it.

Millie, a servant, stepped forward to fill her cup. When she turned to Jestine, her sister waved her away. "I prefer sparkling waters." She seemed to be putting on airs. She may prove to be a difficult nut to crack.

"I will take some lemonade, please." Odette hoped it would alleviate the situation. "I heard you have been busy with a governess and other tutors; I am happy the duke permitted your absence," Odette said, trying to make small conversation.

Jestine eyed the food with tight lips. "Let us hope it does not put us behind." A very tough nut indeed.

"I for one appreciate the break," Grace said matter-of-factly before eating one of the sandwiches.

Perhaps there was hope yet. "Do you enjoy your studies?" Odette asked, taking a sip of lemonade.

"They are exhausting," Grace said with a groan. "But I do enjoy the dance lessons, though we have only just begun. And the piano is quite nice. Really anything but book study is…well wonderful."

"You're rambling," Jestine hissed.

Grace suddenly ducked her head, her cheeks turning pink. Odette tried very hard not to scold Jestine for her bad behavior. Truly, she wasn't wrong, but why was a reprimand necessary when Grace was only eight? It seemed rather harsh.

"I prefer rambling to silence." Odette tried to be reassuring. "Please speak freely. Have you tried any other instruments beyond the pianoforte?"

"The harp—but I do not like the strings. They hurt my fingers and are so hard to pluck. Plus, Jestine is much better at it." Grace seemed encouraged by Odette's words but was picking at the tablecloth.

"That is because you give up too easily." Jestine rolled her eyes before picking up a cookie.

"I would very much like to hear you both play," Odette said, genuine in her enthusiasm.

Jestine sighed. "Grandmother does not have a harp."

"She has taught me a little on her piano," Odette said. She'd been too busy with other things to focus on learning instruments, though she would have to start soon. "Perhaps you can show me more later?"

"I would like that," Grace said but Jestine gave her a look. "That is, if there is time."

"Let us hope that there is," Odette said, but felt the chasm Jestine was trying to make between them.

The next ten minutes was spent discussing the weather and reflecting on the color of the tablecloth and napkins. They discussed dresses, but Jestine said very little. Her sharp eyes watched them closely, deterring any conversation that built any sort of future between them. It did not take long for Odette to surmise the duke had not kept the truth of her birth to himself. Part of her was afraid Lady Minerva would put her out on the street, while another part of her wished to return home. It was only the promise to her mother that kept

Odette's temper in check. She repeated it like a mantra, focusing on making a future for herself.

"I'm full," Jestine declared, glancing at a servant. "As it is a few hours back to Wolf Castle, we should leave now."

Odette was taken back by this declaration. "I had thought you were staying the night. That is what our grandmother said."

When Jestine stood, Odette did as well, moving closer to her. She swallowed down her hurt as her stomach twisted into knots. How much could Jestine dislike her?

"My father said to return before nightfall," Jestine replied, her nose in the air. "Come along, Grace."

"Wait!" Odette put a hand out, to try and waylay them.

Although she was far from actually making contact with either of them, Jestine screeched like she'd been burned. "Don't touch me with your dirty hands." Her entire body shrank away from Odette's fingertips.

"They aren't..." the protest died in her throat when she realized what Jestine meant.

Suddenly, the doors flew open, and Lady Minerva was standing there. "What has happened?" She sounded alarmed, but Odette couldn't look at her.

Jestine grabbed Grace's hand. "My father said we didn't have to stay if we didn't want to. We are going home." Without waiting for an answer, she stormed through the open door past their grandmother.

"What happened?" Lady Minerva asked, before following her granddaughters. Odette only shook her head.

The servants left and for a moment she was alone. Her fingers reached out and blindly felt the arm of the chair Jestine had been sitting in. Her vision was blurred as the emotion of disgust swarmed into her senses, tears falling down her cheeks in angry droves. She had never done anything to her sisters to warrant such treatment. That is why she knew it really wasn't them; they hadn't formed such emotions on their own. It was the duke, her so called father. She may only be twelve, but she knew that children didn't hate naturally—they were taught to hate. That was the lesson the duke had taught her—to hate.

-Present-

To her surprise, she found Jareth waiting for her at breakfast. His nose was buried in a long letter and his brows furrowed so tightly it made him seem years older. His plate was empty and the tea no longer steaming. So absorbed was he, that she sat down before he even noticed she was there.

"Good morning," she said as he set the letter down.

"Did you sleep well?"

"Yes." When she'd finally been able to fall asleep. "And you."

"Well enough." He cleared his throat. "I need to do an inspection of the wall and see to a village nearby that is having trouble."

She nodded, trying not to let it upset her. "How long?"

"Two days, maybe three, if things go poorly." He sighed. "I'd hoped to put this off, but I'm afraid it can't wait. It may be a major issue in the foundation."

"I understand." She forced a smile.

He seemed relieved as he sat back in his chair. "Jay and I finalized the finances last night. Kenith will show them to you, and then give you a more thorough tour after breakfast."

When he stood, she was caught off-guard. "You're leaving now?"

"It is unavoidable," Jareth replied, stiffly. "Sir Lex will be remaining to oversee a few tasks. Should you run into trouble, and Kenith is busy, Sir Lex is also at your disposal."

"Is Sir Mance also staying?" Odette asked hopefully.

A few unrecognizable emotions passed over his face before they settled behind a blank mask. "He'll be accompanying me."

"I see. Please do wish him well. And you also, have a safe journey," Odette managed, feeling suddenly awkward. It was as though the man from last night was a different man this morning. What had caused him to be so changed?

Jareth moved towards her then stopped. He stood there, looming over her a moment before she looked up at him. His eyes appraised her, searching desperately for something. She lifted a hand, offering it in the hopes he wished to bid her farewell. At a loss, she felt the soft brush of his lips before he abruptly dropped her hand.

"Take the time to settle in," Jareth said. Then he left so quickly she felt like he was fleeing her.

Had she done something wrong? Her chest felt so tight that after a few bites she abandoned her meal. Feeling guilty at the waste, and overcome by Jareth's sudden change in mood, she fell upon Kenith when she saw him.

"My husband bid me find you so we might review the ledgers." Odette was overcome with nervous energy, and she hoped staring at rows of numbers would quell it.

"Certainly, my lady," Kenith said, and led her into a massive study.

Unlike other places she had gone, this place reminded her of Jareth. It had been modernized with simple dark woods and rich maroon colors. There were two paintings on the wall, one of a mountain and the other of the ocean. Both seemed surprisingly lonely to her—almost desolate.

She carefully took a seat as Kenith began explaining the financial books. She found them in perfect order, but that was no surprise. The black, maroon, and blue books were all for different operations within Vallerdale Hall. When he showed her the newly created purple one, designated for her, she wondered if the garden could be done in one year.

"And if I needed to increase this amount for a project?" Odette asked, tapping her finger on a number.

"The master instructed I provide whatever funds you need. Should that not be enough for this month, you need but ask," Kenith answered patiently. "Is there something you had in mind that I might assist with?"

Odette swallowed heavily, nearly choking as she inhaled. "This is my monthly stipend?" She'd assumed it was an annual figure—the amount far too generous.

"Yes, mistress." Kenith shifted at her words.

She cleared her throat and smoothed her expressions. "Is that separate from the grounds work? I had hoped to see what might be done about the conservatory. Lord Jareth indicated it was an area of great need."

"The lord also asked that funds be set aside for such an effort," Kenith said, shifting to the maroon book.

"May I see it?" Odette asked, suddenly curious.

"Happily, mistress," Kenith replied, taking a few loose papers out and laying them before her.

She read through them, surprised at how substantial the total was. It made her wonder at the current state of the conservatory. Did it truly need that much? She'd never been put in charge of anything but refused to let her grandmother's efforts go to waste.

"Perhaps it would be best to see the state it is in," Odette said, standing. Her skirts hit the papers, knocking them from the desk. "Oh my!"

Kenith hurriedly picked them up as she blinked in surprise. "How clumsy of me." She bent to help retrieve some of the papers. "What are these?" She asked, as her eye was caught by a sketched picture on one of the pages.

Kenith set most of the bound papers back onto the desk. "When Lord Jareth returned, he ordered his steward to conduct an inventory and look into a few matters. These appear to be his reports."

Odette eyed the stacks of papers, wondering how much reading Jareth would be buried under when he returned. "Shall we go and see the conservatory now?"

"Certainly." He led her through the complex maze that was the castle. She knew eventually these halls would be as familiar to her as Wolf Castle was, but as with most things, it would take time. "It has been closed for decades but every few years the master would have us clean it. Mostly this was done to ensure the tree roots and branches didn't cause further damage."

"There is a tree?" she asked. Her father's estate had a very small conservatory, more of an indoor courtyard really. "Vallerdale Hall's conservatory must be extensive."

"The entire castle was built around it; here in the north there is a longer winter and the conservatory used to be used to host lavish parties prior to Master Rupert." Kenith paused and glanced back. "Have you not had a tour of the estate?"

"I have not." It was something that should have been customary after her arrival, but had been delayed.

"Lord Jareth had wished to do it himself. Would you prefer to wait for his return?" Kenith asked, continuing towards their destination.

"He wanted to show me himself?" She hadn't heard anything about it until that moment. He'd only mentioned something about Kenith doing it.

Kenith nodded. "We discussed it when reviewing the ledgers."

"Please, let us continue on to the conservatory, but after that I may wish to explore the estate while he is away." Odette very much wanted Jareth to show her. She wanted to see his home through his eyes. Yet he was gone and there was work to be done. Not to mention Kenith seemed so eager to show her—she would likely request he be her guide.

"This way."

They approached the massive doors made of glass, and it was easy to see they had been neglected, since one of the doors creaked loudly when Kenith opened it. The smell was of old earth, forgotten and abandoned. As she stepped onto the path, she saw most of the stonework was intact. Small blue tiles that seemed to be in a wave-like pattern. At the center was a massive area with a tree reaching up into the dome of the conservatory like fingers inside a bowl.

"I'll explore alone," Odette said, suddenly wishing to explore without an escort. "I am sure you have much to attend to."

"Are you able to return on your own?" Kenith asked, clearly worried.

"Even if I get lost, that will be part of the adventure." Odette couldn't help but laugh, feeling suddenly so free.

"Lunch is in a few hours. I shall return then if you have not found your way back." Kenith bowed and left.

Taking a deep breath, she closed her eyes and imagined the possibilities. Then she began to explore, taking a tally of broken or cracked planes and examining the plants that were no longer green or lively for further examination. She had never been drawn to fauna, so most of the plants were unfamiliar to her. Yet here, she felt protective of their existence. They had lived and seen lives of people who were gone. History within their very roots. When she reached the far side, she found a smaller secondary room that served as a sunroom. Old furniture was covered in drapery and the floor was slabbed. Plants had been hung from the ceiling but there were only barren potters now. In spite of its desolate state, Odette liked the potential the room held. It was large enough to host an intimate tea party but could also serve as a place to escape to. As her fingers brushed against the sheet covering one of the couches, she was certain this place would become her sanctuary.

Chapter 20

Sitting behind Jareth's desk, Odette's pen scraped against the parchment. With the last number written, she set the paper on the stack. Three days had passed since her time in the conservatory and in that time she'd accomplished much. She'd placed orders for replacement glass, new tiles, and plants from merchants, and found an artist to repair the broken statue in the fountain. Once she'd seen to that, she'd gone through the steward's notes to summarize them. She hoped this might help Jareth, but even more so, she needed to keep her mind occupied. The first two days hadn't been so painful, but now, on the third day, she wondered what delayed Jareth. Had something happened to him?

The sun was shining happily through the windows behind her, casting the warmest light into the study. Since she'd been spending so much time in this room, one of the maids had brought in flowers, and tea was always at the ready for her to drink. Mostly she took short strolls in the gardens and ate her dinners in the dining room; the rest of the time she'd spent walking between the study and the conservatory. In fact, she'd already visited the latter this morning, proud at the cleaned windows and tidied feel of the place, despite its unhappy plant residents.

By midmorning she had run out of tasks. The ledgers were updated, and the reports summarized. What in the world was she going to do with herself now?

A knock at the door interrupted her thoughts. Disheartened that it couldn't be Jareth, since he would not knock, Odette straightened. "Come in."

She'd expected Kenith to come in, or even the steward, Jay, but it was Sir Lex. Since learning of his story, and the friendship Jareth shared with him, Odette found his presence comforting. He was dressed down, in simple armor, opposed to the full battle armor she'd last seen him in, with a pale long-sleeved shirt. She realized in all the sunshine that his darker complexion had hidden some of his finer features; he was actually quite handsome. Odette had been so focused on Jareth, she'd failed to notice until that moment.

"Good morning, my lady," Sir Lex said with a bow.

"Good morning to you. It is very nice to see you," she said genuinely happy to see him. "Has there been any word from Lord Jareth?"

"Afraid not, but that is why I am here." Sir Lex strode closer to stand on the other side of the desk. "Imagine my surprise when I asked how you were settling in, only to discover you'd been practically living in here." He gestured around at the study.

Odette felt her cheeks warm. "Jareth left me in charge of the conservatory. That is, to oversee its restoration."

"Are you at a place you can take a break?" Sir Lex asked, his tone charming.

"As a matter of fact, I am. Is there something you need assistance with?" Odette asked, almost desperate to find another project.

Sir Lex barked out a laugh. "I'll be honest. I had my doubts as to why Jareth would be taken with a woman he'd only met once. It seems you are cut from the same cloth."

His honesty both startled and warmed her. Perhaps it was more the words than his frankness, but she felt suddenly closer to both him and Jareth. Already she felt more at home here than she ever had at Wolf Castle. Then the context of his words struck her—Jareth had met her before?

"What ever do you mean?" Odette asked.

"Come," Sir Lex said as he held out a hand. "I shall tell you while we walk."

Despite his informal way of speaking, he took her hand and held it aloft before placing it atop his arm. It was a very formal way to walk side by side, while still showing others that there was a closeness to the two. Like a brother and sister or a pair of friends. This implication was something Odette liked very much—she hadn't had a friend in a very long time.

"Where are we going?" Odette asked, suddenly aware as they turned into the hall that she'd never agreed to anything.

"It is somewhere Jareth asked me to show you, if you sought me out," Sir Lex said with a smile. "You shall see it when we arrive."

"Then shall you explain your earlier statement in the interim?" Odette did not want to admit how excited she was. Jareth had made so many arrangements for her comfort before he left. Perhaps her secret wish wasn't wrong.

"Ah, yes." There were those perfect teeth again, smiling coyly at her. "When Lord Rupert first took ill, Jareth spent every morning and night seeing to the estate—mostly from behind that desk. Sometimes he'd sleep for but an hour or two at night before rising again to handle matters. Despite that, whenever someone asked him for anything, his response was always about how he could help them. He never wondered how that person could instead provide assistance to the struggling little heir."

Odette stayed silent even though he had misunderstood her earlier question. "Did he struggle much?" Odette asked. "When he was younger, I mean."

Sir Lex's expression became solemn. "Yes, but his ability to endure and grow inspired all of us."

"I'm sorry." The words caught in Odette's throat. "How thoughtless of me. I forget you all came from difficult upbringings."

He patted her hand. "Do not pity us. Lord Rupert cared for all of us and gave us hope where we had none. I am better for it." He turned them to stop in front of a pair of large ornate doors. "Let us dwell on that no longer. We have arrived."

Odette laughed at his showmanship as he swept his right arm out. "Pray tell where here is. The suspense it truly too great."

Her hand dropped away from his arm as he stepped forward and opened both doors with a flourish. "I present, madam, the library."

A gasp escaped from her as she stepped into the massive room. It ascended into one of the castle's great towers. Rich wooden spiraling staircases and several levels filled with books. Some tombs were behind glass cases. She'd never seen anything like it in her life. Wolf Castle's library was larger than most, to be sure, but it was only two levels with bookshelves standing in the middle of the room. In this one, there were four levels, and all the books were against the wall on ornate shelves with sitting areas in the middle. A statue of a seated man, his chin upon his fist and an open book at his feet, was against the back wall. It took her a moment to realize that it wasn't candles but light stones that were placed in the lanterns. That's when she noticed the reason for the mostly empty center; a massive clock ticked away the hour, embedded in the floor. It was difficult to read from ground level but she imagined it was quite ingenious further up.

"It's beautiful."

"Jareth told me your favorite pastime was reading. He thought you might like it." Sir Lex came to stand beside her. "It seems he was right."

Odette nearly started crying, tears pricking her eyes as she fought to keep them at bay. First the peaches and then the library; did his kindness know no bounds? Now her own wishes felt so greedy. Did she need him to love her, when he cared for her so well? Perhaps it was time to re-evaluate that his actions were more powerful than his words. That she might consider showing him in the same way, to make him understand how much she cared for him through her conduct. Then he might understand how dear he was becoming to her.

The spines of the books were of every color, but most were muted gray or black. She reached out and touched one she'd read before as a child. The memories of her life before the duke came back to her. Even when the man who'd raised her had nothing, he ensured they'd have a happy home. He'd read to her before bed most nights; she'd fallen asleep many times to his smooth baritone voice.

"This is wonderful." She turned away to wipe at an errant tear. "I cannot thank you enough."

"I am, but the messenger," Sir Lex said proudly. "It is Lord Jareth's doing."

She cleared her throat to erase the emotion from her voice. "Yes, he is wonderful as well."

Chapter 21

-Past-

Odette was hunched into a ball, trying to disappear. Night had fallen, and with it, the barest of light penetrated her fortress of solitude. She was sandwiched between the windows and the curtain, her face pressed into her knees, and her dress acting like a pillow as her arms encircled her head.

She heard her grandmother enter the room. After a pause, she felt the curtains stir before the cushions shifted as her grandmother sat on the bench. Opening her eyes, but not lifting her head, revealed candlelight and an aged hand.

"What happened?" Lady Minerva asked softly, her voice the gentlest Odette had ever heard it.

Odette didn't move; she didn't want to vocalize what had happened. That would make it real and dash her hopes all over again. Perhaps in the future, when she was wed, this might all be worth it, but for now it was not. For now, she was cut deeply by what had happened. An ache so deep even her nose tingled painfully from the heartbreak.

"Odette?" Her grandmother pressed her to respond.

"They *hate* me." The word cut, as biting as the bitterest cold. After a pause, Odette expected words of comfort.

"They are the not the first to hate."

Odette sat up in shock, meeting her grandmother's earnest gaze.

"Nor will they be the last."

"Grandmother…" Odette said, but lost all notion of how to continue and instead settled on the truth. "I cannot change who I am."

"Your father will not bar you from entering society. As his eldest daughter, you bear a burden that is different from the rest. In a few short years you shall present yourself to society, but you also set a precedent for your sisters." Lady Minerva set the candle down on the windowpane. "My son recognized you will be helpful in forming alliances and bolstering the Wolverson name. He is not so foolhardy as to ignore that it is easier to legitimize you into our family, than to subject the family to ridicule by casting you off. The issue lies in his manner."

"Will he ever accept me?" Odette asked but part of her already knew the truth.

"Do not hope where there is none. It is better to accept that you shall be risen above your station and given opportunities that others dream of," Lady Minerva replied, and Odette's suspicions were confirmed. A hand covered her foot; it was warm and gentle. "I shall love you in your father's stead. I shall be your family, standing beside you when you show everyone that you're as much the duke's daughter as the rest of them."

Odette launched herself at her grandmother, throwing her arms around her neck and holding her close. Sobbing, she clung to her, feeling relief and love wash over her. For a moment she had felt alone in the world, separated and abandoned. Now she felt as happy as she'd been in her mother's household before death had taken her stepfather.

"I'll make you proud," Odette said, before burying her head into her grandmother's neck.

"Oh, dear girl," Lady Minerva said, her hand patting down the back of Odette's hair in a soothing fashion. "You already do."

-Present-

Another day had passed without news of Odette's husband. Sir Lex had checked on her in the morning and she'd insisted he join her for lunch. When it had been time to eat, he'd been called away to deal with a matter. So, she found herself back in the library, having seen to all other matters for the day. Today she'd decided to explore as much as she could instead of trying to discover the books. The spiral staircases and many reading nooks had clearly been designed by a brilliant mind. One that understood the heart of a bibliophile.

Odette explored all four levels of the library. The oldest books were at the bottom and received the most attention. The second level held modern books that focused on current events and other non-fiction writings. The third floor was every kind of fictional work from every era. The top housed magic and religious works. By the time she reached the uppermost level, night was settling in. Glancing at the ornate clock that lay under the floor on the ground level, she saw it was nearly time for dinner. If she didn't leave now, her food may be cold, or worse, she'd keep the cook waiting.

Grabbing a nearby book on the basics of magic, and adding it to the other book she'd picked on farming in the northern climate, she hurried back down the stairs. Clutching the books to her chest, she hurried towards the dining area. She'd decided against changing after the first day, determining that making Kira come and find her every day was inconvenient. After Kira had discovered her project, her lady's maid had been busy overseeing the tidying of the extra sunroom off the back of the conservatory, including restoration of the old furniture.

When a servant opened the door to the dining hall, Odette rounded the corner with a smile. She stopped dead in her tracks at the sight of Jareth seated at the head of the table. He was speaking with Kenith and a young man not much older than the lord was. She took a few hurried steps towards Jareth, excited to see him, but then remembered herself.

"Lady Chadwick." Kenith was the first to notice her.

"See to the preparations," Jareth commanded before dismissing them as he stood to pull out her chair.

"You're back," she managed before sitting down.

Jareth smiled as he retook his seat. "I am."

Odette had so many questions, but they all felt lost in a swirl of emotions raging within her. Had he always been so handsome? His facial hair had come in, giving him a more rugged look. He appeared no worse for wear despite the delay, perhaps even invigorated.

"Did you just arrive?" Odette asked, wondering how long he'd been back. No one had come to find her so she might greet her husband.

"Not even an hour ago," Jareth confirmed as the servants set their food in front of them. "I apologize for the delay. There was a goblin nest we had to root out and the repair took longer than expected. We were able to scout along the rest of the western wall so it will just require we do the same on the east."

"Then you are leaving again?" Odette asked, her heart sinking.

"In a few days. I expect to be gone longer, perhaps ten days since this length of wall is twice as long," Jareth said, partaking of the food.

Odette stared at her food, suddenly not hungry. The cook would be upset if she didn't eat anything, so she tried a bit of everything, even though most of it was flavorless to her. The wine caught in her throat as Jareth finished eating. She'd noticed he didn't like to speak and eat, doing one task or another but rarely mixing the two.

"Kenith and Taleb tell me you've been busy with the conservatory." He sounded excited and that helped ease her tension some. "May I see it?"

She shook her head. "It is far from ready. It would be best to wait for the supplies to arrive."

"Were you able to see the grounds?" Jareth asked, taking a drink from his wine glass.

Odette swallowed. "I've waited for you to show me."

He paused as he was about to take another drink, then very slowly he set it down. "You waited?"

She nodded. "Although Sir Lex showed me the library and Kenith provided a tour of the manor."

"Good," he said, his gaze intense. "How did you find the library?"

"I liked it very much." Odette felt a rush of excitement. "I have never seen so many books arranged so beautifully in all my life."

"I am glad," he said. "I wish for nothing more than your happiness."

Her admiration for Jareth mingled with more complicated feelings. "You seem devoted to it." The words were spoken thoughtlessly, but in earnest.

"I am." A dark expression flickered across his features and it was quickly gone, making her wonder if she'd imagined it. "I shall be busy in the morning but can take you around the grounds in the afternoon. There are a few things I must show you—and a surprise."

Odette felt like she was floating. "A surprise? What kind of surprise?"

He laughed loudly, startling one of the servants. "If I told you, it wouldn't be much of a surprise."

"That is true." Odette felt a little foolish. "Can I expect you after lunch then?"

"I shall meet you here for lunch and then we can begin our adventure," Jareth confirmed.

Suddenly, Kenith appeared carrying a tray with a single letter. "An urgent message."

Jareth picked it up and read who it was from. She couldn't see from where she sat, but whoever it was immediately caused Jareth's jaw to clench. He opened it hastily and read a few lines before his complexion became darker.

"Jareth?" Odette asked, suddenly concerned. "Is it bad news?"

"It is nothing to concern yourself with." He tossed it back onto the tray before speaking to Kenith. "Take it to the study; I'll read it later."

Odette didn't know why but the way he'd said it made her feel rejected. It wasn't the first time she'd been excluded, but this felt different. Jareth was so willing to give her the things she liked, that it felt horrible to be disregarded. Knowing Jareth, it was likely something he felt he could solve without her. Which meant it was either dangerous or a secret. Why did she suspect it was the latter? A quiet corner of her heart suspected her husband had many secrets.

"Did you go into town yet?" Jareth asked.

Odette shook her head. "I shall do so while you are away. I am sure Kira can show me around." Part of her had wanted to ask him, but she didn't want to be burden.

Jareth frowned at her words. "Let Lex know when you wish to go. He'll escort you both."

"I will," she conceded, setting her fork down.

He leaned towards her and she looked up hopefully. It was like he was on the edge of saying something, but stopped at the last minute. Her tongue felt heavy and her throat tight when he leaned back without a word. Why did she always feel like he wanted to share something but decided against it? Perhaps that feeling about him having secrets wasn't far off.

Clearing his throat, he stood, the chair scraping against the stone floor. "If you go into town, please be careful." He kissed the top of her head before leaving the room.

It dawned on her that he was treating her like a houseguest. She didn't think he was doing it to hurt her, but his actions kept giving her hope in ways she was beginning to suspect they shouldn't. Furthermore, it threw her emotions into constant confusion. For the first time in her life, she realized that kindness could be cruel.

Chapter 22

In the morning, she was slow to rise. When Kira tried to rouse her, Odette suggested they have breakfast in her private parlor. After weeks of mostly leaving Kira to do whatever she wished with a few exceptions, her lady's maid chatted excitedly, her face beaming as they shared the meal. Odette realized she should have spent more time with her and made a mental note to do so in the future.

"Everyone cannot stop talking about the Flower Festival that is taking place in a few weeks," Kira said, stirring her tea. "Do you think you and the lord will attend?"

Odette's stomach lurched. "Perhaps. Though Lord Jareth may not be back from his inspection by then."

Kira frowned deeply at her response. "Surely the lord will take you to such an important event. It is the largest one of the summer season; many call it the love festival."

That caught her attention more than anything. "Why in the world is a flower festival called that?"

Kira cleared her throat. "My mama says it is because more babies are born nine months after the festival than any other time."

Odette felt her cheeks warm. "Perhaps they should change the name then."

Kira laughed so hard she started to cough and had to drink some tea to clear her throat. Odette just shook her head, trying to think of a way to change the subject. She very much doubted her husband would care about a local festival, especially one about love. After crying herself to sleep the night before, she'd decided it was time to stop waiting and start doing something about it. It wasn't as though Odette had ever been very good at holding her tongue—a trait that will come in handy when her husband returned. It was time she faced her fears and started asking the difficult questions.

"Has there been any news about the orders I placed?"

"I haven't checked this morning, but I'll corner Taleb."

Did Odette detect a twinkle in Kira's eye? "Do you know Taleb well?" Odette inquired, trying not to sound too interested.

"My older brother is friends with him," Kira replied, sounding a little too indifferent. "We've known each other most of our lives."

"You've told me about your younger brother who is in the academy; what about your older brother?" Odette felt like she learned new things about her lady's maid every day. The day before, Kira had revealed she couldn't eat strawberries because they made her face swell up. Now she was hearing about an older brother for the first time.

"Nigel is in service to the king." The way Kira's lips went into a thin line implied there was much unsaid.

"As a guard or a knight?" Odette asked. She remembered most lower ranking families sent their children to serve the king in hopes of raising their house's name.

"No…" her voice trailed off. "He's a clerk."

Kira's uneager tone had Odette expecting her to say something dire. For a moment she sat there baffled. Wasn't a clerk a good profession? How was it any different from what their father, Kenith, was doing? After a moment contemplating, she just decided to ask. "And that's...bad?" Odette questioned gently.

"He was on track to become a justice." Kira's words came out in a rush. "Then he suddenly declared he was going to be a clerk. When father asked him why, he refused to give any explanation. I barely saw him the two years I was in the capital."

Odette agreed that it did seem like odd behavior. "I do not know your brother, but I'm sure he had his reasons." The words felt hollow, even to her own ears.

Suddenly there was a knock on the door and Odette sat up straighter as Kira went to answer it.

"Oh!" Kira's exclaimed.

Odette leapt from her seat, thinking something was wrong. But it was only Jareth who entered, carrying a bunch of crocuses. Their vibrant purple blended nicely with the rich blues of her room. His smile caught her attention; she felt as though he'd been distracted for days now, but there he was, looking at her intently again. Her heart started thudding in her chest. *Today would be the day,* she told herself. Today she'd muster the courage to speak her mind.

"Good morning, Odette. Kira. I hope you both are doing well." He held the flowers out to his wife. "I saw them in the garden on my way in. I thought they might be a welcome adornment to your living quarters."

"Thank you," Odette said, taking them from him. Her husband was truly a kind and thoughtful man.

Kira suddenly sprang forward. "Let me put them in a vase." They were out of Odette's hands in an instant as her lady's maid quickly rushed away.

"Shall we?" Jareth asked and Odette took his hand.

He swept her through the castle, showing the kitchen, the dining hall, the ballroom, and even the armory. Her head whirled as she tried to remember even half of the historical facts he was hurling at her. The fifth marquess of so-and-so helped modernize the ballroom three hundred years ago. The third marquess had a cellar built that was also used to hide contraband from the crown. It felt like her old governess, might demand a quiz on the history of Vallerdale Hall at the end of the tour.

The best part was Jareth was very animated; he spoke with such passion that Odette couldn't help but be transfixed. She was hanging on his every word, for no other reason than he was the one speaking. Finally, he took her up the wall and to the battlements; the wind was cold and slapped against her face as she stood at the top. Instinctively, she turned into him, trying to shield herself from the harsh winds.

"Perhaps this was a bad idea," Jareth said with a shake of his head. "I shall show you on a calmer day."

He turned them back towards the stairs.

Tears in her eyes from the biting wind, Odette tried to wipe them away as she sniffled. Reaching into her pocket, she retrieved her handkerchief. Wiping at her eyes and nose, she tried to compose herself.

"Is that mine?" Jareth asked.

Odette's surprise turned to shock—she'd completely forgotten it was there. In her hand was the handkerchief he'd given to her for the raspberries. It had become a memento for her. To remind her of that day at the temple.

"Yes." Her quiet voice shook from embarrassment.

"Why?" His words were gentle, hopeful even—or had she imagined that?

"Because it is yours." Her chest was tight.

He shifted closer to her, his hand against her jaw and his fingertips whispering across her hairline. He coaxed her towards him and she closed her eyes. His lips were sweet and soft against hers. She put her hands on his chest as she leaned into him, wishing to meld into his very being. She was at his mercy and yet eager for what he offered—this man who had given her yellow raspberries and peaches. She wanted every part of him to know every part of her. He deepened the kiss, his mouth wide and his tongue probing. Warm and fuzzy feelings tingled down her spine and fogged her brain. Yearning overtook every sense, matched quickly by passion.

Chatter from the bottom of the stairs caused Jareth to pull away from her. He was breathing as heavily as she was, their gaze locked. He took an unsteady step back from her, further down the stairs, but he didn't look away.

"By the gods you are beautiful," he said, his voice sounding hoarse.

Confidence surged through her as she smiled at him. "Jareth, I want this to be a true marriage."

He froze at her words, uncertainty flickering in his eyes. "It is a true marriage."

She swallowed heavily, trying to find the words. "Can it not be as it was while we traveled? Can we not have the same closeness?"

Was that confusion she saw? Her heart sank.

"Is that what you want?" The words were so low she almost didn't catch them all.

Odette suddenly steeled herself, expecting him to reject her. "Only if you want it too." She would not force her love onto him; that would be unfair. Yet it was he who had asked for her hand.

"Why do you look so sad?" He drew closer to her again and his tenderness made tears spring to her eyes. "Odette?"

"Do you regret your choice?" Odette's nose tingled painfully as she tried not to let a sob escape.

"Oh, Odette. Absolutely not," Jareth said, drawing her against him. "I believe there has been a fundamental misunderstanding. Did I not say before that I had wished we'd court normally?" She nodded, still pressed up against him. "I had wished to give us both time to come to terms with this marriage. To court as it were."

Odette jerked back in confusion. "But we're already married!"

"Yes, but though we may be married, we do not know each other well. I only wished to try to rewrite..." He hesitated, his face furrowed in concentration.

"What is it?" Odette urged him, thankful they were talking at last.

"To rewrite our first night." He seemed to glow in a soft blue, his entire posture crestfallen.

"Why did you cut your thumb?" she asked in a whisper.

His surprised expression met her own determined one. "How did you know?"

"I didn't; I guessed, but now you've confirmed it." She felt triumphant that her ability had led her to the right conclusion. "Now tell me why."

"You didn't bleed." He sighed heavily. "I thought your father might stop us, even though you were…pure. I didn't want to risk it. Risk anyone challenging our marriage."

She kissed his cheek. "Thank you for protecting my honor. And please, if you wish to do something, like court me even though we're married, please talk to me so I'm not confused."

He chuckled and leaned his forehead against hers. "Forgive me. I am used to just doing what I wish and issuing orders. I don't mind explaining myself, but the situation to do so rarely arises."

"There is nothing to forgive," Odette said before they kissed again. She was so happy she'd mustered up the courage to talk to him. "Can we discuss this more when you come back?"

"Why wait?" Jareth asked. "Let's talk all through dinner. I'll send the servants away so we're not the center of any scandal." His laughter was merry as he took her hand, and they went down the stairs together.

"They can be trusted," Odette said, her heart bursting with joy. "And we're married; what kind of scandal could we possibly cause?"

Chapter 23

-Past-

"Are you ready?" Lady Minerva asked.

Odette turned; her hair was piled on top of her head and her dress a deep purple. She was fourteen and already to be presented amongst the women. Her debut wouldn't happen until sixteen, but it was not uncommon for a maternal figure to introduce a young lady into society early. This was particularly true during the early or late season when some members of high society were not in residence.

"I believe I am." Odette felt like a goddess in the heavy fabric and the pearls at her throat.

"You are more than ready." Lady Minerva took Odette's hands and gracefully moved with her across the room. "You are a vision of grace and beauty."

Odette felt warm as she touched a hand to her cheek. "Grandmother!"

"But I believe something is missing," Lady Minerva said, before waving a servant over.

Odette glanced down, expecting to see something out of place. "What is it?"

Her grandmother opened a box and within were hairpins set with amethyst and pearls. "The final accent so that everyone knows you are a Wolverson."

Odette felt tears form and had to wave her hands to try and dry them. Without hesitation, her grandmother put the pins into her hair, setting them at the front and left side of her bun. Her grandmother kissed the top of her head, before framing her face with her gloved hands.

"You have surpassed every expectation," Lady Minerva said as the servants brought their cloaks. "Remember, above all else, you are a Wolverson."

"Thank you, Grandmother." Odette kissed her cheek. "I will honor the Wolverson name."

They exited the manor and went towards the carriage. Odette waited for her grandmother to enter when suddenly the older woman swayed. Odette's arms went around the older woman as Lady Minerva shook her head.

"Grandmother?" Odette asked as people surged around them. "What's wrong?"

"I was suddenly lightheaded." Lady Minerva rightened herself out of Odette's arms, waving off those around her. "Excitement and not enough lunch, I am sure. We must leave or we'll be late."

"We should cancel," Odette said, fear overtaking her. "Call a physician."

"You're overreacting. We shall do no such thing," Lady Minerva said, patting her hand.

"At least eat something in the carriage," Odette insisted, feeling helpless in the face of her grandmother's determination.

"Very well," she consented, as a maid hurried to comply. "But we mustn't delay a moment longer."

Despite the slight interruption they arrived at a fashionable time. Her grandmother had eaten and seemed better than she had earlier. She tried to focus on the coming dinner party, but her grandmother's dizzy spell weighed heavy on her mind. However, when Lady Minerva emerged from the carriage, she was regal. The house seemed to glow with light as they entered. The entrance had a small line with a man making announcements. She fished their introduction card from her bag.

"The honorable dowager Duchess Wolverson and her granddaughter the Lady Odette Wolverson." All heads turned in their direction and Odette tried to remember to breathe.

They entered a hall that was packed with people. It was a rather small parlor, but was lavishly decorated. The momentary hush at their entrance quickly ended, as an elderly woman rushed up to them, her eyes wide with excitement.

"Minerva!" The woman threw her arms wide.

"Dorothea!" They embraced and Odette struggled to keep her face from belaying her shock. "How have you been, old girl?"

"Sadly, not getting any younger," Dorothea replied, with a dismissive wave of her hand. "I had hoped grandchildren would mean more energy, but I just fall further and further behind."

"It makes one wonder if we were ever that young." Her grandmother had a merry tone in her voice. "Speaking of grandchildren, this is my eldest granddaughter, Odette."

"Charmed! I am the Baroness Vander." Dorothea barely curtsied, and all but ignored proper etiquette as Odette followed every rule. "I had expected a sickly thing. Born prematurely and then ravaged by scarlatina. Yet she is a vision of health."

To work with the timeline of the duke's marriage, which was rushed after the mishap with her actual mother, she'd have to be born at least seven weeks prematurely. Not many, if any, babies survived such circumstances. Instead of doing that, they moved her birthday a month so that she was only three weeks early. Their story went that her birth had made her susceptible to all sorts of illnesses, so she'd been removed from the household when the duchess had conceived again, bearing Jestine. She had expected to return to the household, but when she was three, the Duchess conceived again, this time with Grace. At five she was slated to return to the duke's household, only to contract scarlatina, which made her very ill. It had only taken her grandmother a few visits to weave such a story, explaining why no one knew of her until she was ten—when she finally overcame all her illnesses.

Such a story they had woven to cover her illegitimacy—that scornful stain she could never erase if it were to come to light.

"After being sick nearly my entire life, my body became exceedingly robust," Odette replied, and then saw the watchful eye of her grandmother and tipped her head down.

"What excitement!" Dorothea replied. "You must sit next to me at dinner."

"I wish I could, but the viscountess requested we sit near the front." Even a dowager duchess wielded power among the elites.

"Ah well, always second cello!" Dorothea said with a chuckle, before launching into a story she'd heard from someone else.

Not long after, they were called to dinner, and just as her grandmother said, they were seated in a place of honor. The kingdom had but three duke's—a royal title in the capital for the king's brother, one in the east, and her father. Of the three, her father's family was the oldest, and therefore, the most respected next to the crown.

"Lady Minerva," Viscountess Mansfield called upon her, the first lady in rank at the affair. "Please do me the honor of by sitting next to me."

It was not long until they were seated and the first course of soup was served. As was proper, Odette partook of the soup, as did everyone else. Though she noticed her grandmother only swept the spoon through, politely playing with the soup, as was appropriate if not consumed.

To her surprise, the Viscount Mansfield was a warm man with kind eyes who said very little. His wife, by contrast, spoke constantly. She chatted away to everyone about anything. It should have been annoying, but instead, her enthusiastic nature was infectious. Her husband seemed quite pleased to simply eat dinner, drink wine, and nod as his wife's voice rained down on them all.

Odette was able to enjoy the conversation more after the second course when her grandmother actually ate some of the food. Perhaps she was worrying for nothing! The viscountess was regaling them with a story about the most recent hunt. Odette hung off her every word, hoping to be able to take part in future events.

There was a startled sound further down the table. A chair clattered on the ground as a larger man stood, his hands at his throat. Odette was frozen as the room erupted into chaos.

"He's choking!" the equally portly woman beside him screamed. The sounds coming out of the man were horrible and his face was turning red.

A man slapped his back as he fell forward against the table. A woman further down the table fainted. Odette stood on impulse as the viscount caught his wife as she also fainted. The man was now coughing, and a moment later, after he was hit on the back again, the man spat out the food. Odette rushed around the table, pulling her smelling salts as she went.

"When I was younger, I fainted often." Her voice shook as she knelt by the unconscious viscountess.

A sharp inhale and suddenly she was roused. Many were clapping and cheering as the viscount helped his wife to her feet. The viscountess was thanking her and asking after the man. Her temporary state did little to stop her stream of chatter once she was awake again.

"You are a remarkably quick thinker," Viscountess Mansfield praised her. "Oh, don't worry dear; it seems all is well."

Relieved it was over, Odette turned back to her grandmother. Her entire world froze as she saw her grandmother slumped in the chair. It took her a moment to realize someone was screaming. She rushed to her grandmother's side, shaking her. Someone was trying to pull her away as she started crying, realizing her grandmother wasn't breathing.

"Grandmother!" It was the only words she could manage as she knelt by her grandmother's too still form.

Her grandmother's hand was still warm as she lifted it to her own cheek, her vision blurry from the tears. "Please wake up." It couldn't happen again. First her stepfather, who had treated her like she was his own, now her grandmother who had taught her everything she knew.

"Don't leave me." Her fingers reached out, feeling for even a whisper of breath from the older woman's lips. When she felt none, she collapsed into her grandmother's lap, sobbing uncontrollably.

Eventually someone was able to coax her away. They were holding and soothing her as Odette felt separated from herself and reality. A physician was checking on her grandmother, and then she heard him clearly pronounce that she was dead. The words punched a hole in her heart as Odette collapsed to the floor.

-Present-

It had been four days since Jareth had left, promising to return as quickly as he could. After four days of summarizing reports and ordering a few pieces of furniture for the conservatory, she was out of things to do. The idea of going into town, simply did not appeal to her, but there was something that had been weighing on her mind.

She found Sir Lex in the training ground, running drills. Spears thrust into the air with deadly force, their bright tips shining in the sunlight. They moved forward in formation before thrusting again. Odette knew she should leave and wait, as was proper, but was absolutely fascinated by it.

"Lady Chadwick," Sir Jonas said with a bow. "What brings you here?"

"I had hoped to speak with Sir Lex, but he appears quite busy," Odette said, trying not to sound as embarrassed as she felt at being caught somewhere she shouldn't be.

"I'll let him know."

Sir Jonas left her before she could stop him, only mustering a stream of unintelligible words as he made his retreat. The charming young knight strode up to Sir Lex, and they had a brief discussion before he looked in her direction. She waved, unsure what else to do. He nodded to her before finishing his conversation and walking towards her.

"My lady, what do you need help with?" Sir Lex didn't seem annoyed at all—she was instantly relieved.

Odette cleared her throat. "I have a request. That is, I need your guidance on something." This was going to be a difficult subject to broach.

"I have no skill in interior design or preparing a menu for the kitchen." Sir Lex seemed to be joking with her. "But I will do what I can."

"It is good that my request is neither of those things. I would like you to teach me how to shoot an arrow." Odette had been contemplating this for days. When she was very young, her stepfather had shown her how to shoot a bow one time. Her mother had forbade it after that.

"Forgive me. I must have heard you wrong." Sir Lex seemed perplexed. "I thought you just asked to learn how to shoot a bow."

Odette nodded her head. "I did. Though a crossbow would also serve."

"A lady…that is," —he paused, inhaling sharply—"it isn't…no…" Sir Lex shifted his weight so hard his armor clanked. "What I mean is it is uncommon for a lady…"

"I know I'm making an almost ignoble request, but I felt if I knew how to manage at least one weapon, I may not be so vulnerable if we should encounter a monster again." Odette was going to have to press him. "I am not from the north; it seems things are done differently here."

Sir Lex scratched the back of his head. "Not *that* differently."

"Was it not the third marquess' second wife that held Vallerdale Hall against the Nightwing attack?" Odette had come prepared for every argument he could make. "Or the sixth marquess' daughter that won an archery competition to convince her father to let her choose her own husband?"

"Aye," Sir Lex replied, his face contorted as though he were in pain. "You haven't even been here a month and how do you know all of that?"

"I like to read," Odette replied with a slight shrug. "A lot."

"Perhaps you do need something to keep you occupied." Sir Lex eyed her. "It won't be archery though."

"I see." Odette's mind raced.

Sir Lex seemed relieved. "I'm glad you understand."

"I do. I'm going to have to figure out a different way to convince you." Odette felt a newfound determination as Lex shook his head and waved his arms to try and dissuade her. "I'll be back tomorrow!" Then, with pep in her step, she left.

"There is nothing you can say to convince me!" He called after her, but she just waved over her shoulder.

Chapter 24

-Past-

"Ashes to ashes, we mourn a life well lived." The priest's somber tone provided little comfort.

The priest stood next to the bed where her grandmother was tucked in. Lynn had helped prepare the body to the point that Odette could almost imagine she was sleeping. After the priest performed the final rites, he left the room, leaving only the three girls and the duke.

Lady Minerva's home, the one that had become *their* place over the last four years, was so empty now. The furniture remained, but without the person who had made the house a home, it felt as hollow as an abandoned building. A part of her couldn't accept the reality, couldn't accept that her grandmother was gone.

"Stop your crying," the duke's voice was hard. "Be worthy of your name."

Odette sniffled as Jestine and Grace watched with oddly stoic eyes. Detached. Why couldn't she muster such restraint? If it weren't for the red rims around their eyelids, she'd almost believe they didn't care.

The grief suddenly swirled within her and coalesced into anger. "She was your mother."

Odette, not seeing the hand coming, suddenly found herself reeling, and on the floor. Gripping her stinging cheek, she looked up wide-eyed and gape mouthed at the man who was supposed to be her father. He'd hit her; struck her with the back of his hand as though it was the most normal thing to do.

"Don't speak to me with such insolence, girl. I told you to stop crying and be worthy of your name. It seems my mother didn't train you to be obedient. An oversight I shall rectify." The duke's words were menacing as he sneered at her. "Tell me what must a wife be above all else, girls?"

"Obedient to her husband," his other daughters parroted like trained pets.

"Good girls." He patted their heads with affection. "My mother may have been right that the more alliances we can make the better, but that is all you are, child. A tool. Remember your place and don't bring shame to the Wolverson name."

"Yes, sire." Odette cast her eyes to the ground.

"We're leaving." With nary a glance back, the duke left the room with her half-sisters in his wake.

Slowly she lifted herself from the floor and stood next to Lady Minerva. She put her hand over one of her grandmother's ice cold ones. "Watch me, Grandmother. I shall make you proud." Then she kissed her hair and whispered a prayer to the gods to watch over her soul, before accepting it would be two years before she could debut. What nightmare would she live until then?

-Present-

"Wait, you have to notch the arrow a certain way?" Odette asked, lifting the arrow up to inspect the feathers.

"Yes, the fletching is a certain way." Sir Lex sounded as begrudging a teacher as someone who has been asked three days in a row to do something they were against; which he was…on both counts.

Odette twirled the shaft until he pointed at one of the three feathers. "This one?" she asked, touching the one he indicated.

"Yes," Sir Lex replied with a heavy sigh. "You put it into this part."

She picked up the already strung bow and tried to pull the notch across the string. "Like this?"

Sir Lex stood up. "Let's put the finger guard on."

He set the bow into the rack and the arrow in the quiver before putting the odd three-fingered glove on her. He buckled it to her wrist, tightening it slightly to ensure it stayed. Then he pulled out a bracer and slid it onto her other arm, before tightening it as well.

"What is that for?" Odette asked. She'd read about the finger guard but not this.

"It is an arm guard," he replied before putting his hands on his hips and sighing again. "You do realize Jareth is going to have my hide the moment he learns about this?"

"I realize that I politely insisted for three days straight to have you teach me," Odette said, quite pleased with herself. "The arm guard…" She hesitated, then smiled. "It's to prevent the string from hitting my arm when I fire the arrow, right?"

"You *loose* or *shoot* an arrow of this type. Only an incendiary arrow is fired." There was a sudden worry in Sir Lex's eyes. "Something you will never, ever try."

"Certainly not." At least not yet, she thought to herself.

She picked up the bow, but Sir Lex stopped her before she could pick up the arrow. "You get to pull a few times to get the stance down first."

"Why are you giving me a longbow?" Odette asked, thinking of the archery books she'd read. "Aren't recurves a stronger and more accurate bow?"

"Yes, but longbows are easier on the joints and aren't as loud." The irritable lines in Sir Lex's brow eased for a moment. *Good*, she thought, pleased he'd stop being grumpy with her.

"That makes sense." Odette replied, walking up to the archery lane and taking a stance. "Is this right?"

"You should use the square stance." Sir Lex stood in front her, his left side facing the target and his body perpendicular to it.

She adjusted her stance. "Like this?"

"Yes," Sir Lex said, turning around. "Now raise the bow."

Odette hesitated for a moment. She'd used a bow before, as a young girl, but had decided to say only that she'd read about them in a book if asked. Clearing her throat, she lifted the bow, gripping it in her left hand as her right hand pulled on the string. To her surprise, it yielded to her demands with only slight resistance.

His eyes narrowed but she pretended not to notice. "Is this right?"

"Raise your right elbow and anchor it better against your jaw," Sir Lex said. "When you are ready, release by slowly letting the tension out until it is back in its original position."

Odette took a deep breath and did as he asked. He had her repeat the movement two more times and already her right arm was starting to feel tired. She'd remembered this being much easier when she was younger.

"When can I use an arrow?" Odette asked.

"When Jareth returns and says you can."

Odette quickly let the tension out. "That may be days from now."

"Yes, and in that time you will build your stamina and control." He didn't look at all influenced by her protest.

"Very well." Unhappy but resigned, Odette continued until Sir Lex told her to stop.

Chapter 25

-Past-

Odette had never been to the capital, but with how little she'd seen since her arrival the week before, she might have well stayed at Wolf Castle. At least here her father wasn't hitting her and mostly ignored her. To her surprise, all three of the Wolverson sisters were restricted to quarters like prized horses. The only time they were allowed outside was when they went to the private gardens, where only women were permitted.

Glancing at the clock, Odette closed the book she was reading, as it was just about that time for her walk. In a way she was relieved not to be paraded around or have to socialize at events like her grandmother had planned. It had been a year since the passing of Lady Minerva, and all her hard work was locked behind a door. One that the duke had made clear wouldn't open again until he turned eighteen and her sister turned sixteen. She would debut in the shadow of her younger sister. That wouldn't be so terrible, but it meant three more years of misery.

There was a knock at the door and she quickly moved to open it. The maid curtsied and then lead the way. It was a silent routine she was used to after the sixth day. The only other place they were able to go was to the temple to pray. Thankfully she had books to read and some embroidery to do or this would be akin to torture.

Jestine and Grace followed. Grace still had a very childish appearance with a round face, big eyes, and a boyish figure. Jestine, on the other hand, was blossoming into a refined, young lady at thirteen. She was starting to fill out in the right places and even Odette couldn't deny how beautiful she was becoming with her pale skin, green eyes, and ebony locks.

"Morning," Jestine said pleasantly, though her eyes were annoyed.

"Good morning," Odette said, forcing a smile. "It seems to be a warmer day."

It was late summer and the day before it had started to sprinkle, so they'd had to cut their afternoon walk short. Yesterday had been a very long day trapped indoors.

When they arrived outside, Odette quickly headed for the small hedge maze. It was the only place she could be alone and not feel suffocated. Everything was the happiest shade of green, alongside beautiful rock formations and stonework. Trees and hedges were trimmed into submission and bright red flowers sprung forth, punctuating the green.

When she reached the center of the maze, she was greeted by a plumeria tree with vibrant flowers, encased in a glass house. The structure's windows were open, and the sweet scent of the blossoms wafted out. Taking a deep breath, she moved towards the back bench and sat down. Watching the clouds, Odette thought of her other siblings and mother. More than once she'd considered running away, but knew that if she tried, the duke would hunt her down again. He may be cruel, but he was not a stupid man.

Half dozing, she was startled awake when a leg appeared through the hedgerow. Leaning back into the bench, she gasped as an arm followed. Then suddenly a boy, covered in leaves, was on his knees inside the center of the maze.

He stood, and as he was dusting himself off, Odette realized he wasn't a boy at all but a young man. He was older than she'd first thought, at least three to four years her senior. His hair was dark, and he appeared rather skinny. Part of her was shocked at how inappropriate it was for a man to be in that garden. Another part of her was curious; it had been some time since she'd seen anyone that wasn't her family or their servants. She'd resolved to say nothing and hoped he'd just leave, but then she noticed his hunched posture and furrowed brows. When he started rubbing his forehead, she knew exactly what was going on. That was a level of distress she'd recognize anywhere—it was someone desperately trying not to cry.

"Hello?" It had been more of a question than a greeting. "Are you all right?"

The young man whirled, reaching for his hip even though nothing was there. When he spotted her, he immediately relaxed his posture. But his eyes were guarded, like the feral cats she'd seen as a child—acting like they belonged, yet ready to lash out at a moment's notice.

"What did you say?" The words had come out as a hushed command, even though he was the one who wasn't supposed to be there.

"I asked if you were well."

His eyebrow shot towards his hairline. "I'm fine."

Odette uncurled from her post and walked towards him. He took a step back, like she was something dangerous, which made her stop and eye him. Despite his attempt to conceal his emotions, she could see right through them. Her powers may not let her actually see what others were feeling, but the ability had made it so she could read the expressions. A mouth twitch here, an eye shift there, and she typically could decipher one's emotional state. Not to mention this young man was terrible at concealing his feelings.

"I don't think you are." She pointed up at him. "Your forehead screams distress." She was being bold to the point of recklessness. The freedom, though temporary, was going to her head. "So, what happened?"

"Why would I tell you?"

"I'm just a girl in a garden. I don't know who you are, and I have no one to tell anyways." Odette did the most unladylike thing imaginable—she shrugged. "Plus, someone used to say that sometimes a stranger's ear is easier to talk to than a familiar one."

His eyes narrowed as he seemed to be appraising her. "They were very wise."

"Yes, they were." She missed her stepfather terribly. "It isn't often I get to socialize. I promise to be a good listener."

"You wouldn't understand," he replied, his eyes hard.

"I wouldn't understand what?" Odette pressed, knowing that it wouldn't be long before their maid called her to return inside.

"You aren't illegitimate." The words were biting and for a moment her heart stopped. "You can't imagine what it is like to be on the outside."

"To never quite belong? To never be good enough at anything for anyone?" Odette replied, feeling the words resonate with her. "Pretending to be something you're not?"

He inhaled, confusion knitting his brow. "Yes…"

Odette took a shaky breath. "I am keenly aware of those feelings. That, and feeling you've been abandoned by the ones who actually loved you because they aren't here anymore." It was a secret she'd never shared with anyone and immediately covered her mouth, as though to hide it.

"You lost someone?" His voice was gentle.

She nodded. "My grandmother." And the only man who had ever been like a true father to her.

"That must have been hard."

"It was." She sniffled and fought down the tears that were brewing. "What about you? Why did you escape through the hedge row?"

He sighed and shook his head once. "My real father is here. I thought he'd be proud that I'd been selected as heir. I thought he'd see everything I'd done, and he'd finally accept me." His jaw was as tight as his voice.

"What happened?" Odette asked, leaning closer, wishing to comfort him but unwilling to cross that line of propriety.

"He barely acknowledged me. Instead, he said it was the Nuvian blood in my veins. His blood, that had made me great." His fist pounded against his chest. His voice was passionate, but he'd kept it quiet somehow.

"We are more than just our blood." Odette wished she wasn't the duke's daughter. If given the chance, she'd leave but knew it would only cause hardships for her mother. "We make choices and sacrifices. Those are not blood, but our souls. And, our souls are our own."

He chuckled and she blinked in surprise. "You must be much older than you look to spout such insightful prose," he said. She giggled at his words and her cheeks hurt from smiling so much.

"Odette!" the maid called.

She gasped. "I have to go." Her fingers dug into the ridged fabric of her skirts.

He put a hand up, as though to stop her. "Thank you," he said, radiating genuine gratitude. "I shall never forget your kindness."

"I really must go," she said, rushing towards the maze's opening. "Farewell."

The maid was waiting, as was an impatient Jestine. "Where were you?"

"I'd fallen asleep reading in the maze," Odette replied as her sister scoffed.

"Father is asking for us." Jestine turned her nose up. "Try not to embarrass us."

Odette bowed as they followed the maid who led them to a waiting servant. The young man took them down one hallway, then another. She didn't think she'd be able to find her way back when they took another turn. Lavish hallways and beautiful paintings depicting past battles and royals lined the hallways. Before she could blink, they were standing in front of a thick wooden door.

Within, there were three men at a table. "My daughters," the duke said. Then, as expected, each girl curtsied as he announced their names, "Lady Odette, Miss Jestine, and Miss Grace."

"They are all very lovely," the one who was about their father's age said. "Miss Jestine, might I introduce my son, the Honorable Valter Nuvian."

Odette's head snapped in his direction. That was the name the boy from the garden had said. Was he also a son of Duke Nuvian? That's when she noticed a different young man sitting on the couch. He appeared younger than the boy she'd met earlier.

"I am honored to make your acquaintance," Jestine said, the picture of charm.

"The honor is mine." After standing, the boy bowed stiffly.

"As you can see, unlike her mother, Jestine is the picture of health," Duke Wolverson said to Duke Nuvian as though the girl were not in the room.

"A little thin but you are right. Quite healthy." Duke Nuvian seemed pleased. "It seems we have an engagement to plan."

Jestine beamed as Odette glanced at the last man. He was much younger than her father, likely in his early twenties. When he met her gaze, she noticed his dark features were so handsome that they felt almost sinister. The two dukes were chatting away happily and hadn't noticed their third member was focused on Odette. She wanted to look away but felt if she did, something bad would happen.

"Your eldest has such vibrant hair," the mysterious man said. "A beguiling trait."

"From my mother's side of the family." Her father was displeased, his lips tipped down in a slight frown. "It was darker as a child but lightened with each passing year. Nothing that interesting, Morran."

Odette took stock of the last man. The recently appointed marquess of the south, Lord Morran. It was as though he could see right through her. Why did she feel like he knew what she was? Almost as though he could read she was a Mystic right on her forehead.

"I don't find her uninteresting," Lord Morran said, leaning forward.

Odette fought the urge to squirm under his penetrating gaze. Jestine seethed beside her; the moment that had seemed to be hers had been stolen. Odette knew that even though it wasn't her fault, she would pay later. She wished very much she'd never met Lord Morran or his scrutinizing eye.

"That is enough, girls," their father said sharply. "Go back."

-Present-

"Just one?" Odette asked, clenching the shaft of the arrow in her hand.

"For the thousandth time, no," Sir Lex replied, frowning. "If Jareth finds out, he'll strike me down where I stand."

"How will he ever know?" Odette asked, desperate to try out her new skills. Jareth had been gone nine days and for the last two she'd spent every spare moment practicing with or without Sir Lex. Her arms were tired, but she was invigorated.

"I'll tell him," Sir Lex replied, raising an eyebrow.

Odette wanted to pout, more to tease him, but she didn't have it in her. It felt too childish, so she swallowed the impulse down. Instead, she put the arrow away before rocking back on her heel. A breeze pushed her hair over her shoulder, its reddish hues more prominent against the crimson dress.

"Should I have you show me the crossbow next?" Odette finally said, watching him out of the corner of her eye.

He was already shaking his head. "One was bad enough. You won't talk me into a second."

She laughed aloud at his words. "I suppose with only one day left, you are right. Though I could wear you down if I had a few more days."

Sir Lex simply let out a heavy sigh in response.

Glancing at the blue skies, Odette wondered what the future might bring. More days bothering Sir Lex? It could be a fun prospect since he was an upstanding man she felt oddly safe with, but she wanted her husband back. After their last conversation, Odette wanted to deepen their relationship, a difficult thing to accomplish if he was on expedition.

"Is Lord Jareth often away?" Odette asked, wondering how many more days alone it would be. She couldn't believe how much she missed her husband.

"Aye, he has trouble staying still," Sir Lex replied, then quickly added, "Though I expect that to change with you here."

Would it though? So far, she hadn't seen that. She understood why he'd left, but it hadn't made it any easier. Perhaps in the future he would let her accompany him. One day she would like to see the land they were responsible for.

"My lady?" Sir Mance's voice cut into her thoughts.

"Sir Mance?" Odette turned and saw his scruffy face. "Welcome back." Her eyes naturally searched around him for the one she wished to see most of all.

"What are you doing here?" Sir Mance asked, his bag still over his shoulder. "Lord Jareth just went inside the manor to find you."

Odette paused and looked at the bow then back at Sir Lex. Thrusting the weapon at him she lifted up her skirts as she darted past them. Someone called to her, but she wasn't listening as she hurried towards the manor.

Jareth was back!

He was coming down the steps when she approached. Out of breath she stopped and stared at him. His even thicker facial hair shadowed his face and his hair had grown longer. His clothing was rumpled but he appeared unharmed. Had he always been so handsome? How was it possible that she missed him more now that she could see him again? It crashed down around her like a storm.

When he reached the bottom step, he looked towards the barracks and stopped. "Odette?" Jareth's brows furrowed.

She didn't wait, instead rushing towards him, stopping only when she was a few steps away. "You came back early." Her chest was rising and falling so rapidly she could hardly catch her breath.

"Yes," Jareth replied, his eyebrows furrowed as many emotions flashed in his eyes leaving her feeling uncertain. "I didn't want to keep you waiting."

"I missed you." Odette wanted to hug him but stood on what was proper. When she took another step towards him, he took a step back. Her heart clenched in confusion.

He must have seen it on her face because he shook his head. "I need to wash. I just wanted to see you first. Make sure you were well."

"I'm well." Odette bit her lip. "Better now that you're here."

He took a step closer, his voice pitched low. "I couldn't stop thinking about you."

"I had to do everything and anything not to keep thinking of you," Odette replied, closing the gap.

"I really must wash," he said, clearly conflicted. "Yet I don't want to leave you. Even for a moment." He held out a hand. "Come with me?"

"To the bath?" she asked with a laugh. "In the middle of the day? You really are trying to cause a scandal!"

Then he was kissing her, his lips demanding her full attention. She eagerly returned it, pressing herself against him as his arms went around her. He smelled of horse, pine, and sweat—the combination not as terrible as he supposed.

When they parted, he put his forehead on hers. "Is that enough scandal for you?"

"Maybe just once more, to be sure." Odette kissed him soundly, laughing when he picked her up and twirled her around.

When he set her back down, he took her hand. Leading them through the hall to his chambers, a line of maids with empty buckets were leaving. Inside was a large ceramic tub, but it did not seem large enough for the pair of them. Odette's cheeks were stained red as Jareth closed the door and came to stand in front of her.

Caressing the side of her face, Jareth put his other hand on her shoulder. "We'll only bathe."

"Forgive me; I find that my words are bolder than I am." A weak laugh bubbled up out of her chest.

"Do not worry," he said, starting to undo the clasps on her dress. "Focus on me."

"It is not worry that we may become…intimate…that makes me hesitate," Odette replied, remembering her promise to be honest. "I find I do not know what to do with my hands. Nor where to look."

He chuckled. "Do you trust me?"

She nodded.

"Close your eyes," he said, his voice gentle.

"What?" She turned slightly away from him.

"Close your eyes," he repeated.

Odette hesitated, but she did as he asked. Although tense, she decided to put her trust in him. She felt him strip her heavy clothing off. The air wasn't cold, yet she felt exposed. Her fingers itched to cover herself but only put a fist against her chest for comfort.

He firmly gripped her hand. "Take a step forward."

She nodded. With his gentle guidance, she entered the tub. The water was still warm, but thankfully not too hot. Once she settled down, she heard a rustling of clothing and then the water level rose a moment later. It caused her to open her eyes on impulse.

"See? That wasn't so bad." That charming smile was back.

She laughed. "No, it wasn't." Her legs were pressed up against her chest and her arms around her knees as she forced herself to focus on Jareth's face and not his sculpted body. "What now?"

"Now I enjoy the warm bath and then wash." Jareth grinned. "While admiring the view."

Her eyes darted down to his corded shoulders and the dark hair on his chest. What she saw caused her to sputter out a laugh before burying her face in her arms as the tip of her nose touched the warm water. She heard him moving and realized he was cleaning himself. When the silence stretched out, she felt a sudden need to fill it.

She lifted her face and said, "You've been wonderfully patient with me." Odette felt the words were coming all at once. "I'd always thought about marriage, but never focused on the husband aspect. I mean I certainly thought about what my husband might be like, but that wasn't the only thing. Well, that is, I…" He was just beaming at her, utterly amused with every word as he draped the washcloth on the washtub's edge. A sense of calm passed over her. "How does a woman ask a man to be her lover?"

He tipped his head, the amusement gone, his eyes were two black coals burning with desire. Leaning forward, he put his wet hand against her cheek and his fingers around the back of her head. He shifted her head before kissing her gently. Then the kiss deepened, leaving her gasping for air. Her arms wrapped around his neck, then her chest was against his. She felt him coax her towards him and she gave in to his gentle request.

Was it the warm water that was making her lightheaded? Suddenly she realized with a start she was straddling him, and he was leaning back as she was pressed up against his strong chest. When she caught sight of the sizable appendage between his legs as she glanced over her shoulder, she immediately brought her hands up and covered her face on impulse.

His laughter rang out. "That won't do." He carefully peeled her hands away from her face. "I can't have you running away every time you see me naked."

"I don't know what to do," she said, boldly moving her fingers to touch his chest. "How do I...please you?"

He groaned and his head went back. "By the gods, you're going to break my sanity."

Jareth shifted her forward, his left hand gripping her hip and back, while his fingers moved towards her womanhood. "Look at me." Jareth's eyes met hers as his fingers touched her most sacred place.

Odette tensed and brought the back of her other hand to her mouth. He was just feeling along her opening, and she found it sent tingles through her body. She'd expected pain, but instead felt eager for him to touch more. His head tipped forward, capturing one of her nipples between his lips. She arched, gasping as he began to shift his fingers more vigorously. She felt a sticky sweetness crawl up her core and take hold of her senses.

Sounds she'd never made before were coming out of her as he kept up with his ministrations. When she felt her legs start to shudder, she shifted back. Something pressed against her opening and Jareth stopped, moaning as his hand tightened on her skin. She felt herself tense as power coursed through her. She reached back and touched where his hand had gripped earlier, feeling Jareth's desire mingle with her own building want.

Emboldened by the struggle happening on his face, she shifted slightly, taking more of him into her. His eyes popped open in shock as he tried to move back but had nowhere to go in the small tub.

"Wait," Jareth's voice was hoarse and tight. Something about him trying to control himself caused her to tighten her core. "Odette." Her name was a groan as he gripped her hips with both hands. "You need to be prepared more."

"I don't want to wait." Had she really said those words aloud? She knew she should feel shame, but instead she only felt courageous. "I want us to be joined."

His grip on her faltered and she took even more of him into her. She felt herself stretch, but it only felt like pressure not pain. Gasping, her hands flew to his shoulders, feeling full already.

"I'm nearly in." Was his voice shaking? She couldn't be sure; she was so focused on the feelings in her own body. "I'm going to start moving. Hold onto me."

Odette nodded and leaned forward, wrapping her arms around his neck. He helped maneuver her hips, moving deeper into her and stretching her to almost painful limits. Although he was slow as he pulled out of her, he plunged into her in a calculated fashion. With each movement, she felt herself expand and accept him, then a sense of pleasure started to wash over her. As his thrusts became a little faster, her own body started to shake. Sensations she'd never experienced came in waves, corresponding with each thrust.

"Jareth," Odette exclaimed as he suddenly started going wild.

One of his hands fisted in her hair before pulling her head back and kissing her. It was a sharp kiss as he grunted. His body shuddered as he buried his manhood deep within her. After a moment, he relaxed back, taking her with him. A sense of euphoria washed over her as she lay against him.

Suddenly aware the water was no longer as warm, she shifted, trying to move the stagnant water. She'd been expecting to feel the same soreness as their first night but was relieved when she didn't. Perhaps, like before, she'd feel it later. Regardless, it was worth it. Being joined with Jareth made her feel incredibly close to him.

"Odette?" Jareth's voice cut through her thoughts.

"Hmm?" She shifted her head up to look at him, seeing a purplish haze around him.

He kissed her before leaning back. "You do not know how happy you've made me."

Suddenly, she knew what that purple glow was: it was love. She was seeing an aura around him that highlighted his emotions. Shocked by the realization that she'd unlocked her second ability and was now a Mage, Odette just stared at him. Should she tell him?

"Odette?" He seemed confused and the faint purple around him vanished. "What's wrong?"

"I just want to remember this moment," Odette felt the words tumble out. "I'm so very happy." She hugged him close but then shivered in the rapidly cooling water.

"Let's clean quickly," Jareth said, as he returned her hug and kissed her neck. "The bath is getting cold."

Chapter 26

Odette sighed contently as she stood in the middle of the bustling conservatory. She was staring at the tree, but her thoughts were elsewhere. More than two weeks had passed since Jareth's return, and they'd spent a considerable amount of time together. They took meals together, discussed the lands and its people, and fell into each other's arms each night. Yesterday, he'd gone to the academy, but should be back that evening. Despite it only being one day, she felt lonely without him. Perhaps the loneliness was so acute because her ability to see emotions was another secret she was keeping from him—physical distance only served to remind her of how her omissions kept her isolated.

"Lady Chadwick?" Kira touched Odette's arm causing her to jerk with a start.

"Oh!" Odette tried to quiet her beating heart. "What is it?"

"I didn't mean to startle you, but I called your name." Kira's eyes shined. "A few times, actually." Kira shifted back and pointed towards the corner where an older man stood with Kenith. "A messenger came for Lord Chadwick."

"He isn't here," Odette replied immediately.

"We told him as much, but he insisted that an important person was only a few hours behind him and that whoever was in charge should be notified." Kira glanced in the messenger's direction.

As the Lady of the house, the responsibility fell to her. "An important guest? Whoever could it be?"

Odette crossed the conservatory, it was nearing completion with only a few unfinished garden beds, some missing decorations, and a few custom furniture pieces left outstanding. The older man wore a crest depicting a sword, surrounded by octopus tentacles. It was one she'd seen as a child: Duke Nuvian.

Apprehensive, she approached the group. "My Lady, this messenger just arrived." Kenith seemed annoyed to the point of being almost hostile to the man. The four guards around them didn't create a welcoming atmosphere either.

With obvious agitation at not being presented to the Lord, the messenger handed the scroll to Kenith, who handed it to Odette. "This contains all the information you need," he said curtly. One of the guards promptly escorted him away, so she presumed there was no need for a reply.

"See that he is cared for," Odette said absentmindedly, remembering it was courtesy to care for messengers.

The letter was direct and to the point. There was no warmth from Lord Nuvian to his illegitimate son who had raised himself from nothing into a marquess. Apparently, her husband had been ignoring their summons. It was customary for a newlywed couple to visit the husband's family soon after the ceremony. As a lord in his own right, Jareth could refuse, but it could cause issues down the line since it slighted the family. Instead, Jareth's birth father wrote that his sister would be coming to talk some sense into him.

"Jareth has a sister?" Odette asked, caught off-guard. She knew about the two brothers, both competing for the dukedom, but had never heard about a sister.

"Yes." Kenith seemed embarrassed. "The only family he still writes to."

Odette tried not to be hurt by the words. They'd only been married a little more than a month. Time would eventually unlock all the doors that her husband had. For now, she tried to council herself to be patient; they had years to share themselves.

"Kenith, ensure a message is sent to Jareth and prepare a room. Have a guard find Sir Lex. I want him to assemble a proper welcoming committee to help me greet our guest," Odette continued. "Kira, let the cook know to prepare tea upon Lord Chadwick's sister's arrival. He should also make a lavish meal for dinner, as befitting such an honored guest." With that, she lifted her skirts, and started heading towards her room to change from her simple gray clothing to more suitable attire. "I'll need to change immediately."

"I'll send Dotty to assist you, my lady," Kira replied before hurrying off to fetch the maid.

After taking care of her task regarding the cook, Kira rushed to help Dotty with Odette's clothing and hair. Thankfully, Kira began filling her in on why Miss Nuvian was not well known. When she was sixteen, she'd been involved in a small scandal with a lesser lord, a lowly baron who had been married once before. When her father had forbidden the match, she'd run away with him. They married and eight months later a baby boy was born. It had all been quite scandalous. Odette was surprised she hadn't heard about it until she realized it happened when she'd been new to her grandmother's household, and barely eleven years old.

"That means she isn't Lady Nuvian. What is her name?" Odette asked, glancing at Kira.

Kira appeared worried. "I don't remember." Dotty shook her head before leaving.

"We'll need Sir Lex to make the introductions, then." Odette smoothed the front of her maroon and golden dress. "Let's make haste."

Odette, with Kira at her side, rushed towards the front entry. They passed a pair of servants carrying linens and a fresh bouquet of flowers. They blushed when Odette thanked them, and Kira giggled behind her hand.

"What is it?" Odette asked, eyeing her lady's maid.

"Everyone is very happy for you and the lord." Kira's eyes shined. "For your newfound closeness."

Odette cleared her throat and sent Kira a disapproving expression. It was not hidden knowledge that they dined, bathed, and slept together. They typically ended up in her room and her bedding had to be changed, while his remained untouched. She thought perhaps it was because her room had been modernized with every comfort, while his was barely decorated and only sparsely furnished. Apparently, he'd cleared out most of Marquess Rupert's items when he'd passed, finding it too painful.

She knew she was trying to think of other things so her already rosy cheeks wouldn't be so bright when they reached the main doors, yet a smile crept into her face. She and Jareth were extremely happy. Although they hadn't discussed this growing closeness, Odette knew with each new piece of information she learned about her husband, she was falling deeper and deeper in love with him.

"Not an appropriate subject right now." Odette censured her as two guards opened the main doors. "Our guest shall arrive any moment."

No sooner were the words out of her mouth, and there was a strange humming in the air. Sir Lex had gathered a small group in shiny armor. They were on the steps, near the bottom. Something crackled as Sir Lex ordered them to clear the area before running towards her. Odette was frozen as she watched a pinkish red color fill the air around everyone—fear.

Sir Lex moved to shield her as a loud crack sounded, much like a whip. Odette instinctively put her hand on Sir Lex's shoulder, hoping to stay his hand as he drew his sword. It must have seemed odd to others, but Odette had occasionally traveled by enhanced carriage with the duke and she was familiar with the oddness of its arrival. When a strained calm followed the commotion, she glanced around the knight. As she expected, a massive carriage sat in the entry area where there had been none. She could see the same crest with the octopus entwined around the sword on the side of the contraption.

The stunned silence was interrupted by someone retching from within the carriage. Odette glanced up at Sir Lex, who appeared as confused as she was. Uncertain about what surprise Duke Nuvian might have sent, Odette kept her hand on Sir Lex's armor. They moved down the steps in tandem as the carriage door opened. A woman leaned out, gripping the door as she hunched forward.

"Baroness Dymus?" Sir Lex said to the distressed woman.

Hearing her name, the woman in question lifted her head and Odette saw some of Jareth's features looking back at her. Despite being older than her half-brother, she looked more youthful. Round cheeks and large eyes would have given her a childish appearance, were it not for the long Nuvian face and serious nose. Her face was positively haggard as her brows furrowed.

"Lex?" She stepped off the carriage, her gaze sweeping around before landing on Odette. "Where is my brother?"

Odette was surprised to hear her say that word; it was rare for an illegitimate child to be referred to as such. Her shock doubled when the lady stepped off the carriage and straightened. When her thickly layered skirts settled, they revealed a very prominent belly. She was with child!

Outrage blinded Odette as she rushed down the rest of the steps to help her sister-in-law. "They had you travel in your condition? What were they thinking?"

Baroness Dymus laughed aloud but let Odette link their arms and help her up the stairs. "They were thinking that Jareth's obstinate nature wouldn't listen to anyone else. Where is he?"

"He was visiting the academy, but I have sent for him," Odette managed, trying to cool her temper as Kira fell into step behind them.

"You must be Duke Wolverson's eldest daughter," Baroness Dymus said, which caught Odette off-guard. Her manner and speech were lacking in refinement, leaving Odette off kilter. "First time my brother has shown any interest in a girl, and he marries her."

Kira bristled at the words. "You should address her ladyship appropriately."

Baroness Dymus raised her eyebrows as her lips curled into a coy smile. "Is this your secret?" she asked Odette as they reached the parlor. "Do you simply incite loyalty in everyone you meet?"

Odette felt a blush rush to her cheeks. "I may have once been a duke's daughter, but I am now the wife of a marquess."

"Yes," the Baroness said, eyeing her scrupulously before she curtsied. "Forgive my impertinence, Marchioness Chadwick."

It was the title she much preferred, yet a part of her felt unworthy. "It is no bother." Odette found it easy to forgive her; she seemed quite the opposite of anyone she'd met so far in polite society.

"Might I have a moment of your time..." — the Baroness fixed Kira with her stare — "unaccompanied?"

Kira shifted uncomfortably, and although Odette felt the same twinge at her request, she concealed her emotions and nodded. "I am certain we have much to discuss." She patted Kira's hand, to try and comfort her. "I can manage the tea."

Kira reluctantly left, and an awkward silence descended. Baroness Dymus had this funny way of staring, as though she could see beyond the exterior and into the makings of a person. Would all Odette's secrets be undone by a single woman's inquisitive stare?

She began to pour the tea, trying to keep her hands occupied. "Milk and sugar?"

"Milk, lots of milk. No sugar."

When it was blended, she handed a cup to the baroness. Unwilling to be intimidated by the stillness, Odette decided to be as frank as her sister-by-marriage. "What was it you wished to discuss?"

"I am sure my father and brothers ventured to guess at Jareth's sudden nuptials. No doubt their summons and insistence to see the happy couple stems from the fact that you've legitimized him. Yet I can see why my brother would be drawn to you," Baroness Dymus said, taking a sip of her tea.

Legitimized him? Odette felt the walls slowly close in. She hadn't thought of that. As a legitimate daughter of a duke, their marriage erased the fact that Jareth was illegitimate. Any children born from their union would also be considered legitimate. All this time she'd thought of herself as the same as Jareth, but in the eyes of society she was not. Though there had been some questions over the years, her father had never addressed her origins outright. Instead, treating her as the eldest to all manner of people, *outside* the

Wolverson's estates, that is. Is that why Jareth had married her? It made too much sense not to be at least partially true.

She tried to keep the emotion from her voice. "Why do you suppose he would be drawn to me?" Anything to keep the other thoughts at bay.

"Jareth is a protector in his very soul. He can be stern and even cold at times but must have looked at you and seen what I see." Baroness Dymus smiled brightly, catching Odette unawares. "You and my brother are kindred spirits." She set her teacup down. "You asked why I came in my current state. It was to talk to my brother at the family's request, but I also wanted to meet you. Jareth is very dear to my heart. He cared for me when others turned away at my very name. I know too well the ridicule he endured, as I suffered something similar. I wanted to see the woman he chose for himself. As luck would have it, he has chosen well."

Odette's heart was pounding wildly in her breast. "I am the lucky one."

Suddenly, the door opened, and Jareth stepped into the room. Startled, Odette put a hand to her already racing heart. How in the world had he returned so quickly?

"I didn't expect you for some time, brother," Baroness Dymus struggled to her feet. Jareth hurried to help her stand.

"I was already on my way back and wanted to get here as quickly as I could," Jareth said, kissing both of her cheeks. "What brings you here, Mavis?"

Lady Mavis gave Odette a knowing smirk. "Grandfather wishes to see you. He has tasked father with ensuring you both come, as is tradition."

"I received his letters," Jareth said, his voice frigid. "I shall tell you the same thing what I told him; I have no intention of bringing my wife anywhere near the East, or that place."

Odette loved the way he said, "my wife," but she was not as thrilled by the rest of it. He was well within his right to decline the current duke, yet it was considered poor taste to decline a request from a former duke. As she knew the former Duke Nuvian was still well known and considered one of the closest friends of the rulers of the neighboring kingdom across the ocean.

"I thought you might say as much. Which is why I am here to propose a compromise." Lady Mavis put her hands on her swelling stomach. "Dinner, in two days' time, at my estate. My husband has already agreed, and it has been too long since you've seen your nephews."

"As much as I'd like to see them, I am unwilling to subject my wife to an evening in their company." Jareth seemed rooted in his spot, but Odette saw no harm in a single night.

"I have nephews?" Odette asked, standing as she imagined playing with children again. "How many?"

"Three. My eldest and the twins." Lady Mavis touched her stomach. "I am hopeful this one is a girl. I have given my husband more sons than he ever dreamed of. For once, I'd like a daughter."

Odette whirled on Jareth. "May we go? I wish to meet them."

Jareth seemed unhappy, almost pained by her request. "You do not know what you are asking."

Odette steeled herself. "You forget, as the duke's daughter, I met Duke Nuvian as a child. We should go."

"Steadfast, caring, and wise," Mavis said before clapping Jareth on the shoulder. "You really hit the jackpot with her." Then she laughed before plopping down. "What do you say, brother?"

Jareth appeared conflicted, but Odette wouldn't backdown. This was the best possible outcome, a single dinner with his family. "Will my brothers be there?" The way he said it almost broke her resolve.

"Of course." Mavis sighed. "Though I tried to persuade father otherwise, he insisted it had to be the entire family or it would not be honoring tradition. You know how he feels about tradition."

"All too well." Jareth's voice was full of bitterness.

"It is one night," Odette said, folding her hands together as she wished to rush over and comfort him. "We can manage one night, can we not?"

Jareth sighed heavily. "We shall."

Chapter 27

-Past-

It was the last day at the capital. After all of the excitement with the mysterious boy and meeting the other heads of the most prominent families, she'd forgotten they would be presented in front of the queen. They were supposed to do it when they first arrived, but the queen had been unwell and thus it had been delayed.

Now they were standing in front of their father, dressed in their finest hand-painted silk gowns, ready to walk through the throne room doors to meet the queen. Depending on what she saw, the queen could bestow favor onto them for their debut into society. Odette should be making her own that year, but due to the betrothal Jestine already had set with Duke Nuvian's eldest son, the duke had announced his two eldest daughters would make their debut together in two years.

The doors opened and Odette tried to remember to breathe. She thought of her grandmother and held her head high as they walked. All of those she loved may have left her or died, but she could still honor them. She could still prove that she was as worthy as Jestine and Grace. The throne room was full of rich reds with golden crests of griffins sewn into the banners. Keeping her lashes lowered as they reached the dais, Odette curtsied with her sisters.

"You may rise." A soft, almost fragile voice commanded.

The woman on the throne was beautiful, with pale skin like newly fallen snow. She appeared dignified, but there was an air of exhaustion that Odette recognized. It reminded her of her grandmother the day she died.

"Blessed be the star of our kingdom," Odette said, her voice shaking as the emotion from thoughts of her grandmother surfaced.

"May you reign always," Jestine added, her voice strong and confident.

"Bring prosperity and peace to our kingdom." Grace's voice was as soft as the queen's, nervous with every syllable. Father would scold her later.

"What lovely daughters you have, Olier." The queen's informal use of her father's name surprised Odette. "Your eldest takes after your mother, rest her soul. Your youngest takes after your lovely wife, what a youthful face she had. I see Jestine received most of the Wolverson features. A true beauty. I had heard you'd finalized a betrothal to Valter's second son." Despite her frailness, the queen's eyes had an intelligent shine to them.

"Yes, your highness," the duke replied. "A second son for a second daughter."

Out of the corner of her eye, Odette could make out Jestine beaming radiantly. Pride seemed to radiate off her like she was secreting a powerful scent. The queen only nodded as her gaze fell on Odette, piercing her in place.

"No plans for your eldest, who is nearly of marriage age?" the queen asked, addressing the elephant in the room.

"As you know, my eldest suffered many illnesses. She is quite behind and will not be ready to debut until she is eighteen," the duke replied. It was odd hearing him sound so...charming. "I am sure you can understand how protective I am of her."

His fingers curled around her shoulder and Odette forced her face to remain emotionless. The queen nodded and then laughed slightly. "I honestly was beginning to believe they were imaginary; you kept all of your girls under such tight watch growing up. Whatever will they do when they no longer have you watching over them?"

"Our husbands will care for us," Jestine said, proudly.

"Is that right?" The queen smirked coyly. "Do you agree Lady Odette?"

Odette's tongue felt leaden in her mouth. Had the queen caught her disagreement with Jestine's statement? The duke's hand tightened for a moment as she struggled to find the right words. What would her grandmother say?

"We shall have Father's teachings to guide us, protecting us wherever we are. Just as you protect this land, your grace." Odette shifted into a curtesy, moving out of her father's painful grasp.

"Clever you are. More forthright than I originally thought. I shall watch your progress with great interest." The queen lifted a hand. "You are all dismissed."

Odette felt relieved to have apparently passed whatever test that was, but as she turned, she caught the look of absolute hatred on Jestine's face. What should have been Jestine's shining moment of speaking directly to the queen, had been overshadowed by the one person who shouldn't have spoken at all. Odette followed her father from the throne room knowing that he may spare her a lashing, but Jestine would get back at her through the servants. She'd already suffered due to the fact Lord Morran's had paid attention to her—this would only make it worse. Odette felt sick to her stomach at the prospect as they returned to their rooms.

-Present-

Her father's face was dark with fury. He was telling her she had to marry, had to surrender, to be submissive. Odette was trying to get away, aware it was a dream but unable to wake herself. He kept hitting her, over and over again. She tried to fend him off, but his words cut into her with each horrible name he called her.

"Odette."

Her eyes opened as Jareth was holding onto her. He looked worried in the moonlight. They'd forgotten to close the curtains again; they'd been so quick

178

to fall asleep, exhausted by thoughts of what was coming. Then the memory of the dream came back, and she felt the tears on her cheeks.

"Jareth?" Odette asked.

"What was hurting you?" Jareth asked, smoothing her hair back from her forehead and thumbing her tears away.

"I don't remember," Odette replied, not wishing to reveal how horrible her father had been to her. One day she would tell him, but not now. Another secret—how did they fester and grow so easily?

"Whatever it was, it is over now." Jareth kissed her forehead. "Do you think you can sleep now?"

"I don't know," Odette replied, feeling an emotional ball slide into her chest, blocking her throat. "Will you hold me?"

"Is something bothering you?" Jareth asked. "Is it this dinner?"

Odette shook her head. "I have sat through worse; I promise you." She recalled the horrible dinners at the duke's house that she'd had to endure. "I think it is something your sister said. I told myself it wouldn't bother me, that I wouldn't ask, but…"

Jareth had lay back next to her and pulled her close, but he went onto his elbow as her voice trailed off. "What is it?" His face was mostly lost to the dark, so she could barely see his expression. "You can ask me anything and I shall answer as honestly as I can."

"Why did you choose me?" Odette asked the question that had been following her like an ill wind—pregnant with dark omens. The only way to overcome the fear it had wrapped around her, was to ask it. "Was it to legitimatize your children or your claim?"

He went very still. "What gave you that idea?"

"Your sister mentioned it. She said your family thought that was why you wanted to marry me." Odette's voice shook, yet she tried to remain calm.

He sighed heavily. "I made a promise that if I was ever in a position to help you, that I would. You helped me more than once with your words—they carried me, saved me." His expression seemed so soft and yet his gaze was so far away. As though he wasn't there with her anymore, but in his memories.

"I wish I could remember," Odette whispered, touching his cheek. "Where did we meet?"

"At the palace. In the gardens," Jareth said, his gaze thoughtful.

Odette tried to search her memories. "I remember a boy in the hedgerow. I do not remember much else. Only that you were a taste of freedom."

"You reminded me that blood is only so important, that the soul matters more." Jareth kissed her forehead. "Have I answered your question? Are you calm enough to sleep now?"

Odette nodded, sliding further under the covers and turning against him as he joined her. Without asking, he held her against him, holding her hand against his chest. As she drifted off, Odette realized that she wanted to tell him how much she loved him. How he had saved her as well. When she glanced up at him, the words on the tip of her tongue, she saw he was already asleep. Nestling against him, Odette decided she'd tell him in the morning.

Odette shivered when she woke, and tried to move closer to Jareth for warmth. Opening her eyes in surprise, she found the bed empty. Where had he gone? Sitting up, she glanced around the room, finding herself alone. She was still in a state of undress from the previous night's...coupling. After donning a robe, she called for Kira to help her dress. It wasn't as early as Odette had first thought—breakfast had already been prepared and she was running late. It appeared Jareth had asked that she not be disturbed, but Odette was determined to tell him how she felt. She wanted it to be clear before they faced his family.

"Lady Dymus requested you join her," Kira said, setting a card on the vanity. "She gave this to me before joining Lord Jareth for breakfast."

As Kira started arranging her hair, Odette opened the letter. The content was simple and straightforward—she wanted Odette to join her in town to find presents for her three sons. It was a perfectly normal request, but it would take her away from Jareth. Smoothing her frayed nerves, she knew they had the entire evening. Furthermore, she wished to know more about her newly acquired sister.

"Tell the baroness I'd be happy to join her." Odette set the letter down, standing so Kira could help dress her. "No, not the pink one; let's put on the dark green one." She wanted to look her best, like that first night at the inn when he'd complimented her.

"It is such a lovely color," Kira said, retrieving it from the wardrobe.

"It is one of my favorites," Odette replied.

After she was dressed, she ate her food in her rooms while Kira made the necessary arrangements for the trip into town. She didn't like the idea of taking a carriage down to town, it would take longer, as it would take longer, but she also knew she couldn't put a pregnant woman on a horse; especially one as far along as Jareth's sister. So, carriage it must be. She was nearly done picking at her food, daydreaming about what Jareth's reaction might be to her confession, when Mavis joined her. Trailing behind her was a befuddled Kira, who looked quite done for. Odette was beginning to suspect that the eldest daughter of Duke Nuvian was more of a handful than most could manage.

"Is it true?" Mavis asked, sitting down beside her.

"Is what true?" Odette replied, looking to Kira to help clarify the situation.

"That you haven't been to town," Mavis explained, quite emphatically. "I asked your lady's maid what you might wish to visit. She said she wouldn't know because you've never been to town."

"I've only been here a month." Odette laughed at how put out Mavis appeared. "Jareth said he would take me eventually."

"I'll not hear of it," Mavis stood, gesturing for Odette to join her. "Come, come, we shall visit every shop until you have inspected every good and ware yourself."

Odette trailed behind Mavis as Kira hastily tried to catch up as well. It was like following a raging horse that was galloping ahead. There was little time to think of anything except to act. As though she'd lived there all her life, Mavis expertly led them down to the carriage. The footman hurried to open the door, then turned to face them. Odette was surprised to see it was actually Sir Jonas, and even more surprised by Mavis's reaction.

"Jonas!" Mavis threw her arms around him, much to Odette's surprise.

"Cousin," Sir Jonas laughed, returning her hug. "When Lord Jareth suddenly recalled me yesterday, I thought something might have been wrong. I didn't expect to see you here."

Mavis kissed both of his cheeks. "You have gotten so handsome. Really quite rugged and dashing." Her tone was teasing. "Are you to escort us today?"

"Yes, it will be my duty to protect you ladies today." He bowed to her, then turned to address Odette. "Marchioness, we are ready to depart when you are."

"We are ready to depart, Sir Jonas." Odette had no idea they were cousins but now she could see he and Jareth had the same nose. That was where the similarities ended.

Once they were loaded into the carriage and it started off, Mavis seemed ready to burst with excitement. "Where do you think we should go first?"

Hours later, they wearily climbed back into the carriage. Even Mavis's glow of earlier excitement seemed to have dimmed. Three dress shops, two milliners, two jewelers, a bookseller, a shoemaker, and the draper. Odette fervently wished there was nowhere else to go.

"Where to next?" Sir Jonas, who had mostly stood guard, didn't seem as spent.

Odette groaned inwardly, glancing at their guest.

"I could eat a whole chicken," Mavis grumbled, rubbing the side of her stomach. "To the bakery!"

Odette perked up at that. "That sounds lovely."

"I promise it shall be our last stop," Mavis replied, causing both Odette and Kira to sigh in relief.

When they arrived, the smell of sweet bread filled her nostrils and washed over her—a buttery, sugary aroma that reminded her of her mother. Odette had always been fond of her mother's baking when she was a child. It made her wish she could do it herself, but it had become beneath her station when she'd gone to live with her grandmother.

Mavis waddled inside and quickly pointed at a litany of items. She paid, all while chatting with the poor shopgirl. Mavis really was a force to be reckoned with. It was obvious after just a few hours in her company that she was used to getting her way. It also explained how she was able to marry the baron even against her father's wishes.

By the time they loaded the bags into the carriage, intent on returning home, Odette was exhausted. No sooner had she sat down before a piece of bread was thrust into her hands. "You must try this." Mavis shared her tasty treasure with them. After a while, she sat back and sighed contently. "That was just what I needed. Oh!" She snagged Odette's hand and pressed it to her belly. "The baby agrees!"

Suddenly Odette felt something press against her hand. "It's kicking!" Odette was breathless. It was the most amazing feeling.

"Wait until you have one of your own," Mavis said. "There is nothing like it in the entire world."

Odette felt the baby move again before withdrawing her hand as Mavis leaned back and rested her hands atop her belly. A baby? She'd never given it much thought. She knew it was entirely possible; they had been performing the act that could lead to conception. Yet the notion hadn't occurred to her. Did Jareth want children? Did she?

To her surprise, she did. The idea took root within her, spreading into every part of her being. She hoped their marriage might soon be blessed with a child of their own. She began to imagine the traits they might have.

Then a sudden realization struck her. What if they inherited an ability? It was not uncommon for a daughter of a powerful bloodline to pass it on, even one who showed no signs of having an ability, but it was rare. One child she could see…but what if more of them inherited an ability? Unlikely, as far as she knew. As far as Odette knew, she was the only one who had any real powers, as Jestine and Grace had never exhibited any special talents or abilities.

More secrets. She was going to have to tell him about her abilities. Perhaps like her grandmother, he could help her now that she was a Mage. Glancing at Mavis's resting figure, Odette wondered if any of her children had abilities. Should she confide in her sister-by-marriage? No, not before talking with Jareth.

Suddenly, the baroness inhaled sharply and sat up. "Oh my." She took a few deep breaths. "That was a painful one."

"A contraction?" Kira asked, her face suddenly as white a sheet.

"It can't be," Mavis replied, waving her off. "I'm not due for another month" Despite her words, she winced again. "I'm sure I've just overdone it."

"When we return, I'll have a surgeon brought to you." Odette held her hand. "Is there anything I can do to help?"

"You really have an unusual ability to sense what I need before I ask," Mavis said, breathing rapidly as she squeezed her hand. "Just don't let go."

When they arrived, Odette helped Mavis from the carriage. "Help! Sir Jonas, have a surgeon called. The baroness is in pain."

"Right away!" Jonas rushed off.

"Kira, go and find Jareth, he'll know what to do," Odette commanded once they reached the top of the stairs.

"They are getting closer together." Mavis had seemed so sure in the carriage but now she was clearly distressed. "It is too early." A tear slid down her cheek, as she whispered. "I can't lose another one."

Odette's heart nearly stopped at the pain in her sister-by-marriage's voice. "I won't leave your side, no matter what," Odette replied, determined to bring her any comfort.

"I want Nigel," Mavis wailed as they reached the parlor. Odette helped her onto the couch as she started to undo her laces. She remembered her mother needed help with them when Caden was born.

"Your husband?" Odette asked, realizing that even with her continuous chatter, she knew very little about Mavis's marriage. She'd heard everything about her nephews, but no mention of the husband until that moment.

"Yes," Mavis replied, tears streaming down her face as Odette finished with the laces and dug into her pocket for a handkerchief. "He's always been my rock. My patient, steady rock." She gritted her teeth and held her stomach before panting. "That was a bad one."

"What can I do?" Odette asked, wiping the streaks off her face.

Kenith entered with a pitcher of water. "Madam, drink this."

"Water?" Mavis asked, but took it.

"Yes, it helped my wife when she went into labor early." Kenith appeared nervous.

Odette moved close to him. "Where is Jareth?"

"He went riding," Kenith replied quietly. "I sent Sir Jonas to retrieve him."

Odette knew that meant he could be anywhere for miles around. "And the surgeon?" she asked.

"He's in town performing a delicate procedure. It may be an hour before he can come." Kenith appeared even more anxious.

"Do you have a midwife at home?" Odette asked, suddenly realizing they were running out of options.

"Yes." Mavis's face scrunched up in pain as she took strange, measured breaths. It seemed to be helping, so Odette encouraged her to keep doing it.

"How do you operate the horseless carriage?" Odette asked, gripping her hand.

"That horrible thing?" Then she groaned. "It just needs to be activated by someone with Nuvian blood. The return destination is already set. A child could do it."

"Good," Odette replied. "Because we're going to have to use it." She turned to the butler. "Kenith, please have the carriage brought around front. We'll need help carrying Mavis to the carriage."

"Mistress do you intend to…" Kenith seemed seriously concerned.

"Don't leave me," Mavis cried, gripping her hand again.

"She's family," Odette replied. "Please do as I ask."

He nodded before rushing off. Odette turned to Mavis and comforted her. They walked, drank more water, but the contractions kept getting closer together. She watched the clock and realized they were typically seven to eight minutes apart.

Kenith returned, his face grim. "It is ready."

A few servants appeared to help carry Mavis to the carriage. Kira helped put a cloak on her. When she tried to come as well, Odette waved her off, she would risk her own life by going into uncertain circumstances, but not Kira's. Not again.

"Mistress," Kenith said, glancing at the carriage. "Although Lady Dymus has always kept a close relationship with Lord Jareth, you are going into another's territory. Please be careful."

Odette tried to put on a brave face. "I will." There were so many things she wanted him to tell Jareth but only one thing seemed appropriate. "Tell the lord his lady will be waiting for him."

When she went to enter the carriage, Sir Jonas appeared. "After you, Mistress."

Relief at not going alone flooded through her. "Thank you."

Settling in next to Mavis, Odette's hand was quickly in a death grip as Jonas closed the door. Before she could say anything, Mavis reached out and touched a strange sigil. There was a soft glow inside as the carriage began to shudder. Odette shut her eyes as she felt a pressure squeeze in around. Her stomach did somersaults as she held on. When she opened her eyes, Mavis was panting, then leaned forward and heaved out her food onto the carriage floor.

Odette helped Sir Jonas move Mavis from the carriage as she shouted. "Call for the midwife!" Unfamiliar people rushed in around her as she stood awkwardly in the middle of a house she didn't know. Kenith's words suddenly hit her full force. She had jumped headfirst into a world she didn't understand. Glancing at Sir Jonas, he appeared just as lost. At least she wasn't alone.

Chapter 28

Someone had enough foresight to pack a bag with a few essentials. If she were to venture a guess as to whom, it seemed she owed Kira an extra thank you. Mavis was with the midwife and Odette was in her room, anxiously awaiting news.

A soft rap at the door drew her attention. "Yes?"

"Baron Dymus wishes to see you, Marchioness," a soft female voice said.

Odette hurried to the door. "How is the baroness?" she asked the moment the door opened.

The older woman blinked in surprise. "She is resting. It would be best if you spoke to the baron."

"Right," Odette said, remembering that although Mavis refused to follow proper protocol, she should not be so hasty to forget. "Please lead the way."

The hallway was dark as was the day. Apparently, the magic of the carriage wasn't instantaneously like she presumed, it placed those inside in a sort of suspended time, but actual transportation took about an hour. Considering it was normally two hundred times longer, that still seemed like quite an improvement.

The baron was in his study, smoking a pipe. He was older than Odette thought he would be, at least twice her age. When Odette had heard the story about the younger Mavis, she had assumed the baron was about the same age as Mavis. Young foolish love that had brought scandal, not this man who appeared in his late thirties.

The gray in his beard and hair made him appear distinguished, yet the creases at his eyes portrayed a man who enjoyed laughter. Uncertain what to expect, she opened her ability in an attempt to sense his emotions. All she found was happiness, in the form of a pale green aura. So, she quickly closed the door on her talent, realizing it might be too underdeveloped to be of much help.

"Mavis tells me of the great service you rendered her," The baron said, smiling at her. "I thought you might like to know it was a false labor. The midwives were able to calm it enough to stop all contractions."

Odette felt a great weight lift off her shoulders. "That is wonderful news."

He nodded and stood up. She was surprised at how short he was, standing at about her height. She thought Mavis must tower over her portly husband. Yet he walked with a spring in his step and a twinkle in his eye. Odette was surprised when he held his arms out, as though to hug her.

"You have done my family a great service. I wish to formally welcome you to our household as family." The baron waited patiently.

She took a tentative step forward, as the baron pulled her into a hug. It was a fatherly embrace, one filled with guileless appreciation. Odette felt she understood what might have drawn Mavis to him. He did feel as steadfast as he'd been described.

"I have sent word to your husband that you arrived safely but I'm sure he has his own means of travel and will join us shortly. For now, I have a proper room made up. Sir Jonas has also been seen to." He squeezed her shoulders. "I am sure Mavis will wish to see you in the morning."

"Thank you for the gracious welcome," Odette replied, genuinely warmed by his behavior.

He laughed, patting his belly. "I have no doubt I owe you more than Mavis lets on. She has always been more than most people can handle. Yet she speaks so highly of you."

"She is unlike anyone I've ever met." Odette couldn't admit how in awe she was of her free spirit.

"I felt the same way all those years ago. Didn't think this old ticker would work, until I met her." The baron chuckled. "Now, I'd do anything for her." He grinned from ear to ear. "You had better sleep while you can; this household has an early start thanks to my boys."

He ushered her to the door as she said, "I can't wait."

As she followed the maid to her new residence, Odette stifled a yawn. It wasn't until she was changed and slipping between the covers that she realized she'd never told Jareth how she felt. With a heavy sigh and no small amount of disappointment, Odette hugged a pillow to her, certain the opportunity would present itself soon.

Odette felt like something was holding her down. She could hear something clattering in the hallway as she opened her eyes blearily. When she tried to move, she felt something across her waist. Shifting the blankets, she nearly screamed when she saw a masculine arm.

"Don't get up," Jareth grumbled.

"Jareth!" Odette exclaimed, throwing her arms around him. "When did you get here?"

He hugged her to him and tried to burrow both of them deeper into the covers. "It took me most of the night to get here. I'm still tired."

Odette giggled as she tried to cover him with kisses, but he refused to let go of her. Her fingers weaved through his hair, hugging him against her. How was it possible that she loved him more each day?

"I'm happy you're here." She kept stroking his head. "I wasn't sure when you'd arrive."

"I couldn't leave you to the vipers," he muttered, already half asleep. He did look tired, like when she'd been injured. Her sudden departure must have worried him.

"Jareth," Odette leaned forward, intent on telling her what was in his heart. "I—"

There was a loud crash in the distance that startled the rest of the words from her. One of Jareth's eyes opened, he waited patiently, listening, and then snuggled deeper. Before she could recover, a sharp knock on the door interrupted the second building of her courage. Resigned that the time was beyond her, she cleared her throat.

"Yes?" Odette called, unsure who would be there.

"I've come to tend the fire and help you dress, Marchioness." A loud voice practically vibrated the wood.

Jareth's head raised. "Narsa, is that you?"

Suddenly, the door swung open, and the bear of a woman stood in the doorway—a very short bear. Odette was taken back by her appearance, two braids stuck out of each side of her head, she seemed to be no taller than a child and yet her shoulders were as wide as any man's. A jovial expression broke up an otherwise harsh face.

"When did the cat drag you in?" Narsa asked, before bellowing out a laugh.

"A few hours ago," Jareth waved at her. "Which reminds me, I'm tired." He retreated into the covers, leaving Odette with the intimidating woman.

"Seems you've grown lazier." Narsa shook her head with her hands on her hips. "Are you trying to hide your plump self under those covers?" Without waiting for a response, which was a halfhearted chuckle, she strode in and started tending to the fire.

Odette had to wiggle free of Jareth, who reluctantly let her go. "I only have the dress from yesterday." It was still laid out over the back of the chair.

"Nonsense." Narsa went to a wardrobe and opened it. "The mistress had dresses brought for you to wear."

Two navy dresses, a lavender, and a mustard dress with beautiful embroidery hung inside. Two of them were a style that Odette didn't recognize, but the others were decently fashionable for a married woman. Yet one of the navy dresses with long ribbons and lace caught her eye. As though sensing her interest, Narsa pulled that one out.

"My! Aren't you just a picture?" Mavis said from where she sat in her bed.

Her sister-by-marriage was fully dressed, her hair loose and over her shoulder, but she seemed tired. Odette took her offered hands and sat beside her. It seemed that childbearing was very taxing for the mother—not at all the bountiful blessing many seemed to preach. She was sure it had its rewards, but was nervous for her own future experience.

"How are you faring?" Odette kissed her cheek affectionately.

"Better now that you are here to divert my attention." Mavis giggled. "Nigel won't let me lift a finger until we're sure the baby is staying put." She rubbed her protruding middle. "Little angel gave us quite a scare. Though not enough to stop my father's visit."

"Jareth's here," Odette blurted out.

Mavis's face brightened as dimples appeared on each cheek. "Good. He'll need to prepare you for our lovely family. Bunch of vipers, the lot of them." She waved a hand as though she hadn't just insulted her entire family. "Don't worry dear. Just be yourself."

"I worry that won't be enough." Odette sighed.

"Understand that there is nothing you can do to please our father, the duke, and you'll be much happier. I adopted that philosophy ages ago. The man is a walking privy. Instead, focus on grandfather." Mavis's flippant behavior caught Odette unprepared, and she had to stifle a laugh behind her hand. "Oh, don't hide it. Father knows he's made of lemons on the inside and any idea of reform was abandoned long ago."

"What about your grandfather?" Odette asked, trying to change her focus.

"He's the real backbone. My father merely plays at being duke." Mavis seemed quite smug at the declaration. "When father denied this marriage, it was grandfather that approved it. I was always his favorite. Being the only girl, I knew it, but he made me promise to never leave this marriage. That it was for life. An easy agreement, but he knew my changeable nature. He thought it was a fancy and didn't want to be shamed by it later. Prudent, really."

It was strange to hear her talk about her family so openly. Odette was used to speaking very little about family matters. Everything she knew said these types of discussions just didn't happen. It oddly, yet equally put her on edge and made her feel included.

"Thank you for sharing," Odette said, her throat tight.

Mavis suddenly pulled her into a hug. "I'm so happy you're part of the family now."

Odette melted into her. "So am I."

Unlike further north, summer was in full swing there. The sun shone so brightly that Odette was temporarily blinded as she stepped into the gardens. When Odette had asked Mavis where her children were, she's been told the gardens, to try and wear them out. It was a bit improper of her to go with only a maid showing her the way, but she had only a day to get to know them.

It was the laughter she heard first. When she rounded the corner behind the maid, they both stopped at the sight. The baron was standing with a ball in his hand. There was a strange track with different colored balls spread around. When he tossed the ball, there was tense silence followed by a cheer.

"You can go," Odette whispered to the maid, who curtsied and left.

That's when she noticed that Sir Jonas and Jareth were also there. Each paired off with a young boy. The oldest was stocky and the spitting image of his father, expect for his darker hair. The twins reminded her more of the Nuvian family, clearly taking after their mother. The oldest was about five and the twins were somewhere between three and four. They were all so absorbed in their game that none of them had even noticed her.

"Your turn," the baron said, ruffling one of his sons' hair.

With a gap tooth grin, he stepped up and tossed the ball. As before, they all watched it, eyes fixed as it flew through the air. They all celebrated when the ball landed. Odette watched them play a round, half hidden at the end of the hedgerow. It was lovely to see them all laughing and having fun; she'd been right to insist they come.

Jareth went last, tossing the ball. His partner in crime whooped loudly. "We gonna win!"

"Toss the ball," the oldest boy grumbled, though he didn't look all that upset.

Without any hesitation, the young boy hurled it through the air. When it plunked down there was stunned silence followed by Jareth exclaiming and lifting the boy onto his shoulders before spinning him around.

Wide-eyed the boy cheered in excitement. "Faster!"

His twin immediately reached up and demanded, "I wanna go!"

"Me too!" the oldest said, abandoning the game without a second thought.

Jareth gathered the boys under each arm while the first twin held tight to his head. He spun them around laughing as they threw their arms wide like birds.

"My that's making me ill just watching," the baron said, hand on his portly stomach before he turned. That's when their eyes met. He immediately perked up and held a hand out. "Lady Odette, how kind of you to grace us with your presence."

Odette glanced at a surprised Jareth—his hair was mussed in a charming fashion and the boys were demanding he keep going. Instead, he set them down one at a time, and sent her a rueful grin. Much like Caden when he'd been caught eating her mother's berry pie before dinner. With a sudden realization, Odette knew why she loved this place so much; it reminded her of a home. It was warm and loving like the one she knew as a child. Like the one she wanted to make with Jareth.

"I didn't mean to interrupt when you all were having so much fun." Odette was the one who felt sheepish now, having been caught spying on them.

"Nonsense, my dear," the baron hurried to her side, "I am excited to introduce you to my spirited offspring. Boys! Meet your aunt, Odette."

They'd been watching her with curious eyes but were a little guarded. Taking a peek at their emotions revealed yellow swirling with green. Excitement and nervousness—but what was causing the second emotion?

"I am very excited to meet you all," Odette said, trying to smile in a comforting way.

One of the twins whispered to the baron rather loudly, "Is she like our other aunts?"

"She is nothing like your other aunts," Jareth cut in, his gaze sharp. "She's my wife."

Odette felt herself stand a little taller—feeling both cherished and complimented. She couldn't have kept the smile from her lips even if she wanted to.

"Good, I don't like them," the first twin said.

"She looks nice," the second twin commented.

"Will she play with us?" the oldest asked.

They really were a whirlwind of activity. "If you'll show me how, I'd be happy to play." Odette said as the twins took each hand and led her towards the smattering of colorful balls.

"That's my cue," Sir Jonas said, waving as he hurried in the other direction. Laughter followed his hasty exit as three very eager boys began to explain the rules of the game.

Chapter 29

Odette collapsed into bed that night. Once they finished playing the bowling ball game, they filled the rest of the afternoon with other games. Although the baron left at some point, she and Jareth continued playing with them until it was time for dinner. They supped like they'd been together all their lives. The boys were put to bed and Mavis told stories from their childhood, mostly about the trouble she got into or Jareth's occasional mishap.

All the stories swirled around her as she settled down into the covers. Jareth would return soon; he'd stepped out with the baron for a nightcap. She very much wanted to tell him all the wonderful feelings he brought out in her. All the future plans she was building in her head that she wanted them to work on together.

She rested her eyes for just a moment when suddenly she was being woken up. She expected to see Jareth but instead found Narsa peering down at her. Odette gasped and clenched the sheets to her throat, which only caused the bear-like woman to chortle.

"I've seen worse in my day," Narsa said glibly as she lifted up two dresses. "The mistress said you looked too stunning in blue not to offer these two dresses. One for today and one for supper."

She barely glanced at them. "They're fine. Where is my husband?"

"He's assisting the Baron with some matters," Narsa replied, already preparing one of the dresses.

Odette tried not to be crestfallen at the news as she slipped from the covers and stood in the middle of the room. "Was there any indication when they might return?"

Narsa shrugged. "Before the guests arrive."

Words fell away as she let herself be dressed and made presentable. Not only was the stress of facing his family weighing on her but also the fact that she'd been trying unsuccessfully to confess her love for days. For some reason her lack of progress made her feel like a failure. Silly as that notion was, it persisted.

"Is my sister awake?" Odette asked, hoping to at least spend time with Mavis.

"Not last I checked. Did you need something?" Narsa's curt manner never wavered.

Odette tried to keep the improper eagerness from her voice. "I thought to join her for breakfast."

Narsa tended to the fireplace and gathered the dirty washing bowl from the night before. "It was my next stop. I'll ask."

"Very well," Odette said, collapsing into the chair as Narsa left. She watched the clock tick as a growing impatience began to claw its way up her back. She couldn't speak to her husband and she couldn't tend to Mavis. Her foot moved restlessly as she chewed on her thumb. Is this what caused madness?

Her eyes narrowed on the clock. How could a minute take so long?

Unable to stand it any long, and unwilling to let the clock win, she hurried after Narsa.

Mavis had occupied most of Odette's day. It seemed very little time had passed when she was being draped in the finest fabrics for dinner. She'd seen the Nuvian family arrive from the safety of Mavis's room. The eldest son had his wife with him, a Lady Yeamon that Mavis reported was "pretty but snobbish." Even though Jestine's engagement had been finalized with the second son, but he was unaccompanied. The third son was still completing his studies in the capital and would not be joining them. Despite his age, the former duke appeared the most prominent figure, more handsome than his son and thrice as dignified. Actually, he reminded her of Jareth the most; they had a similar bearing.

Now, she was nearly ready to leave the room and Jareth had yet to appear. If she didn't know how much he was dreading this, Odette might suspect he was avoiding her, although she hadn't given him a reason to do so.

Yet.

Odette groaned internally. She practically fell out of her seat when the doors opened without anyone knocking. Jareth strode in, every bit the nobleman. It was as though the warrior were gone and had been temporarily replaced.

"What do you think you are doing, you foolish boy?" Narsa censured him as though speaking to a child and not a powerful lord. "She could have been in a state of undress."

Odette expected a glib response but instead he was solemn. "Are you ready?" His question was directed at Odette.

Without responding, Odette stood, thanked Narsa with a nod before taking her husband's offered hand. He was so tense that their short walk to the dining area felt stiff and uncomfortable. She tightened her hold on his hand, hoping it would comfort him.

He seemed to shake himself out of it. "You need not worry. Whatever happens, you are a marchioness and a duke's daughter."

"I am not worried," she said, and was surprised that in spite of slight nerves, she was more concerned about him. "You have always protected me. Know whatever happens, you are still my husband." He gripped her hand as they stood in front of the doors. "Ready?" Odette tried to appear confident.

"Thank you for doing this," Jareth said, leaning over to kiss her cheek. "I love you."

She inhaled sharply at his words, overcome with emotion. "I love you, too." She felt giddy as she tried to keep from crying. "I've been trying to tell you for days."

"It is as though your heart knows mine." Suddenly a deep red encircled him. "Always sensing what needs to be said." He leaned in, nose to nose with her. "I wish to leave so that I can ravage you."

Instead of embarrassment, she only felt desire and a giddiness in her chest. "You will not escape dinner that easily." She tapped his nose with her own.

He chuckled before kissing the tip of her nose. "I had to try."

Odette lifted her head and nodded to the very embarrassed attendant who was trying desperately to blend into the wallpaper. He cleared his throat and opened the door before announcing them. As they entered, Odette's gaze swept across the room. Duke Nuvian had gray in his hair where there had been none only three years earlier. To his left, at the head of the table, sat the former duke. His hair was entirely gray and cut short, his face cleanshaven and his blue eyes calculating. They took the two open seats to his left, as the honored guests.

"Welcome Marquess and Marchioness Chadwick," the former duke said. "Forgive me for not standing." It was then that Odette saw he was in a wheelchair. "Let me have a look at you."

Jareth quickly pulled her seat out instead. "Forgive my impatience. We have had a long, trying day."

Mavis patted her protruding belly. "It was thankfully a false alarm."

Many laughed politely as they took their seats—all except Duke Nuvian, who seemed rather annoyed. His face was emotionless but the bright yellow around him belayed his irritation. Odette's head started to hurt as she glanced at Jareth's grandfather before switching off her ability. She was still unable to process so many people's auras at once. Yet she'd seen the haze of green that had whispered a pride. The old man was proud, but of what?

"Earlier the marchioness was regaling me with a story about how she was slow to adjust to the colder temperatures in the north. Do you know they are only now getting buds on their flowers?" Baron Dymus, being the good host, broke the silence.

"Did you have trouble adjusting to the cold? I imagine it was much warmer in your childhood home," the former Duke asked.

"I am adjusting, though it may take more than a year if my husband is to be believed," Odette replied, gripping Jareth's hand. The servants began dishing out the soup.

Jareth's features softened. "I believe I'd said it would be two years in your case."

"Perhaps I am simply being optimistic. What do you think, Grandfather?" Odette asked, purposefully using an informal reference, which would be considered appropriate among family.

There was a stunned silence as she stared intently at the former duke. Unlike the current duke who had a cold streak as frigid as the North, the former duke seemed to have a sense of humility about him. As though time had changed entitlement to tolerance. Time did have a way of changing one's perspective on things.

"These old bones wouldn't go anywhere near the North," he said, his eyes shining, "Unless it was at your invitation, Granddaughter."

"By next summer I shall finish renovating the conservatory," Odette replied as she picked up her spoon and began to move it elegantly through the soup. "It shall be the warmest place in all of the North. Perfect for your comfort."

"You do not leave such matters to your steward? How uncivilized," Lady Yeomon, the first son's wife, commented.

"The estate is my responsibility," Odette replied, proud of the fact. "I personally see to its restoration."

"How barbarous," Lady Yeomon said, aghast.

"Not all ladies can be as refined as you, Yeomon," Duke Nuvian commented.

Jareth held fast to her left hand, glaring daggers into the duke. "My wife has my full confidence."

"I should say," the former duke replied, glancing at his son. "It seems Jareth found a more suitable wife for himself then you found for your sons."

Everyone was struck dumb by his statement. Odette nearly dropped her spoon in shock. She'd never imagined that the former duke would come to their aid. His frank manner of speech and the way he set the tone showed why many considered him still the power behind the Duke of the East.

The baron's face flushed as he stammered. It was Mavis that came to their rescue. "Grandfather, each lady has her own charms, wouldn't you agree?" Despite her conversational tone and pert smile, her eyes were sharp.

"How could I forget?" the former duke replied before turning to his soup.

Odette glanced at Jareth, who appeared just as confused as she was. When she furrowed her brows and tilted her head, he simply shrugged slightly before returning to their meal. The rest of it was light conversation, mostly initiated by their lovely host and hostess. No heavy topics: instead, they focused mostly on the coming hunt. One Jareth had mentioned he intended to take part in.

Chapter 30

Although Odette felt utterly exhausted after the dinner, she was oddly giddy. Not only had Grandfather Nuvian praised her but Jareth loved her. Their feelings were mutual! Her happiness only increased when Jareth snatched up her hand the moment they were out of sight and kissed the inside of her wrist.

"I shall escape them as soon as I can," Jareth said, his eyes ablaze with desire. "Wait for me."

Breathless, she nodded. Thankfully, the women had insisted upon retiring when Mavis declared she was positively asleep on her feet. When he went to leave, he paused, glancing around. Odette was confused until he turned back and kissed her square on the lips. How could they be so soft and welcoming?

"You have bewitched me, my wife," the words were hushed and sent a tingle up her spine. He was gone in an instant, leaving her reeling.

She heard a clatter behind her before she rushed towards their room. She did not want anyone to stop her in case it kept her from Jareth for even a moment. He would finish seeing his family off and then he would come to her. She touched her warm cheeks, reminding herself their couplings were normal.

Though she doubted that so many nobles shared their beds with their wives every night.

The only time they were apart anymore was when he was away from the castle or when she'd left to help Mavis. She'd grown accustomed to his presence beside her. This was the life they were building, and she liked it. Craved it.

Odette dismissed the maid after she helped her out of the dress and corset. Once she took off her stockings, all that remained were her bloomers and shift. Washing herself in the bin, she arranged her hair, and removed her jewelry. Once everything was settled, she sat by the couch. Was there something else she could do to make herself more appealing?

Glancing at the bed, she considered stripping off her clothing and settling in. That would certainly be daring of her. Despite the thought, her courage deserted her. It didn't matter how she looked in the past, Jareth had always acted as though she were desirable. Without removing a stitch of her remaining clothing, she crawled under the covers to wait.

Had time always moved so slowly? With a heavy sigh, she rolled over and stared at the door. She didn't feel tired and yet her eyes were heavy. It had been an eventful day; perhaps she was just trying to convince herself she wasn't tired because the bed was suspiciously comfortable.

Jerking awake, Odette searched for the sudden sound that had roused her. Jareth was stripping off his dinner jacket with a scowl on his face. Alarmed by his anger, she sat up and was about to speak when he tore off his shirt and tossed it onto the closest chair with his jacket. Flinging a letter onto the desk, he slid his fingers through his hair, muttering to himself.

Odette was caught between the urge to help him and the uncertainty of how she might do so. No doubt his family had caused the change in her husband's demeanor. She was afraid it would take her husband away from her, after they'd just connected.

With that thought, she slid from the bed. He stiffened when she approached but didn't turn. "I didn't mean to wake you."

Her arms encircled his chest, the bare skin warm and comforting. Pressing her face against his back she inhaled and then sighed heavily. One of his hands covered hers and she felt him relax; the tension leaving his body as she held him.

"Let's go to bed," Odette whispered.

When she tried to move around him, Jareth's arm encompassed her waist, drawing her closer. "You won't ask what has upset me?"

"It does not matter tonight. All that matters for now is it keeps you from my bed," Odette replied boldly.

Jareth's eyes flashed with desire before he pulled her against him, pressing his lips against hers. It was not a sweet kiss; it was fire and it made her feel alive. Wrapping her arms around his neck, she went on her tiptoes to get better access to his lips. He lifted her up off the ground and instinctively she wrapped her legs around his hips.

His fingers caressed her legs, sending a jolt through her body. He stopped mid-thigh when her underwear got in the way. With a grunt, he walked her over towards the bed, his fingers digging into her bottom. When he reached the bed, he swung her up and she gasped in surprise as her feet landed on the mattress.

He stripped her bothersome bloomers off and pressed her nightgown up until he could kiss her stomach. Her hands gripped his head and shoulders, feeling lightheaded with anticipation. She expected him to keep undressing her, instead he nudged her legs apart. Odette's eyes flew open when she realized what he was going to do, but her protest turned to a gasp when his fingers touched her slit.

"You're wet," his voice was hoarse.

Embarrassed by how loose that made her sound, she tried to move her legs together, but Jareth's hand prevented complete closure. Instead, he leaned back and glanced up at her. Her cheeks burned and she felt shy.

He smiled softly at her, as though to reassure her. "I want only pleasure for you. Will you let me?"

Odette's heart was pounding wildly, but even with her embarrassment, she nodded. It was not hard to place her trust in this man, this man she loved. Tenderly, he helped her lay down, moving her nightgown so it pooled around her waist.

Instead of moving to touch her, he just stared at her. Her legs shook as she fought the urge to cover herself. Her fingers tightened in the fabric of her clothes.

"You're beautiful," he finally said and some of the tension immediately left her.

Then he moved forward, and she expected him to touch her again. Instead, he wrapped his arms around her legs and shifted her towards the end of the bed. At first, she didn't understand what he was going to do until he bent his head.

With sudden clarity she caught his head in her hands. "It's dirty!"

"I assure you; it is not." His grin was lopsided before she felt his head press against her protesting hands. "It is anything but dirty."

Her last barrier was gone as she let him slide between her fingers to her most sacred part. When he licked along the length of her, she moaned. At the noise, he fell upon her with earnest; she writhed as pleasure blinded her. She felt like she was caught in a storm; nothing mattered but what he was doing. Squeezing her eyes closed, she felt her legs start to shake as something was building within her. His tongue slid into her, and she jerked in surprise. He continued his ministrations as she gasped his name. She tensed, losing all sense of reason, which only caused whatever was building to burst. Waves of pleasure assaulted her every sense as euphoria wrapped around her like a blanket.

"What are you doing to me?" he muttered against her bare stomach.

"That is what I should be saying."

Jareth stiffened at her words. Then he moved up the length of her and kissed her square on the mouth. Her fingers went up to touch his chest and found hot skin. It was soft to her touch but unyielding.

"I love you," he said as she felt him press against her folds.

"And I you," Odette gasped the last word as she felt herself open for him.

He pushed into her slowly at first, finding a rhythm that made her grip his shoulders. His lips found hers as his thrusts became furious and her body clenched in wanting. How could his powerful penetration feel so wonderful?

It left her dizzy, and she could barely focus as he thrust into her. With a grunt he stilled within her, cradling her head against him as he buried himself deep.

"Odette," he said as he maneuvered her head around to kiss her. "You shall be terrible to part from."

She was breathing heavily as she met his gaze, her heart clenching as what she suspected came to pass. "Then take me with you, so we'll never be apart."

He kissed her again, this time on her forehead. "I shall take you only where you are safe."

Her arms wrapped around his broad chest. "If I am with you, I shall be safe."

"Then we shall go to the capital tomorrow," he replied. "Together."

Chapter 31

The capital was not at all what she remembered it to be. Though if she were being fair, there was little she had seen in her visits as a child. Too often the three of them were hidden away, left in their rooms or sequestered to carriages. Jareth did nothing of the sort. Instead, he asked her often what she wanted to visit or see. Even though the capital was wonderous, a bigger part of her wanted to go home with Jareth in the North and never leave. A silly notion to be sure.

"Perhaps you should get fabric. You can have any dress made once we return home." Jareth leaned back in the carriage and looked out the window.

They'd used Duke Nuvian's carriage to get just outside the capital limits. The wards kept any teleportation in or out of the main city. They'd quickly switched to a horse drawn carriage, but Odette didn't remember most of it, feeling too ill from the transition. Apparently, further distances had a greater affect at times.

"When can we go home?" Odette asked, perking up.

Jareth seemed surprised and then laughed. "That's the most excitement I've seen from you all day."

Odette felt her cheeks warm. "I miss our home."

"I like hearing you say that." His posture relaxed. "Our home." They shared a kiss. "I shall hurry so that we might return today." Then he called up to the driver, to have her brought to a local haberdasher after dropping him off. He departed for his meeting with the king with a kiss on the back of her hand when they arrived in front of the palace.

Odette sighed, but thought it best to make use of the day. He would be at least an hour if not more and there was a good distance back to the teleportation location beyond the walls of the capital. She could at least secure lunch and perhaps a gift for Kira.

The capital was exactly what she remembered from the safety of the carriage. They had so few people with them that she'd use the footman Jareth had hired to see to their needs. She would remain within the safety of the wooden walls. Perhaps it was better that way; it was what she was used to.

Glancing down at her hands, she nearly laughed. How easy it was to fall into old habits when Jareth wasn't there to hold her hand. She would go and see to the fabric herself while she sent the footman and coachman to fetch lunch. No doubt a ribbon or pin would make a perfect gift for Kira, both of which could be found at a clothier.

When they arrived, the footman opened the door for her. "Lady Chadwick, we have arrived."

"Thank you. Please secure a basketed lunch from a local place and return within the hour." Odette said, before entering the fine shop.

Fabrics and dresses lined the room. There was a small group of women within who quieted when she entered. Holding fast to her calling card, she walked up to the counter and quietly set it upon the wood. The shop owner called to an assistant and continued to see to the group of women.

Odette immediately began viewing the ribbons and thinking what would fit Kira best. She was just settling on a pale blue silk one when the shopkeeper approached her.

"Marchioness Chadwick," the shopkeeper said, just loudly enough to be overheard. "How may I assist you?"

"I wish to have enough fabric to make a few dresses," Odette replied, well aware that those around them were paying close attention now. "I'd also like to review your pin boxes."

"This way." The shopkeeper led her to a private room. They brought tea, and a lady she'd never seen joined her.

"I am the owner, Julia Sheffield. I wished to welcome you to my shop personally and see to your every need, Marchioness Chadwick." Her voice was smooth and held a professionalism that was impressive.

"Which fabrics would you recommend?" Odette asked, suddenly recalling that she too had a part to play. She was a marchioness after all and it would not do for her to be any other person.

Despite the endless options, Odette concluded her business in just over an hour. Two ribbons, a pin that reminded her of Kira, nine new fabrics for dresses, and one for a nightgown. The purchase was likely modest for someone of her stature, yet she felt extravagant.

When they arrived back at the palace, it was another hour before her husband emerged. She was just considering eating without him when he practically leapt into the carriage. He hugged her and kissed her. Then he pulled the curtains closed.

"Jareth, what is it?" Odette was suddenly overcome with giggles.

"I have been thinking about your words and wishing nothing more than to be at home with you." He knocked on the side of the carriage. "Back to our personal carriage." Then he kissed her again, this time more passionately.

"Jareth!" Odette gasped, breathless at his enthusiasm.

"I know," he whispered, kissing along her sensitive neck. "I cannot seem to keep myself away from you."

His hands explored, gripping at the fabric in such a way she felt lightheaded, and she tried to stop him by grasping his upper arms, but wished for him to continue against her better judgement. He'd never been so brazen before. Especially when there were people passing the carriage just outside; it was all so uncivilized.

"Why does the scent of you do this?" Jareth groaned and she found herself opening to him without hesitation. "It drives me mad."

She whispered his name, breathily. Pressing the back of her hand to her mouth she stifled every trembling sound he elicited. He was kissing along her breasts, his tongue teasing beneath the fabric towards her nipples. How she wanted him to take them in his mouth. It was as though all reason had left her.

Suddenly, his forehead rested against her collarbone as he let out a long sigh. "I had better stop before all reason leaves me." He kissed her forehead before settling in next to her. "I promise, once we return home, we shall continue."

"It shall not take too long I hope," she said coyly.

Jareth laughed as he intertwined their fingers. "If it were not the middle of the day, such a statement might make my good sense abandon me."

"You are too much a man of discipline, I should think," Odette replied, feeling quite powerful after his many compliments.

That caught his attention. "If I were to hazard a guess, I'd almost say you were antagonizing me."

"You were the one who started something we cannot finish until later," Odette replied, her cheeks burning.

Jareth sounded surprised but amused. "So, you wish me to suffer?"

"No," Odette replied immediately. Then thought for a moment. "Perhaps a little."

"I assure you," he said in a husky voice, tilting his face closer. "I am suffering. Being so near you and being unable to have you."

She leaned against his shoulder, embarrassed beyond words. Instead of responding, he put an arm around her and drew her against him. Kissing the top of her head, they continued in contented silence. Regardless of their playful banter to the contrary, neither were truly suffering, knowing that within the hour they would arrive, then soon after, they would travel home, and the privacy of their bedchamber would be waiting for them.

"How much longer?" Odette asked as the carriage jostled.

"Impatient?" Jareth asked coyly but answered without further prompting. "We're already beyond the capital's outer wall, so we're a quarter hour from the teleportation platform."

"Good," Odette replied, twining her fingers with his.

They faced each other and Odette closed her eyes, preparing for the press of his lips. She felt the barest brush of them when something slammed into their carriage. It didn't tip them over but they quickly came to a halt.

Jareth's arms went around her as they heard yelling outside. Suddenly fire exploded on the side of their carriage as glass shattered. Odette was terrified as smoke filled the interior, she clung to Jareth in absolute horror as he stood. Why were they being attacked?

"Hold on," Jareth whispered, cradling her head against him.

Just as quickly as the sounds began, they vanished. Odette opened her eyes and leaned back to a serene forest. She took a startled step back as Jareth glanced around, his eyes sharp as though assessing the situation.

There was only one explanation Odette could draw from their sudden relocation. "You're gifted?"

Jareth's head slowly turned in her direction. Instead of answering, he merely nodded. It wasn't that much of a surprise, not with his fame and heroics. Especially not when she thought about her own experience with the wyvern. Yet it troubled her to know he'd never deemed it a topic for discussion. Odette had been trying to determine how best to share her own ability with him, considering he'd never asked, and it was not considered polite to bring up. Though she was finding herself less likely to stand on social etiquette.

"A Mage?" Odette pressed.

"Magician," Jareth countered, scratching the back of his head uncomfortably. "I don't like to talk about it."

"I see." Odette really didn't, it just seemed the right thing to say. "I'm a Mage."

That caught his attention. "What?" He appeared troubled by her confession and that made her uncomfortable for some reason. "For how long?"

"Just recently. I was a Mystic until…well until I fell in love with you." Odette met his gaze, challenging him to respond to her heartfelt confession, though she feared he would reject her.

"What can you do?" Each word seemed strained.

"See emotions like auras," Odette replied. "And you can teleport without the carriage?"

Jareth nodded. "And slow time. Those are the essence of my abilities."

They assessed each other and then Odette remembered why they were standing in the middle of the forest. "Who attacked us?"

"If I was to wager a guess," Jareth replied, his expression suddenly filled with fury. "I'd say it was one of my jealous brothers."

Odette was startled for a moment, though she shouldn't have been. There was only one slot to become a duke and Duke Nuvian had a few sons. Though the North did well enough, the East was rich in resources and had the largest fleet of ships. Just as the West was the center of trade with other countries, and the South fed the whole country with its long growing seasons.

"Will they try again?" Odette asked, suddenly afraid as she shifted closer to him.

"I have no proof, but this must be reported and investigated," Jareth replied before drawing her against him. "Hold on."

With a sudden pressure, they were standing just beyond the capital walls. Their sudden appearance startled a man with hay stacked tall on a cart. He glanced around and scratched the back of his head as they started walking.

"I demand an audience with King Enry." Jareth's voice held a level of commanding authority she'd never heard him use. There was a sharpness in his tone that unnerved her.

"May I inquire as to the reason?" responded the esquire, a tall man with a halo of white hair and a bored expression.

"My near assassination," Jareth shot back with clear annoyance.

Odette tightened her hold on his hand, remembering the fire and the smoke. Surely those poor men had been killed. She put a hand to her throat.

"Are you well?" Jareth asked, his voice soft with concern.

"Shaken," Odette replied, but put on a reassuring smile. "Nothing time cannot assuage."

He nodded but pulled her closer against him. They waited, hand in hand, for the esquire to return. To her surprise it did not take long for him to reappear with the same stiff lip.

"The King asked that I escort you to his personal study; he shall join you shortly." His voice was as flat as paper before he lifted an arm to show them the way. However, when Jareth took a step forward with Odette in tow, he added, "Just you, Marquess. The marchioness must remain here."

"No," Jareth replied, his shoulders taunt as he leaned forward menacingly.

Odette put a hand on his shoulder. "I am sure I would be of little use. Please go."

Her husband seemed torn and it warmed her heart. "I do not wish to leave you alone."

"I shall have a maid called to serve her."

"See," Odette replied. "I shall have some tea to quiet my nerves and wait for you. All shall be well."

He nodded, though he did not seem pleased. Then after a surprising but welcomed kiss, he followed the esquire. Now alone, Odette lost some of her earlier bravado. In these unfamiliar halls she felt very small. There was little she could do but put on a calm face while she waited, which took longer than she would have thought. She was wondering if she was forgotten when a young woman joined her in the waiting area.

"Marchioness." The little maid approached her. "I am here to escort you."

Odette followed her down the hall. She glanced at the fineries as they walked, wondering how much further it was. She was so distracted that she didn't notice a group of men walking in her direction at first. There was something oddly familiar about the man in front; they all seemed to be following and listening to him. When his eyes locked with hers, she saw his eyebrows lift in surprise.

"Marchioness Chadwick, this is a surprise. Your husband led me to believe you would not be staying in the capital." He may be older, but his voice had not changed; this was Lord Morran.

She curtsied as was customary. "Lord Morran. There was a final matter he had to discuss with his highness."

His appraising eyes made her uncomfortable. It was not that they were full of desire or anything unsavory, but that they seemed to peer into her soul. It was a sensation she remembered from when she was a child. It seemed that her ability had only grown keener in the years since their last meeting.

"I see you are still the most interesting of the Wolverson sisters." It felt like a comment he was making more to the air and less to her.

Regardless, Odette was taken aback by his sudden and brazen comment. "I do not understand what you imply."

He waved his group away. "Finish what I asked." Once they were gone, only the maid and Lord Morran remained. "I meant no offense, only that your father appears to be losing his touch to have let you fall into the hands of his enemy."

"It was at the king's command," Odette reminded him.

"True." He tilted his head as he responded. "Though I doubt Duke Wolverson put up much resistance."

"My father is loyal to the king. He would have no reason to oppose it." Odette felt uncomfortable with this line of discussion. "It was a pleasure speaking with you. Have a fine day, my lord." She curtsied and tried to move past him.

He stepped in closer to her, narrowly blocking her escape. "Tell me, what is it that you see when you look at me?" The words were a soft whisper meant just for her.

Odette sucked in a sharp breath. Though his question wasn't explicit, she had the sudden understanding he was hinting at her ability. She swallowed down the panic clawing its way up her throat.

"I don't..." The words came out sharp and uneven. Odette cleared her throat before continuing, "Whatever can you mean?"

"You know," was his only reply.

Odette felt weak in the knees a moment before Jareth's voice cut through their conversation. "Step away from my wife."

Odette's gaze darted in his direction, shocked by the hatred seething off him. She'd never seen Jareth this way, never seen him so outwardly aggressive as he quickly put himself between Lord Morran and her. Not even with his own family, who'd shown nothing but hostility and likely tried to kill them.

Lord Morran raised an eyebrow. "I was only exchanging pleasantries. No need to be so dramatic."

Odette clasped down hard on Jareth's upper arm when he surged forward as though to swing a punch. She could see Lord Morran was purposely trying to bait her husband. To what end, she wasn't sure but wanted nothing more than to leave.

"He was asking after my health," Odette lied, trying to do anything to stop what was happening. "We should go."

"Yes," Lord Morran replied, rooted to his spot, making no effort to defuse the situation. "You should go."

The poor maid seemed confused as Jareth hastily herded Odette away. He silently dragged her from the palace. He called a carriage and yanked her into it. Once they were seated, Odette tried to project her confusion in his direction, expecting him to explain himself.

Instead, he finally said, "Never speak to that man again."

"He is another marquess. I may have to," Odette replied, wondering at her husband's sudden emotional state. He seemed more upset that she'd had a brief conversation with Lord Morran than about the assassination attempt.

"No," Jareth replied. "I promise you shall never have to speak to him again. I will escort you home before returning to answer questions that may aid the investigation."

Odette nodded quietly, staring at her hands in her lap. She felt like a scolded child who didn't understand what she'd done wrong. For the first time in a very long time, Odette was reminded of her father and Wolf Manor. Perhaps she'd never truly escape so long as she remained in the world of nobility. It made her wonder if all those years ago, she'd made the wrong choice.

Chapter 32

Jareth was true to his word. They'd no sooner arrived at Vallerdale Hall than he'd returned to the capital to deal with the proceedings, after explaining the events to a select few. Kira was immediately attentive and talkative, but Odette was worn down by the events. Although she had not eaten, instead of food, she simply craved sleep.

The next day she was loathed to leave her room, especially when she learned Jareth had not returned. Seeing to only the barest of duties, the entire household seemed to sense she was not her normal self. Everyone kindly let her be for the rest of the day, and it had passed in a blur of thoughtfulness before the oblivion of sleep.

The following morning, she felt no improvement, tired and lethargic. Yet there was one margin of relief she could enjoy. One secret that had created a divide between her and Jareth was gone. She no longer had to hide that she was a Mage and learning that he had an ability like her brought her infinite joy, putting aside their recent interaction.

Kira entered the room, cautiously. "I'm awake," Odette said, slowly rising. "Please help me dress."

"Yes, Mistress," Kira said, appearing relieved. Normally they would have chatted as she was dressed, but Odette couldn't find the energy. It was as though something were dragging her down.

"You'll tell me when Jareth returns?" Odette said as Kira finished her hair.

Mid-pin Kira slowed, her eyes wide for a moment. Then carefully she said, "He arrived late last night."

Odette froze. Why had he not sought her out? It wasn't as though he hadn't come in late before or left early. Was their earlier interaction souring their relationship more than she'd first thought?

Standing, Odette tried to smooth her frayed emotions. "Where is my husband now?"

"He already broke his fast; I cannot guess where he is now." Kira frowned. "Should I ask for you?"

Odette shook her head. "I am sure I can find him."

If he hadn't left, he was likely in his study. When she knocked there was a pause before he called out, "Come in."

When she opened the door, she could see his entire body tense. She thought to see his emotions, but now that he knew her ability, it felt intrusive. They had always been able to discuss matters before; this time should be no different.

"Good morning," Odette said, forcing a smile.

Jareth seemed guarded as he remained seated. How could the space between them in the room feel like a crevasse? Part of her knew it wasn't the room, but the distance between the two of them. Forcing herself to move, she tried to physically close the gap.

"Good morning, is there something you needed?" Jareth asked, his expression and tone formal.

That caused Odette to stop in her tracks a few steps from his desk. She shook her head, uncertain how to proceed. How could so much change in just a few days?

"I am going to have to leave again, to finish the king's first request," Jareth informed her, setting the pen in the inkwell.

"How long?" Odette asked.

"A few days, I hope, but it could be a week or more." He leaned back in his chair, hands steepled.

She folded her hands across her stomach. "I see." She wanted them to be close again and thought of the only thing she knew for sure they had in common. "When you return, can you assist with my Mage abilities? I had help as a Mystic, but these Mage abilities are so new."

Her hope died on her tongue and lodged in her throat at the dark expression on Jareth's face. "Absolutely not. That is entirely unnecessary."

"I don't...can you explain what you mean?" Had she misunderstood?

"There is no reason to spend any time on your ability," Jareth explained, his tone final.

Odette took in a shaky breath; it was like he was rejecting her. Her ability may only be a part of her, but it still hurt. "Is there a reason why?"

"You don't need to become a Magician. Stay as you are."

"But you're a Magician." Her sadness was twisting inside of her. "I can be of use."

His jaw tightened. "It doesn't matter. Do as I say."

A tear slid down her cheek, and for the first time, Odette got angry with him. "It matters to me." He seemed startled by her outburst. "I cannot do what you ask. It would be like denying a bird the right to fly. And you would ask this of me when you yourself can fly?"

"That isn't..." Jareth's voice trailed off as she wiped away a tear.

"Excuse me." Odette abruptly turned as more tears threatened. She shot out the door and quickly rushed to the only place that had been a constant comfort to her. The library was empty and the only light was pouring in from the lofty windows. It was as though she were right back in Wolf Manor and any moment her father would strike her for her insolent tongue. She'd rarely opposed him over the years, but her willfulness could not always be easily suppressed. It surfaced periodically, like a ship thought to be lost at sea that always found its way back again.

Tucked into her favorite alcove, she tried to sort through her emotions—lining them up like the books on the shelves next to her. She hoped that by identifying them she could work through them. She knew the discussion would continue if the last expression on his face was any indication. So, for now she must figure out how best to handle their next inevitable conversation.

Hunger is what drove her out of her sanctuary. She had food brought to her rooms as she settled other pressing matters that nature wouldn't relent on. Once both were resolved, she sat quietly, having calmed her stampeding emotions into a direct course of action. There were only two people in the whole world who knew of her abilities; her husband, and she suspected, Lord Morran. Only one of them she had openly shared that secret with.

The fact that he didn't want to help her with her gift wasn't the core of what bothered her. It was that she'd shared a secret and his first reaction was to deny it. What would he do if he found out she was Duke Wolverson's illegitimate daughter or that she had living relatives she was sending funds to? Add her father's beatings and the fact that she was barely the fine lady she pretended to be—her gift was the least of her secrets and he'd acted like it was reproachful.

Would Jareth abandon her and force her back to the very place that had nearly broken her spirit?

A knock startled her, causing her to drop the book she'd been holding. Shaking her head, she realized it was very likely the maid retrieving her mostly empty platter. It was unlikely Jareth would seek her out so quickly after their earlier spat.

Clearing her throat, she called out, "Who is it?"

There was a short pause, which caused her heart to thump in her chest. "May I come in?" Jareth asked; he sounded resigned.

Odette immediately gathered the fallen book and tried to straighten her dress. Sitting properly on the chair, she glanced at the messy plates and stood. Bringing him to the bedroom that they'd shared on many occasions didn't seem wise. She would rather risk being overheard than possibly fill her room with unhappy memories. Since she didn't wish to do that in any of her favorite places, which left her only one option.

Striding to the door, she opened it. Jareth turned to her, surprised. "I was just going for a walk. Would you care to join me?"

Jareth nodded, then glanced down at her book. "Were you going to read?"

Odette had forgotten she was holding it, and set it down on the entry table. "Shall we?"

Wasting no time, Odette went straight to the garden, Jareth trailing behind her. Once they were safely in the green, Odette slowed and took a deep breath of the outdoors. The scent of lilacs wafted sweetly in the air, mingling with the freshly trimmed lawn. It truly was a lovely day.

"I never meant to hurt you." Jareth's voice cut through her tranquility.

"Yet you did," Odette said, before turning to face him. "I love you, thus your words matter to me."

His expression was pained as he moved closer. "There are many things I cannot tell you. Things that are the very foundation of my decision making. I am sorry if my methods are harsh."

"We all have our secrets," Odette replied, thinking of the mounting pile she carried on her back. "Will you tell me one day?"

"Soon I hope," Jareth replied, nodding. "For now, please trust in me."

Odette moved closer and offered her hands, which he quickly took in his own. "I know you are not thoughtless." She said. "I don't know what drove you to this moment, and I know those words were not intended to hurt me, but I am not a knight to be ordered; I am your wife."

"It is no excuse, but I have lived a long time without an equal. It seems I met my match in you." He lifted her hand and kissed her palm. "Can you forgive me?"

"Yes," she said, moving closer to press her forehead to his. "As long as you promise to hurry home to me."

"I shall use all of my abilities to return quickly. I hope soon my fears will be put to rest and I can finally share with you the truth." Jareth pulled her tightly against him, nuzzling into her. "Then there will be no further secrets between us."

Odette rested her head on his chest, knowing it was time that she shared as well. "Yes. No more secrets."

Chapter 33

-Past-

Odette was hiding in the library, hoping no one would come looking for her. She was constantly wedging herself into the narrowest place she could find, hoping no one would notice. In two days, Jestine would turn sixteen and their debuts would happen. Turning to the book on the herbal remedies she was reading, Odette tried not to squint too hard at the fading picture. If she did it too often it would mean less overall reading time and sore eyes.

Suddenly, there was activity. Someone was shouting. Odette sat up to try to hear better and her stomach lurched when she realized it was her name. With a lump in her chest, she carried the book with her, cradling it against her like a shield as she went to her fate.

"There you are!" A maid found her in the hallway. She scolded her before adding, "Your father wishes to see you immediately."

"The duke?" Odette felt shock and fear.

"Who else?" the maid retorted as though speaking to her equal. It had taken no time at all for the servants to treat her as badly as the rest of her family did.

Her father's normally solemn demeanor appeared almost jolly when she arrived. Grace was clapping her hands and laughing as Jestine appeared pleased.

"What did he do next?" Grace asked, her eyes shining.

"He told the king to cut him off. What a fool!" The duke took the last swallow of his drink. "It was so easy to disgrace him by siding with Lord Morran. The Hero of Mount Vere, more like The Fool!" Then his eyes flicked over in her direction and she instinctively flinched. "There you are!" He stood and held his arms out, as though happy to see her.

"You needed me?" Odette asked carefully, still clenching the book tightly against her.

"I have such joyous news." The duke clapped her on her shoulders in an affectionate way.

She relaxed slightly. "You do?"

"You are to be wed!" the duke announced and held up his hand. "To Lord Morran."

Odette glanced behind her father at the imposing figure of Lord Morran. She tried not to panic at the sudden change in her circumstances. Lord Morran still watched her with that same penetrating gaze that made her uncomfortable. There was something dark about him, like he was a walking raincloud.

"Miss Wolverson," Lord Morran said with a bow.

Unwilling to face her father's wrath, she quickly curtsied. "Lord Morran."

He strode up to her and took her hand. It was very abrupt and she was immediately intimidated by his closeness. He kissed the back of her bare hand, an intimate gesture. It took every nerve she had not to react.

"I would be honored by your hand, should you give your consent." His eyes never stopped watching her.

It was her father's will; what could she do but agree? "It is you who honors me."

-Present-

It was wonderful to have Jareth back after dealing with a border matter at the king's request. He'd promised, once he received confirmation of some news he was awaiting, they'd talk. She'd been feeling run down lately and hoped his presence would improve her overall motivation. He'd also promised not to go away again for a while unless an emergency arose. She'd convinced him to read the reports in the parlor so they could have tea while she lounged on the couch. Although concerned at how he might react to her own revelations, he'd been doting on her, and their earlier amicability had returned.

"Shall we go riding later?" Jareth asked.

Odette hesitated; the idea of going into the somewhat chilly day to ride a horse seemed beyond what she could handle—for some reason she'd been so tired lately. Yet the idea of time alone with Jareth seemed perfect. Before she had a chance to decide, there came a knock on the door.

"Enter," Jareth commanded.

Sir Lex came in. "I have news." Odette immediately sat up at the urgency of his tone—was this the information Jareth had been waiting for?

"What is it?" Jareth asked, standing.

Sir Lex glanced at Odette as though hesitating at her presence. "Assassins tried to kill Lord Morran," he said.

Jareth visibly paled at the news. For some reason that struck her as odd. Jareth seemed like the last person to care what happened to Lord Morran. More than once she'd seen his open dislike of the man. If she didn't know how honorable Jareth was, she might presume he'd had a hand in the attack on Lord Morran.

"You may go," Jareth commanded, sharply.

Odette moved closer. "What is it?"

"It is happening again," Jareth said, his entire being in anguish and his eyes unfocused.

"What is?" Odette was completely confused; not just by the words he was saying, but also the certainty in his voice.

His gaze snapped to her. "We must warn your father. Lord Morran is going to kill your entire family." He stood as though he was going to leave, but she hurried to stand in front of him, stopping him.

"How do you know this?" Odette demanded, her stomach in her throat. She'd always suspected he was keeping something big from her, but not this. Could he see the future?

Jareth hesitated. "When I die, I come back to the moment of my greatest regret: when I'm made the Hero of Mount Vere and King Enry offers me any reward I demand." His voice was level, but it did nothing to diminish the impact of his words.

"When you die?" Had breathing always been so difficult? "How many times?"

"This is my third." His face grim.

"Why would you keep marrying me every time?" She couldn't stop the flow of tears as she collapsed on a nearby chair, overwhelmed by the information.

He shook his head and took her hands as he knelt in front of her. "No. This is my first time marrying you."

"Then how did you know Lord Morran would kill my father and sisters to take over?" His face was solemn. "What is it?" she demanded, her stomach in knots. "Tell me."

"Because it keeps happening. First, he fakes an assassination attempt on his own life and then hires real assassins to murder your family. Once by his hand." He averted his eyes. "Last time you were involved, with Lord Morran's help."

She stared at him in disbelief. "I was involved in their deaths?"

"Yes." His head hung. "Directly."

"I don't...can't understand." She replied with a frown, shaking her head as though to ward off his words.

"I died killing him the first time. When I met you in my second life, you were married to Lord Morran. He is a Magician that taught you everything you knew." His expression was dark. "Together you conquered the kingdom far faster than the first time."

"I couldn't do that." Odette shook her head but even as she said the words something whispered within her that she might have. That she'd consented to marrying a stranger because her father told her to. His face was patient as she looked down at their joined hands.

"The you from that past life did, but when he went too far, you came to me. Told me it had to stop and how to stop him. While we worked together, I came to know what you were under the mask." He touched her cheek with the same affection she'd always known. "I admired you. Before we faced him, you asked that if I truly lived my life again after I died, to promise to protect you in my next life. To show you there was another way."

"Why didn't it work last time?" Odette asked. "You said this was your third time."

"The first time everything played out and we never met. You died when your father was killed. The second time, when I tried to change things, you came to me after you sensed my pity. It confused you and bothered you enough."

"So, you knew I could read auras?" Odette asked.

"I didn't realize you were already in tune with the start of your powers until you told me. I assumed Lord Morran was the one who had awoken you. Once he saw the value of your talents, they became critical to his quick success the second time." He shook his head. "But yes, I knew you would eventually be able to see peoples' emotions, not just feel them on objects."

Odette shook her head. "Seeing auras isn't that valuable of a talent. How could I have been of such great help to such a powerful Magician?"

Jareth sighed. "When you fully tap into your ability as a Magician in your own right, you don't just see them, you can influence them."

Odette pulled out of his hold as she stood and took a step back. "You kept this from me?" She felt betrayed. "You rejected my abilities because of this?" Tears pricked her eyes. "Do you know what I thought? How that made me feel?"

"Odette." Jareth reached for her, but she put her hands up to ward him off.

"I need a moment." She shied away from him. Her chest hurt as she tried to find a path out of her confusion.

"I understand," he said. She turned away as he hesitated only at the door. "I just want you to know that although I may have admired you in my last life, but I love you in this one."

Chapter 34

-Past-

Lord Morran may have been a dark figure, but his large manor was not. She'd expected a gothic structure decorated in monochrome. Instead, she found a rich home with busy servants and well-trained guards. When Lord Morran had insisted they leave prior to their wedding night, Odette had thought her father would protest but he did not. Instead, they were zapped to her new home in the blink of an eye. Feeling a little ill after Lord Morran's horseless carriage had seen them to her new home, she'd been left with two lady's maids who quickly dressed her for dinner.

Overwhelmed, she'd barely tasted the food at dinner and drank far too much wine. Yet that night he'd stayed in the dining hall and sent her to her bed—alone. As he had done for weeks. She barely saw her husband yet her every need was cared for. She'd been unsure and jumpy at first, but it soon became clear that Lord Morran had little interest in the wife he'd just acquired, and the marriage remained unconsummated.

As weeks turned to months, she found her place in the castle. Lord Morran spent time across his providence and at the capital. He was changeable and would suddenly appear for dinner. He would ask her questions about her well-being and her needs, much like she was a houseguest. He never approached her, never tried to touch her, and little by little Odette came out of her shell. She came to know most of the servants and befriended her two lady's maids.

It was a freedom that Odette had never known. One she never wanted to lose and yet there was this quiet fear. Why wouldn't he consummate the marriage? Did he plan to use this against her father? It was the only weight that pressed upon her shoulders, whispering into her ear.

At a dinner like any other, Odette was eating her food as Lord Morran did the same. They had exchanged their normal pleasantries and now ate in silence. At least that is what he'd done until then.

"You may leave us," Lord Morran said, sending the servants away.

Odette went to stand but he waved her to stop. She slowly settled back down, confused by his sudden change in their routine. "Is something wrong, my lord?"

"Have you enjoyed your time in my home?" Lord Morran asked, his gaze appraising.

"Yes. I thank you for your hospitality." Odette tried to be demur, like she'd been taught.

He steepled his fingers. "I am going to ask you a question, and I need you to be honest with me. Do you think you can do that?"

Odette's heartbeat quickened at his words. "I will obey, my husband."

She felt like he was boring holes into her. "What is your ability as a Mystic?"

Odette froze. It wasn't a question if she had abilities, it was what were they. It implied he knew that she was a Mystic. A flood of emotions mingled with the drumming of her heart. She swallowed the lump in her throat.

"I can sense strong emotions on objects." What could she do but obey?

He smiled at that, making his face seem less severe. "Would you like to be whole? To become a Magician?"

She'd never even considered it. "How?"

He stood and held out a hand to her. "Come."

She took his hand, and they went.

-Present-

Odette didn't know what to do with herself. All of this time felt like a lie and yet she couldn't dismiss it. Could she believe his words? Did he really love her or just the former her? Her head was pounding as she paced, trying to make sense of just when her entire world had shifted. She'd thought over his words again and again. Instead of answers, she only came up with more questions.

Even with her uncertainty, she couldn't simply dismiss everything they'd been through together. Despite what he said, she did still love her husband—no matter how foolish that may be. That's not to say she wasn't still angry with him. He could have told her about all this at any time, yet had kept it a secret from her. What other secrets did he have? The idea made her sick with worry and frustration.

A sudden thought struck her, and she froze. If she had revealed her abilities to Jareth what else had her past self shared? Had she told him she wasn't really the duke's legitimate daughter or about her family? Guilt swarmed her insides. Here she was angry at her husband because he'd kept such a secret from her when she was doing the same.

What fools they had both been—but it was time to make it right. Because she knew if they could overcome this, the love they shared would only grow. Her legs carried her from the room and to his down the hall. When she knocked he didn't answer.

"Jareth?" she asked cautiously before opening the door. It was empty within, and dread suddenly filled her gut.

Rushing from the room, she nearly tripped down the stairs, catching herself on the railing. She rushed to his study but found it as empty as his bedroom. The maid she passed was surprised but said nothing. It did little to slow her down as she met the butler in the hall.

"Kenith," she called, breathless. "Where has my husband gone?"

"He saddled his horse half past the hour," he replied. "Is something wrong, Lady Chadwick?" The color around him became green as nervousness mixed with the orange panic.

"I just need to speak with him." She didn't wait for an answer but hurried to the stable, where she ordered her mare be saddled. She wasn't properly dressed to ride, but that wouldn't stop her. If she knew her husband at all, she knew exactly where he was going.

Dark clouds loomed on the horizon as she rode and it didn't take long for her to regret leaving so impulsively. Not only was she not dressed to ride, she was not dressed for the wind or threatening rain. She didn't turn back and, as she reached the bottom of the hill, she spotted his horse; just as it began to sprinkle. She dismounted the moment she was close enough.

Her husband had been kneeling by a grave marker for the former Marquess, his hand still resting on it as he stood. A wave of emotions hit her and assaulted her senses. She shut them out; she didn't want to be swayed by what he was feeling, she only wanted to share with him what she felt.

"Odette?" He took a step towards her as it began to rain. "What are you doing here?"

"To tell you the truth." Her voice came out with more force than she'd intended. "I've been keeping my own secrets."

He hesitated as uncertainty flashed across his features. "What secrets?"

"I don't know what my former self told you, but I am not the duke's legitimate daughter." The words twisted inside of her, but they were so freeing. Finally, the shackle of this secret had been shrugged off. "I was only in his care for seven years before you saved me."

"Saved you?"

"For the three years I lived with him, my father was not kind to me." No doubt her face was as twisted with the emotions she felt. "I was his greatest mistake."

Suddenly his arms were around her, holding her against him. His smell mingled with fresh rain as she buried herself in the comfort of his warmth. She'd never felt so loved as she did in that moment. He accepted her despite the truth. Part of her had always known he would, but fear of what her father might do if she broke her promise had kept her silent.

When he shifted back, she looked up at him. "Can you ever forgive me?" she asked, the rain making her blink as droplets struck her face.

"There is nothing to forgive." His lips met hers and she surged against them. Wrapping her arms around his neck she pressed herself against him, wishing to be one with him. "Odette," the erotic way he spoke her name sent shivers down her spine.

"Join us," she pleaded, and he groaned against her mouth before capturing her lips once more.

He lifted her from the ground and carried her down to the bottom of the hill. Under the closest tree they were afforded some shelter from the rain as neither wanted to break away. She giggled when he nearly tripped and cursed at the offending root. She covered his face with kisses as she wrapped her legs around his waist.

"You're driving me insane," he whispered as he pressed her against the tree trunk.

Odette leaned back and studied his face. He'd lost some weight while he'd been away, but his intensity hadn't been reduced one iota. Even now she was completely caught up in the way it radiated off him. He touched his cheek.

"I love you." Her words felt so right.

The smile on his face was radiant with love. It nearly blinded her as he responded, "I love you, Odette."

The next kiss felt like the joining of two souls. He kissed her cheeks, chin, and eyelids. She felt like he was worshiping her as he kissed down her neck. She moaned, drawing in the smell of rain and the sweet scent of leaves. Her chest heaved as she arched her back. Her nipples slid free of the fabric as he licked at them, the heat of his tongue in complete contrast with her chilled wet skin.

The fingers of her left hand dug into his clothing as her right found purchase on the tree. Curling her fingers around the branch, she ached to be free of the constraint of her clothing. The hindrance of the layers of her dress creating a barrier between them that made her want to tear them off. Instead, she tugged on his cloak's clasp until it fell to the forest floor.

He cursed against her breast as his hands struggled to find flesh. Raising his head, she felt a shudder run through her—like a starved predator craving something to eat. It only served to fuel the raging need within her.

She slowly slid off of him; her legs felt like gelatin as they met solid ground. He seemed like he was trying to reign himself in, but she had no such notion. Pulling at the buttons on her dress her heavy skirts fell around her ankles. All that remained was her stockings and silk panties.

He surged against her. "Jareth!" she cried as he ravaged her. An electrifying tingle rushed over her skin as Odette tugged at his shirt.

He discarded the tunic as she lay her hand on his chest. The raindrops continued to cascade down, causing a faint halo to form around him. He appeared to her more than human, an ethereal presence. The moment his hand found her sensitive junction, pleasure surged through her. No matter how wonderful it made her feel, she wanted more. She wanted him inside of her, buried deep.

"Odette," his voice was husky.

With a gasp, her entire body clenched. She shuddered around his fingers as his thumb continued to move along her sensitive nub. She felt like he was melting her from the inside out and nearly collapsed as her insides spasmed.

"Hold on," he said as he wrapped her arms around his neck. Lifting her up, he sheathed himself into her in a single thrust.

Odette arched at the sudden penetration. His hands and arms were like metal coils as he plunged into her. His hard body was unforgiving and yet so wonderful. Like a ship on stormy seas, she held on and rode the waves. She was lost to his passion; her mind could only focus on their joining and what it was doing to her.

She tried to keep his emotions out, but she was overwhelmed by them. They mingled with her own as she reached her second climax. His name was on her lips as she clung to him. Tears slid down her cheek from the intensity of the closeness she felt. The rain was as relentless as his powerful thrusts. Her head tipped back as her vision became blurry.

"Jareth," she whispered his name, trying to grasp onto reality.

It only made him drive into her deeper and faster. She felt herself reach an edge she'd never experienced. Instead of fear, she only felt liberation. Instead of fighting it, she let herself be carried away an instant before yet another sharp orgasm crashed against every nerve in her body. Suddenly Jareth grabbed her hand, interlacing their fingers a moment before he stiffened.

They were both breathing raggedly as Jareth embraced her. She rested her cheek against the side of his head, smelling the soap in his hair. She leaned back and brought her hands up to frame his face. In that moment, just when she didn't think she could love him more, she did.

"I'll never leave you," she whispered. "I'll always be your wife." A smattering of Jareth's conflicting emotions struck her and she blocked them out, wishing only to hear what he said to her. "I accept you no matter what you say."

She hugged him close to her. Then when she tried to move away, he tightened his hold and said, "Once was not enough."

There was a soft pressure against her and then they were suddenly standing in their bedroom. Odette barely had time to orient herself before he set her on the bed. He hurried to undress her, kissing and licking away the rainwater that was all over her skin.

"Jareth," she tried to tell him how sensitive she was but stopped when she saw how eager his manhood was. Whatever protest she had died in her throat at his gaze—it was as though he were enchanted by her.

He entered her without hesitation or resistance. She felt lightheaded as her depths were impossibly tender. She gasped as he began to slide in and out of her slowly. Immediately overwhelmed by the sensations he was causing, she lost all reason. Words and sounds escaped her; she tried to move away from him but his stone-like weight kept her in place. She was overrun by stimulation, turning her mind into a boiled mess. She became a being only capable of feeling pleasure as he drove into her without restraint.

This time when she climaxed, she gripped his head and pulled it against her lips. She felt him thrust into her one last time before he joined her. Odette's head tilted back at the force of that final penetration; she felt like he was going to break not just her sanity but her body. Something she found overwhelming but not unwelcome.

"Odette?" Jareth's voice sounded far away.

"Hmm?" she asked, trying to open her eyes. Concern riddled his face; it was enough for her to keep her eyes open. "What's wrong?"

He touched her cheek. "Did I…" he hesitated, and she saw the anguish on his face.

"No. I'm not hurt," she replied, trying to stifle a yawn. "Just wonderfully spent." She patted his cheek as she drifted off to sleep.

Chapter 35

"Concentrate," Lord Morran said, his deep voice soothing to her.

Day by day, she had become stronger and learned that she was holding herself back. Many times, abilities manifested themselves in ways that tied directly to what they could do. Since emotions drove her abilities, she would have to learn to control them or experience new ones to unlock her Mage skills.

Very slowly she opened her eyes. Lord Morran was watching her, his normally expressionless face softened. It made him appear almost handsome. He really had been incredibly kind and patient with her. Almost like a friend. She'd always wanted a friend.

Odette's eyes widened as she saw a soft glow appear around him. It was like the color spoke to her, telling her what it was.

"I can see!" Odette said excitedly. She waved her hands around his head. "It is yellow for excitement." It was as though this new ability had always been there.

"Good." A soft smile touched his lips, something that had been happening a lot more of late. "Progress."

"Thank you!" Odette threw her arms around him without thinking, so overcome with joy. When his hands settled against her back, she opened her eyes in shock. Gasping as she realized what she'd done, Odette stepped back, yet he didn't remove his hands.

"You did well." He sounded proud, and she was once again bursting with happiness.

"I couldn't have done it without you." She tucked her hair behind her ear, suddenly shy as she felt something shift between them.

"I believe you would have eventually." Lord Morran lifted her chin. "You are extraordinarily resilient."

When he moved towards her, she didn't move away. Their gaze was locked as he stepped ever closer and his lips captured hers in the gentlest of kisses. She leaned into him as he kissed her, causing her mind to go fuzzy. It was the first time he'd ever touched her in such a romantic way. She braced for more, expecting him to press his claim since she'd done nothing to deter him. Instead, he eased back and cupped her cheek.

"How could I have neglected you for so long?" The question wasn't for her. "You make me question everything."

"Everything, my lord?" Odette whispered, uncertain and yet finding herself drawn to this reserved man.

His expression was sad a moment before he dropped his hand and turned away from her. "Keep practicing." His words were not harsh, but they did feel final as he left. Odette watched him depart and wondered what their future might hold.

-Present-

"Odette."

Her eyes opened slowly and took a moment to adjust. Jareth was sitting on the bed next to her. It was evening now, and the moonlight was streaming through the window. She shifted towards him.

"Jareth?"

"Are you hungry?" he asked, holding up her robe.

Though she should have felt embarrassed by her state of undress, she simply took the garment before kissing him. "Starved."

Once they were settled before a warm meal, Odette studied her husband as they ate in silence. So much about the world had changed in such a short time and yet her love for him was unshakable. It was obvious in everything he did that his affections ran deep for her in the present, and she decided that would be enough.

"Why didn't you teleport us back earlier?" Odette asked, feeling coy.

He chuckled. "I couldn't think straight enough to even make an attempt."

She reached over and touched his hand with her own. He quickly interlaced their fingers, and she could tell the playful banter was over.

"How long do we have?" Odette asked, setting her fork down.

"Two nights at most. I'll have to go in the morning; it'll take me most of tomorrow to arrive at your father's estate." He took a drink of the wine.

"I think you mean we. My father will never listen to you even if men were breaking down the door." Her father may not love her, but at the end of the day, he would listen to her before the man he considered his enemy.

Jareth's gaze was sharp. "I will not place you in danger."

"I won't leave your side for even a moment," Odette promised. Still, he hesitated so she pressed him. "My father is prideful; he'd rather die fighting than follow you. I may not have my father's love, but I do know how to convince him."

Jareth cringed. "Very well."

Odette picked up the wine and took a drink, but it tasted strange. She set it down and drank the water instead. She yawned despite herself. Jareth stood and kissed the top of her head.

"I'll make the arrangements; you should sleep. Tomorrow will be a long day." Jareth squeezed her shoulder.

"You promise you won't leave without me?" Odette eyed him. She trusted him but also knew how protective he could be.

Jareth sighed. "I promise. You are right; my chances of success are higher with you there."

When he left, she stretched and returned to the bed. She wondered if she was coming down with something as she lay down. Between the exhaustion and the aversion to strong drinks, she didn't know what else it could be. She was nearly asleep when a sudden realization hit her.

Sitting up in bed, she touched a hand to her stomach. Her monthly hadn't come in a while. Actually, she'd been so busy and distracted that she couldn't remember the last time it had. Before Mavis had visited, that was for sure.

Could she be pregnant?

A large part of her wanted to rush down to the healer and find out immediately. Yet as the idea took root, everything started to make sense. She remembered her mother had many of the same issues when she was pregnant with Melody. In her heart she knew that she was with a child, but the moment she confirmed it she would let Jareth know. Lord Morran's plan hinged on the duke's death, and she was likely the only person who could convince him.

No. Confirmation would have to wait. She would just have to be extra careful.

Chapter 36

-Past-

In the weeks following their first kiss, Lord Morran had not left. He seemed to check in on her often, giving her gifts, and showering her with his own quiet affection. Odette was unsure how to respond to such a change in her husband and yet she liked what was forming between them.

She'd even heard the servants commenting that he'd never spent so much time at home. He was sending representatives in his stead so he could take her riding. When he did go for an inspection of a nearby farm, most times he took her along.

Despite their kisses, and the way he'd hold her on horseback, he kept her at arm's length in the evening. He'd never tried to be passionate with her and that left her confused. As her feelings for his reserved but caring nature grew, she wanted to become more intimate. She had felt his desire for her, yet he always seemed to pull back. Odette couldn't understand why and felt, with each passing day, the only way she'd find out was if she asked.

Some days she was bored with only the servants and a maid to speak to, never meeting anyone new. It was more isolating than Wolf Manor. At least there, they dined with guests, though she would never wish to go back to such terrible dinners. The judging eyes and subtle way her family shunned her were haunting memories.

Odette glanced out the window; the dreary weather made her less than motivated. It wasn't long before a carriage arrived. A man exited their mansion wearing a hat and long concealing clothing. She was her father's daughter and recognized someone trying to obscure their identity. She was not so naïve that her husband's random questionable dealings didn't catch her attention. Yet she had noticed they came less often, as though he were interacting with them more secretively or just less frequently overall. Closing her eyes, she listened to the rain as it pattered against the glass, the book in her lap sliding closed over her finger as she dozed.

"Odette?"

Jerking awake, she looked up at Lord Morran's concerned face. Immediately stretching, she yawned. "Forgive me, my lord. I must have fallen asleep."

"Do you feel safe here?" His tone surprised her; it was filled with concern.

Odette swallowed the lump in her throat. "I have told you as much before, my lord."

"Are you…happy?" His hesitation was evident.

"I am content," Odette replied as he hovered close to her but far enough away that the gap was apparent. "Yet I seem to have done something to displease you. Is there something I can correct?"

His expression was shock and then confusion. "You have not. Why would you suppose such?"

"Why else would you not consummate this marriage?" Odette had this nagging fear he would never accept her and one day she would have to return to the nightmare that was Wolf Manor.

His eyes searched her face, his brows furrowed. "You are innocent." His response did nothing to explain why, only confused her further. He knelt next to her, taking one of her hands. "You are young and full of life. You do not know the darkness of the world, the death and destruction. You do not see how the poor suffer and how the royalty ignore their pleas. One day you shall be wed to a man worthy of you. For now, I intend to keep you safe."

She touched his cheek with her free hand. "*You* are my husband. I do not intend to take another."

"This marriage can be broken," he said, shaking his head. "Please understand you are far superior—pure and unsullied. You will live in the world I plan to create so that no one will ever suffer again."

Her emotions caused her ability to spill out. She could sense his words were specifically for someone, so she saw his emotions. Love and pain; the kind only a mother could cause. He'd never spoken of his past with her, yet she could see it—this drive to stop something horrible from happening again.

"What happened?" Odette asked softly. When he tried to turn away, Odette made him keep looking at her. "Help me understand."

He averted his gaze. "My mother was carefree and innocent. When my father grew tired of her and she could no longer bear his offspring, he killed her. Deprived her of everything until she withered away so that he might marry again. I couldn't stop it. Although my father didn't pay an assassin, it was murder, and the royalty turned a blind eye because of his wealth and power." His eyes were unfocused but she saw the torment.

Leaning forward, she wrapped her arms around his head drawing his ear to her chest. "I am not dead. Do you hear my heartbeat?" He nodded. "I am a living breathing person who you cannot put on a shelf, my lord." Odette leaned back and put her hands on his jaw. "I will exert my will as you do, but I shall do it to declare that I wish this to be proper marriage. I may be innocent, but I know within you beats a loyal heart. One that could join with mine if you would but let it."

He leaned forward and kissed her softly, wrapping his arms around her. His gentleness became a hunger and she opened herself to him. She was breathless as he pressed against her, driving her back against the glass in her window seat. Odette gripped his clothing as his hands moved along her curves, eliciting a moan.

"My lord!" she exclaimed when he pulled at the laces of her dress.

"William," he replied, jerking at the curtains.

"What?" Odette asked, dazed, peering up at him.

"My name is William and it is what you shall call me from now on." His gaze was as heated as the kisses he'd stolen her breath with earlier.

"William." The name was like a declaration on her lips.

He lifted her up, concealing them behind a set of curtains as he pulled at her clothing. She felt dizzy at the change in him, not as concerned as she ought to be when he exposed her breasts and stripped off her thick skirts.

"You taste as sweet as I imagined."

"You imagined how I tasted?" Odette's cheeks burned, and she was shocked at his admission.

"You have plagued my every thought. Every bit of control I had was deployed in your presence. I felt doomed to this moment from that first kiss, craving you more and more. Coveting you to the point of obsession." His words were mingled with kisses and the slow removal of clothing until all she had left was her last layer, which covered only her legs and sacred area. "You have been my living torment and greatest relief all at once."

"I thought you did not want me," Odette replied honestly, her mind buzzing with his words.

The pressure of him across her body was pleasant. "Let me show you how much I want you." His fingers moved down the length of her, eliciting a gasp. They slid between silk and flesh, touching parts of her that were forbidden except to those who were wed. She did not know what to do with her hands and clung to him, tight with anticipation.

"William?" she said when he slid his finger into her, confused by the sudden feeling.

He stiffened at her words. "I promised I would go slow, yet you tempt me beyond reason." His movements became more persistent as his finger moved inside her delicate folds.

Thoughts left her as she felt him touch and stretch her. His soothing voice commanded she give in. It was not unpleasant, and at times she even felt pleasure, but it was all so scary and new it was hard to completely relax. When he finally positioned himself between her legs she clenched, a part of her wishing to accept but her body too afraid of what came next.

"Breathe," he whispered, and she exhaled. On her next inhale something pierced her. She cried out against his shoulder, trying to shift away from the pain. "It will soon pass," he assured her.

She could feel him moving inside her as he grunted. Tears pricked her eyes, affection for the man at war with the act itself. She was half joy and half agony, wishing for this joining to continue but also for it to end quickly. His movements became almost frenzied, and she felt uncomfortable, gasping at his every thrust. When he finally buried himself all the way into her, she threw her arms around his neck, feeling him shudder as she tried to console herself that next time would be easier.

Then he kissed her, and the confusion created by the animalistic frenzied copulation vanished. He brushed her hair back from her forehead, apprising her with a softness she'd never seen directed at her. This man was not a beast; she could love him and would love him. When he hugged her close, still joined, she knew this was a real marriage.

-Present-

Odette was exhausted. They made multiple jumps together and by mid-afternoon, they had to rest at an inn that was a little more than halfway to their destination. Even though Odette was tired, Jareth looked more so. He ate heartily and then fell into a heavy sleep. The rented room was cramped and smaller than anything she'd ever seen, but it was clean. Watching Jareth sleep, she stifled a yawn.

It wasn't long until she drifted off into blissful sleep as well. When she awoke, Jareth was still next to her and only a few hours had passed. She stood up and donned her coat dress, before going down into the dining area. There was a man behind the bar who nodded at her.

"May I have the dinner we ordered delivered to our room?" Odette asked the imposing man. His look notwithstanding, the green and lavender around him indicated nervousness and insecurity. She realized she caused those emotions in him. Once their meal plans were confirmed, she returned to their room.

When she opened the door, Jareth was sitting up on the bed, appearing worried. "Where did you go?" He slid off the bed and came towards her.

"Just to get dinner," Odette said, surprised at his reaction.

"When I woke up and you weren't here, I thought something had happened." He sat down heavily and ran a hand through his hair.

"I'm not her." Odette could see that far off look and knew what he was thinking. It was odd to talk about herself—or at least a version of herself that did not exist.

That drew his attention immediately. "I know. She may have had your face, but she was...different."

"How?" Odette sat down next to him and took his hand. She could tell it tortured him, the multiple lives he's led.

"She was altered. Like a part of her was empty, broken, and that nothing could fix it. Her eyes were haunting. That was the worst part, that death seemed almost like a relief. I can still hear her making me promise to save and protect her in the next life, no matter what. As though she knew some terrible secret, something she was begging me to stop by changing your fate. A fate she seemed to believe was worse than death." He shook his head as Odette felt tears well in her eyes. "That's why it scared me. I don't know what Morran did to her, but I'm afraid to let you out of my sight until he is stopped."

Odette put a hand on the side of his head and pulled his cheek against her lips. "I'm not her." She nuzzled against him. "And you've already saved me."

He embraced her. "I love you."

"I love you too," she replied. "Once we have dinner, let us make haste before night takes hold and my father goes to bed. It will be much harder to convince him if he is asleep."

Odette shook Grace awake. Her sister's tired eyes grew wide when she saw who it was. "What are you doing here?"

"Someone is here to kill you," Odette said pointedly. "We need to get you to safety."

Grace glanced at Jareth, who held the lantern up further. Instead of answering, she just nodded dumbly before joining them. With the younger girl sandwiched between them, Odette led them through the house and to the carriage. It was good that after all these months nothing had changed.

Grace entered the carriage as Jareth and Odette glanced around to ensure they were alone. "Why are you helping?" Grace's voice sounded so small and afraid.

Odette knew she should be kind, perhaps even refer to the fact they were family—sisters—but Odette was never one to lie. "You don't deserve to die that way." She closed the door and made sure it was secure. "We'll be back."

Jareth followed her closely; she felt him glance at her a few times but said nothing. Finally, as they neared the study, Odette asked, "What is it?"

"I could subdue him and throw him in the carriage." Jareth's tone implied he was trying to lighten the mood, but the words were serious.

She sent him a sly grin. "A good contingency plan."

Despite her bravado, when they reached the door to his study, she hesitated. This was the man who had brought her into this world and rejected her very existence from the beginning. He'd become her torturer, her abuser, and here she was trying to save him.

Jareth's warm hand wrapped around hers on the handle. "I'm here."

She loved this man with all her heart and nothing could shake that. Not after everything they'd overcome. She nodded once before pushing the door open. Her father was smoking a pipe at his desk. He was reclined, but jumped to his feet when he saw them.

"What are you doing here?" The duke asked, his hand on a dagger that was sheathed on the desk. It had been there all her life.

"Saving your life." Odette was surprised at her own steady voice.

Jareth grabbed a chair and barred the door as the duke gripped the dagger and said, "More like come to kill me."

Had he always looked so old? Odette really studied the lines at the corners of his eyes and underneath them. His stature was smaller than Jareth's and not as steady as she remembered. To her surprise, she wasn't afraid of him anymore; he would never hurt her again.

The doorknob turned behind them and someone pushed against the door. Odette and Jareth moved further into the room as the duke's eyes widened. He glanced between them, obviously trying to understand what was happening.

"Those are Lord Morran's assassins, here to end your life." Odette knew they were running out of time as the person on the other side pushed again, this time more urgently.

"What do you want from this? Love?" The duke's comments were humorless.

Odette remained calm, gripping Jareth's hand tightly. "I have never loved you, but I could not abandon you."

"And you?" He jutted his chin at Jareth.

Jareth grimaced. "It is better you live and keep Morran in check than die tonight." He held out a hand. "Your daughter Grace is already safely in the carriage. Will you live or die on this night?"

"I will owe you nothing," the duke replied, as though his life were some debt yet unpaid. "Nothing, you hear me."

"As you've never given me anything before without ridicule, why would you think I'd expect anything now?" Odette was as cold as her father; she felt less than nothing for him now. She was only here to prevent the future Jareth spoke of.

Something thudded against the door, bulging the wood. A decision had to be made and Odette knew that there was only one thing to convince him. The only thing he held onto more than grudges, was the need to win.

"If you die here, Lord Morran wins."

"Choose." Jareth's eyes tempted the duke to do nothing.

With an unhappy grumble, he took Jareth's hand. In an instant, they were transported to the carriage. Grace was huddled within, her face as white as a sheet. Once more, Odette was thankful Jestine was far away in the capital, preparing for her wedding—she would not have been so easy to corral.

"You should go to the one place no one will look," Jareth said as Odette gripped his hand tighter.

"You are gifted?" the duke asked, eyeing Jareth. "I suspected you needed something to defeat a dragon."

"Do not act so surprised." Odette's words were more bitter than she intended. "You are not the only one with abilities." With quiet satisfaction, she watched him recoil; she had never forgotten the secret her grandmother had shared.

"We need to go." Jareth nodded at the duke. "Don't die."

Then they were standing in the fields of peaches. The twilight sparkled and Odette turned to look into Jareth's eyes. She touched a hand to her stomach and decided now.

"Do you need to rest before the next jump?" Jareth asked, his face dulled by exhaustion.

She put a hand on his chest. "There is something I must tell you." Odette kissed his cheek. "Thank you for letting me come." She put his hand on her stomach. "For letting us come."

He glanced at their hands and then back at her face. "Do you mean…?" Before he even finished, he lifted her up and twirled her around. Then he set her down abruptly. "You went into a potential war zone pregnant, and didn't tell me?"

His hands gripped her arms. "I'm not absolutely certain I am, but there is a good chance that is the case. Plus, if I told you, there was no way you would have let me go." She'd known it the moment she found out. "My father never would have believed you. I had to be here."

"I could have forced him," he said then covered her face with kisses. "You reckless beautiful idiot."

"That isn't a very nice name." Odette just laughed and nudged his shoulder playfully. "You super caring prat."

Chapter 37

-Present-

Four Months Later

Odette wrung her hands as they stared up the lane at the home she hadn't seen since she was a child. The house was in disrepair and there were only two old horses, but it was the same place. Her last memories had been fleeing it in the face her father's…stepfather's death. Putting her hand on her stomach she felt the growing child within her, already halfway through her term. It was the earliest that Jareth would let her travel.

A hand wrapped around her own. She glanced at Jareth, whose loving eyes reminded her that she no longer had to face such difficulties alone. Her fingers curled into his.

"Are you ready?" Jareth asked, his voice understanding.

Odette couldn't manage a word, only nodding. With a quick command from Jareth, the carriage resumed moving along the bumpy road. Despite the roof appearing to have been mended, and the main house being in decent condition, the overall disrepair of the estate was disheartening.

A thin maid, bent like a fishing hook opened the door and stepped out. Her eyes squinted at the sight of what Odette knew to be an opulent carriage. Jareth swung the door open and stepped down, turning back to assist her. She took his offered hand and held tight, unwilling to part with him.

"May I ask who is calling?" the maid asked, her voice raspy and thin but direct.

"I'm…" Words escaped her.

Something clattered on the ground to their left and everyone turned to see a tall girl wearing a shocked expression.

"Ettie?" the girl said.

Despite the years, Odette could see the red-blonde hair and button nose that had been her sister's hallmark features.

"Melody!" Odette choked on a sob and she opened her arms as her sister ran to her, throwing herself against Odette as they both began to cry. She heard Jareth saying something, but it was lost to the sound of their joy. They clung to each other as all the memories came back.

"You've gotten so big!" Odette replied with a sniffle. "A proper young lady."

"You've gotten prettier," Melody replied, wiping the tears from her cheeks. "Mother said you wouldn't come until next month."

"We had to travel close to here and Jareth suggested we come now. I couldn't resist." Odette laughed.

"Odette?" The softly spoken word cut through the air like a well-aimed dart. Everything stopped as Odette slowly turned.

The woman in the doorway looked like her mother but her hair had streaks of gray and wrinkles adorned her face. Yet her eyes had the same resiliency that Odette remembered—and complete love. Her mother was suddenly down the steps and wrapping her into a hug.

"Mother." The tears started all over again as the three women babbled words of affection.

"You're more beautiful than I could have imagined," her mother said, framing Odette's face with her hands. "My precious daughter."

Her mother and sister parted so she could see a tall, solid boy who was the spitting image of her stepfather. He was standing breathless on the front steps. Needing no further invitation, Caden trotted down the steps and joined them.

"You are home," he said, wrapping them all in a big hug. "You're finally home."

"I love you all, forever and always," Odette sobbed.

"Always and forever," her family answered, and Odette knew she really was home.

With some coaxing, Jareth had gotten them into the house and into the sitting room. Odette had been peppered with questions and thanked for her support. All of them had avoided talking about what she had experienced in the duke's house, none of them wanting to taint the happy atmosphere.

"Thank you for taking care of my Odette," her mother said, her gaze fixed on Jareth who had taken a seat in the corner of the room to give them space without leaving her alone. It was as though he knew what she needed without her having to ask.

"It is your daughter who has taken care of me," Jareth replied with a soft grin. "Accepted me in ways I couldn't imagine possible."

Her mother patted her hands. "That's my Odette, always doing more for others than herself."

"You are the strongest person I know," Melody added.

"We are very proud of you," Caden said, his open honesty so much like his father.

Odette reached out and took her brother's hand. "You all have managed well on your own. Taking care of mother while I could not."

"You were busy taking care of all of us," Melody interjected before Odette could continue. "We know it must have been so hard. We missed you all the time."

Odette glanced at Jareth with a smile. "Well, that is why I am here. We want to invite you all to come live with us."

There was stunned silence. It was Caden who spoke first. "We just bought our first breeding pair with the money you sent. I'm planning to try and revive father's business."

"This is my home," her mother replied, but appeared conflicted.

"I can't leave mother," Melody replied shaking her head.

Odette blinked at them in surprise. She hadn't expected all of them to agree, but she also hadn't expected a unanimous refusal. Her mother patted her hand. "That is a kind offer, but I think we would prefer to stay here."

Jareth's voice broke through her surprise. "Then at least allow me to be your first investor." Jareth folded up the newspaper he's been pretending to read, and stood. "Caden, would you show me the grounds and the state of the barn? I'd like to assess what is needed to get this place into operation."

Caden jumped up to attention. "Yes, sir!"

Jareth kissed the top of Odette's head before leaving. She watched him go and realized no matter how much she wanted to return everything to the way it was, there was no going back. Her mother took hold of her hand, drawing her attention.

"It isn't that we don't appreciate what you are offering, my love, but you have a family of your own now, and we have an opportunity to rebuild something together, here. Your brother is very excited to rebuild the Baccus name." She sounded so proud that it was hard for Odette to feel hurt for long.

"I'm already thirteen," Melody said as though it was the most important news. "I'll make my debut in a short three years."

"I'll look into a governess in the area who can help get you ready," Odette said, understanding the desire to stay with family. "I'll make arrangements closer to your birthday so we can join the other debutantes in a local presentation first. You are a count's daughter and the sister to a marchioness. You have options."

Melody threw her arms around Odette and pulled her close. "How I have missed you!"

"Promise you will come visit when the baby is born?" Odette asked.

"You can't keep us away," her mother said. Touching a hand to her cheek, her mother added, "Are you happy?"

"Yes, I am," Odette replied, and she meant it.

Chapter 38

-Present-

Fourteen months later

"Look she's doing it!" Odette said, trying not to jump in and help their tottering daughter, Iris, as she pulled herself into a standing position.

She and Jareth clapped as their daughter's partially-toothed grin lit up the room. She was the spitting image of her father, with the exception of Odette's strawberry hair and the Wolverson's green eyes. Iris tried to move along the chair but fell onto her bottom. Letting out a giggle, she looked from Odette to Jareth, as if trying to see who would pick her up first. Jareth lifted her up and twirled her around, placing kisses along her cheeks. Odette had never been happier.

Suddenly, there came a knock on the door. "Come in," Jareth said, bouncing Iris in his arms.

Kenith entered; his face twisted in concern. "What is it?" Odette asked, alarmed.

"Duke Wolverson is here." Kenith appeared worried. "He is asking to speak with Lady Chadwick."

Jareth and Odette exchanged a glance. Slowly she stood. "Where is he?"

"The parlor."

Jareth caught her hand. "You don't have to go alone."

"Yes, I do." Odette kissed his cheek and then Iris's. "He doesn't control me or my actions."

Jareth nodded. "Call me if you need me."

"Play with Iris. I'll return shortly." She did not expect this to be a long conversation. The letters he'd written trying to mend what had never been, went unanswered. Ever since they'd saved his life, he'd been trying to worm his way into her life. No doubt this was his most recent attempt.

The duke turned around when she entered and appeared happy to see her. "How are you doing, daughter?"

She ignored the name he'd called her. "Why are you here?"

"Can a father not visit his daughter?" the duke asked.

It took all her control to keep her voice level. "You may have sired me, but you have never been my father and you cannot imagine yourself to be one now. Not even you are that deluded."

"I only wish to repair what has been done." He sounded almost repentant, but that could not erase the damage he'd caused. "I had hoped to meet my granddaughter."

"You will see her from a distance at court. That is, if you are still alive when she is of age." Odette narrowed her gaze.

The duke took a step closer. "Won't you forgive me?"

She put a hand up to ward him off. "No. You are not worthy of my forgiveness."

"That is all you have to say?" He was clearly offended.

Odette would not be cowed, not by this man who had rejected her as a child. He did not deserve it. "It is. Is that the only reason you came?"

"No," the duke replied, clearly not happy with the conversation's direction. "After the king disavowed Lord Morran, he went to ground. Despite all my attempts, he escaped out of the country." It was one of the good sides to a man who held a grudge; time did nothing to lessen his pursuit of revenge.

The room suddenly felt colder. "What has changed?"

"I was informed yesterday that he reentered the country and is hiding somewhere in the north by the border. As I cannot lead a group of soldiers into another lord's territory, I'm here to ask your husband's assistance." The duke was displeased with having to make such a request; it was all over his face.

"I'll go get him," Odette replied, turning to leave.

"You really will not let me see her?" He sounded confused.

"No," Odette replied, hoping her gaze was as steely as she was trying to make it. "You wanted nothing to do with me as a child. Consider this your repayment. You shall have nothing to do with my personal life, nor hers." Then she curtsied. "I wish you the best of health, Lord Wolverson."

"I must go," Jareth insisted, his hands gripping her arms. "You know this must end."

"If you face him, you will die again and this will all start over," Odette said, shaking her head. "Someone else should go."

Jareth inhaled. "Your father has sent multiple assassins and they have all died. Whatever Morran is using, it keeps anyone but the gifted out. Your father tested it himself. That leaves us with very few options. You know I can kill him; I can end this."

"You do not have to be the hero," Odette said with a strangled cry. "Someone else should go."

"Who else but I can defeat him?" Jareth asked, pulling her close as he pressed his forehead against hers. "If I die, I will choose you again." He kissed her passionately. "I will choose you every time."

"How can you be sure?" Odette wondered if they were doomed to repeat their mistakes—if they would be led back to this moment no matter what.

"When I first brought you to Vallerdale, do you know why I had you ride outside the carriage?" Jareth asked. He waited for her to shake her head. "I did it because I wanted to show everyone you were *my* wife. Don't think for a moment I'm not proud to have you as my wife. If I could, I would tell everyone I meet. So, I know…no matter the outcome… I will find my way to you again."

There was a knock on the door and Sir Lex appeared. "It is time."

"I will see you again. One way or another." He kissed her once more before leaving the room.

Tears fell unabated as she slumped onto the loveseat in their shared room. Jareth had a plan; one that had a decent margin of success. She grieved their life together, knowing that her husband was right. Who else could hope to defeat him?

She could. Odette straightened at the thought.

Wiping her tears away, she realized in their past life, she'd been victorious and paid the ultimate price. Rushing to the nursery, she found Iris fast asleep. Her prefect cheeks, round head, and long lashes made her appear the most beautiful sight.

If Jareth succeeded in killing Lord Morran it would cost him his life, meaning Iris would never be born. It was as though someone had stabbed her in her heart. She knew if Jareth married her again, she'd fall in love with him once more. In her very soul she believed that to be truth. Yet it would not all happen the same, it was impossible to think that their daughter would be the same.

Propelled by that thought, she hurried down the hall to the one person she swore she'd never go. Hesitating only a moment, she knocked on the door. When it opened, her father stood on the other side. The duke's eyebrows lifted high on his forehead.

"Is something wrong?"

"May I come in?" Odette tried to calm her beating heart and keep a level tone.

He took a step back as she entered. The moment they were alone, she turned to him with purpose. "If you ever cared for me at all, even a little, I ask you now for your help. Jareth goes to face Lord Morran alone, and I must stop him."

"I do not know what that has to do with me." The duke's expression was guarded.

"It doesn't," Odette replied. "You are the only person with the means to get me there. I need your teleportation carriage." Then she thought of something else. "And I'll need that." Odette pointed at the ring he was wearing; a ring she knew to contain poison.

Chapter 39

-Past-

Odette kissed William as they lounged after picnicking outside, the sun was shining and it felt like the perfect day. It had been nearly a year since their wedding and spring had coated the land in a layer of cheerful green. Unlike Wolf Manor, they were located further south and it was much warmer earlier in the year. She was loathed to return even though the hour was drawing closer to evening.

"What if it's a girl?" William asked, touching a hand to her protruding stomach.

Odette laughed at the concern in his voice. "You will spoil her worse than me."

He chuckled in response, so transformed in these last months she barely recognized him to be the man she married. "That is true."

"Plus, you have months still before the baby is here." Odette put her hand over her stomach, comforted by the protected layer it provided. It was as though her very body was cradling the life inside, and ensuring its survival.

"It seems so far away and yet so close," William said, shaking his head. "Perhaps a girl would not be so terrible."

Odette chuckled. "Come, the midwife should be here soon to tell us if it is a boy or a girl."

William helped her up before waving a servant over to clean up after them. They walked down the hill as Odette took in the scent of new life. How she loved spring in her new home. Here it was so full of possibilities.

The steward, Marlin, was waiting for them, appearing eager. "She's here."

William took her hand and Odette squeezed it in excitement. It had taken some convincing for the royal midwife to be brought before them. Yet she was the only one with the ability to see into the womb and confirm the child's gender.

Even though she was only halfway through the pregnancy, she would already know if she should sew dolls or warriors. The midwife was sipping tea in the parlor when they arrived. She was older than Odette would have thought, having recently married to a twice widowed viscount.

"Lord Morran," she said, standing and bowing to them both. "Lady Morran."

"Welcome," Odette said warmly. "Thank you for coming."

"I was given little choice," the viscountess glanced at Lord Morran. "Shall we proceed?"

Odette nodded. "Certainly. I wouldn't want to delay you further."

Without any notice, the viscountess put a hand on Odette's stomach. She concentrated a moment before announcing without emotion. "It's a boy."

"A boy?" Odette felt excitement lace through her. "Truly?"

She nodded. "May I go?" The question was directed at William.

"Marlin! See that the viscountess is escorted home." Then he turned his back on her to wrap his arms around Odette.

"A boy!" Odette placed a hand on her stomach, already imagining what traits their growing child would have. "He'll be so handsome."

"I had started to imagine a girl." William chuckled. "Now I must return my thoughts to a boy."

Odette laughed. "You are so changeable! To think you are disappointed it is a boy after weeks of insisting that would be best." She patted his arm. "Do not worry, my love. Perhaps the next one will be a girl."

"Next one?" He asked, raising his eyebrows.

Her heart was singing at his playfulness. "You cannot imagine we would only have one."

William's face nuzzled into her neck. "Now I can imagine this house full of our children."

As she hugged William close, Odette marveled at the change in her husband. Gone was the brooding Magician planning unspeakable acts in the dark. She was not blind to what her husband was, he was a master manipulator, a king maker. Yet whatever big plans he'd had seemed to have stopped in the last few months. No more secret meetings with strange men in robes or masks. No more trips to the capital that would take him away for weeks. Instead, he'd be gone a day or two at most and then hurry home. To her.

There came a knock on the door. "What is it?" William demanded, straightening from her embrace.

Marlin stuck his head in. "Dinner is ready; would you like to dine in the main hall or your rooms?"

"Bring out the best dinnerware," William replied with a twinkle in his eye. "We have much to celebrate!"

Walking arm in arm they made their way to the great hall. The servants rushed to swap dishes and bring out their finest candelabras. William pulled the seat for her himself, kissing the crown of her head before taking his own seat.

Odette reached over and added some wine to her water. She'd been having a hard time drinking just straight water and a little flavor helped her finish it. All the wonders of being pregnant were not as much of a treat as she'd imagined. There were many downsides but so far, all were manageable. Besides, any inconvenience was brushed aside by her and William's excitement.

"A boy," William raised his glass. "How blessed we are."

Odette raised her glass. "To our future."

"To our son," William replied before they both drank.

Odette drank nearly half the contents of her glass before setting it down. "What do you think for a name?"

Cutting her steak, she watched William chew slowly before pausing. A strange look came over his face before he started to gag. Bringing a hand to his throat, he gasped while trying to stand, knocking his chair over in the process.

"William!" Odette screamed, jumping to her feet. As she did so, she suddenly felt lightheaded, and vomited onto the floor.

Stumbling towards William, she fell to her knees, clenching her stomach. Falling to her side she could hear her heartbeat drumming wildly as she struggled to breathe. She couldn't see anything but William opening his eyes and looking at her. That was the last thing she remembered before the darkness took her.

-Present-

Odette found herself in a massive derelict structure. She had followed the path Jareth had taken, feeling the wake of emotions he'd left behind. Since her daughter's birth all of her skills and abilities had amplified. That, coupled with the teacher Jareth had brought in to quietly help her focus and evolve, had made her a master of her abilities. It was good, because she'd need them all today.

Suddenly, a sword appeared, and it was pointed at her. "Odette?" Jareth appeared confused, which was followed closely by anger. "What do you think you are doing?"

He reached out and snagged her hand; the exact hand she'd needed him to grab. "You cannot do this alone," Odette replied, aware she needed to buy herself some time. It shouldn't be long now.

"You need to leave." Jareth moved directly into her path when she took a step forward.

"No," Odette replied. Her father had assured her the drug was fast acting, but she began worrying her plan was going to fail.

At that moment Jareth slumped back against the wall. "What's happening?" He shook his head and relief surged through her.

"You should sit down," Odette said, helping him.

"I can't feel my arms and my legs are rubbery." Odette felt a sudden glance of guilt at his words and how forlorn he sounded. "What's happening?"

She knelt in front of him and touched his cheek. "It's a mild paralytic. I promise it will pass."

The flash of shock and betrayal on his face cut her deeply, but she knew her actions were necessary. "Odette? What have you done?"

Her fingers caressed his face and then she kissed his forehead. "You have to live. If you die, our daughter ceases to exist."

"No," his words were starting to slur as his head lulled to the side. "I would find you again. I'd choose you again."

"I know, but it won't happen exactly the same. You told me everything you did changed the outcome every time. Which means no matter what, Iris will not be born exactly as she is. I can't let that happen." Odette felt a tear slide down her cheek.

His words came out as an unintelligible protest as his eyes screamed for her to stop. She took the warding pendant he'd been wearing off him and placed it around her neck. She would need it to get the element of surprise on Lord Morran. Knowing she was running out of time, she leaned forward to kiss him. His lips barely moved as she poured her love into the act, believing it might be the last time they'd ever kiss.

"I want you to know I'd choose you too, but I can't risk our daughter. I'll face Lord Morran and his curse because you and her will keep existing in the world." Her tears were flowing freely. "And I hope one day you'll forgive me." She kissed his cheek. "I love you."

Jerking away, she hurried down the hallway to face Lord Morran. If she could destroy her father in the past life because of the grief he'd brought her, she could destroy Lord Morran in the name of love. All that remained was to defeat him and pay the ultimate price to keep her family safe.

Chapter 40

-Past-

Odette opened her eyes, feeling empty and fragile. Disoriented, she tried to get her bearings, to remember what had happened. That's when she saw a shape slumped in the chair next to her. It took her a moment to recognize him.

"William?" Her voice was hoarse and barely a whisper. Her body wouldn't respond when she tried to sit up. Moving a hand across the blanket took great effort as she reached for him. She tried to clear her throat.

Her husband stirred but he was not the same man she remembered. This one was haggard, a beard on his face, and his hair a tousled mess. What had happened to make him that way? She couldn't seem to remember.

"Odette?" William appeared uncertain, like he couldn't trust his eyes.

"What happened?" She was having a hard time talking, her mouth was so dry.

When she tried to move, he sprang forward. "Wait…!" Then he called over his shoulder, "Get the healer!"

She blinked at his wild eyes. "What…" Then she started coughing.

He helped her sit up as her body was wracked by the coughs. When she opened her eyes, the barest of tears welled within them. She felt so tired, and yet something seemed wrong. Something was…missing.

Why was her stomach so flat?

"The baby?" Odette asked, the word barely audible. Where was her baby?

The devastated expression that twisted William's face told her everything. She shook her head, trying to pull away, hide from the truth. It couldn't be. Their baby. What had her son ever done to deserve this? What had she done? Who would do such a thing?

William was holding her, stroking her hair. Despite her grief and denial, she heard his words. "I know who did this; who hurt us. When you are well, we'll make them pay. Make your father suffer the way they made us suffer. I promise you. Our son will be avenged."

He was right. What else did she have now but revenge? She would make him pay, make him suffer the same way that he had made her suffer. She would use her gift to make him believe his daughters were monsters. She would make him kill them and then live with the truth.

Yes, she thought as she slipped back out of consciousness. *She would have her revenge.*

-Present-

Odette moved further into the belly of the ancient building; the solemn and blackened walls making the eerie feeling intensify. Once having served as a temple for long forgotten gods, its massive interior boasted of winding corridors and rooms upon rooms. Regardless, she could still sense the lingering remnants of Lord Morran's emotions and previous assassins who had all come this way.

It did not take her long to find him. He was sitting at a desk writing, the room mostly empty with a cracked basin that had been repurposed into a makeshift brazier filling the room with heat as the smoke exited up an old chimney. There was rotting furniture and clothes draped about. Suddenly, he stopped writing and sat up.

"Who is there?" Lord Morran asked, standing.

Odette stepped into the room. "I've come to beg your mercy, my lord."

"Lady Chadwick?" Lord Morran's eyes seemed almost crazed. "Where is Lord Chadwick?"

"He isn't here yet," Odette replied, clasping her hands in front of her. "I've come to plea with you, to spare my husband."

Lord Morran chuckled. "To think I admired you once." He shook his head. "I have no desire to kill a woman today. Leave and do not return."

When he turned, she saw the dagger at his hip and let her ability ooze out of her. It was the most subtle way to make the mood of the room shift, and eventually overcome a subject with emotions; To change the fringes of their reality first, and then close in slowly.

"I know you think I am a fool, but I also know you have a sense of honor," she said. It was the one thing their earlier conversation had revealed. "I ask you now: remember it."

His grunt was humorless. "My honor died with my initial plans."

Gathering up her own emotions, she sealed them away and focused on projecting only one: fear. Lord Morran whirled as she faked a startled gasp, feeding to the illusion. To her right, her husband had appeared, or at least an apparition of him.

"The Hero of Mount Vere," Lord Morran said as he drew his sword. "Here to end things?"

Odette knew her husband so intimately that his image was flawless. Then, more men appeared—men she'd come to know well; Sir Lex, Sir Mance, and Sir Jonas, chief among them. They all marched into the room.

"What is this?" Lord Morran demanded, shock in his voice.

"Did you really think your magic that powerful?" The fake Lord Chadwick asked. "There is no way out."

They moved towards him, drawing swords as Lord Morran drew his dagger. She smoothly transitioned from projecting fear to desperation. The figures drove him back towards the fire in the basin that she'd expertly hid. She'd burn him before he could utter a word. He was cursing at illusions as she vanished from what he could see in the room.

Lord Morran swiped at the imagined figures; the whites of his eyes looking amplified. Odette saw him stumble backwards, trying to keep them at bay. He was yelling but her army of memories was not stopping. He was nearly to the fire when he brushed against its edge and jerked back. His cloak caught the flames and for a moment, in her excitement, the images wavered.

Unexpectedly, he threw the dagger through her illusions and in her direction. She turned away from it and it skittered across the floor. She stared at it in shock as it rested in the corner behind her. Turning back, she saw him throw his charred coat down as he moved away from the fire. She'd been so close to ending it and yet she'd failed. Dread settled in.

He inhaled and rocked back on his heels. "You made a mistake." His voice was hoarse, his eyes sharp, as she took an involuntary step back. "Now that I have tasted your gift, I shall revisit it on you tenfold."

Odette had expected his attack and forced herself to focus. The time spent practicing her illusions made it easy to ground herself. He was conjuring the dead bodies of her family—yet their faces weren't quite right. That was the issue with illusions; the person projecting them had to have the details down perfectly.

"It is not so easy," Odette commented, as her heart raced. "You may be able to use my ability, but you have not mastered it."

He laughed. "You're right." He moved forward, the menace in his eyes fervent. "I thought it would be fun to play, but I think I'll just gut you like a pig."

She caught movement out of the corner of her eye. She turned and saw the duke standing at the entrance to the room. Although the expression on his face was blank, his gaze passed between them, and Odette felt uneasy. Her father may have repented, but that didn't mean he would help her.

"What do you want?" Lord Morran snarled.

"We came to an accord, Morran," the duke said, venturing further into the room. "I only came to stop my foolish daughter." That was the man she remembered, cruel and dismissive.

"What delicious emotions ... so dark," Lord Morran said with a cackle. "Do you regret saving him now?"

The lump in her throat almost choked her. "I'll never regret doing the right thing."

He drew the sword from his hip, the action slow and deliberate. "Your righteousness disgusts me as much as your husband."

Odette stumbled back as he moved forward. A flash of movement came from her right, and Lord Morran froze;, his eyes wide as he looked at the dagger now sticking out of his chest. She watched him stagger backward, shaking his head, as the duke moved to stand in front of her.

"Don't think I ever forgot you tried to kill me," the duke said.

Odette couldn't believe what she was seeing as the duke moved forward. Lord Morran pulled the dagger from his chest before he fell to his knees and his sword clattered on the ground as he gaped like a fish.

"I curse you," Lord Morran muttered. "To die my death."

"You should have made sure I was dead the first time." The duke grabbed the bloodied dagger from the floor. "I won't make the same mistake."

"Stop!" Odette called out, rushing to grab his arm. "His curse is real!"

The duke's normally expressionless face seemed almost remorseful. "Remember, I don't deserve your forgiveness."

As he slit Morran's throat, a matching red line formed on his own. Rubies clattered onto the floor as Odette screamed in horror.

Chapter 41

-Past-

Odette was hollow. Her son was dead. She'd felt him move inside, felt the start of her own miracle that she was growing. When his life had been taken, so had any chance she'd ever bear another baby. Her future was stolen from her by one person.

The duke.

Glancing up at Wolf Manor with apathy, she felt it was oddly unchanged. Yet instead of it feeling as imposing as it had all her life, she felt like it was a mask to the evil that lay within. For what other word was she to give what her own father had done? Destroyed an innocent of his own blood.

One of William's many loyal knights carried an unconscious figure over his shoulder. The sleeping face of her sister Jestine stirred nothing within her. She was to serve as a vessel for her revenge.

"Is there anyone worth saving?" her husband asked.

There was a mirrored emptiness within him, his tone and his eyes were soulless. The only time she saw any warmth was when he was addressing her,

or his plans for revenge brought them one step closer to his goal. He only involved her when it suited him, but Odette didn't care. She didn't care for much of anything if she were being honest with herself.

"No, but I want him to be unsuspecting," Odette replied. "Let me carve a path."

William nodded. "I'll shield us with our own illusion."

Stepping forward, she put some distance between them before she began forming a wave of emotions. She focused on exhaustion, sleep, and suggested they lay down. The guards patrolling were hit first. They slowed, their footfalls growing sluggish and heavy. Then, with a clatter, they slumped to the ground.

As Odette moved through her former residence, she recalled the misery she'd endured. All of it could easily have been avoided if the duke had an ounce of kindness in him. He didn't have to love her, but he'd gone out of his way to alienate her.

Everyone fell to her powers, swayed by the illusion she wrapped them in. She projected emotions onto them, driving them into complacency while she, William, and their guards penetrated the place she'd once lived. When they reached her father's study, Odette stopped. Her emptiness turned to anger in the blink of an eye. She wanted to rage and yell at him. It was only when William's hand covered hers that she realized she'd been gripping the doorknob and breathing heavily.

"Let us end this," William said, a shimmer in his eye. Then he waved his men forward.

The two sleeping bodies of her sisters were laid before the door. Odette stared at them, remembering how cruel they'd been to her. Jestine the instigator and Grace ever the follower. When she roused them, it didn't take long for their eyes to become round with fear.

"What is happening?" Jestine demanded.

"I want you to know that if you were true sisters to me, I could never have dreamed of letting this happen." Odette felt the power of the change of their position flow through her. For the first time she wasn't the one scared and alone. "Unfortunately for you both, you take after our father."

She took a step back as she looked at the door and felt her father within. He opened the door a moment later, no doubt drawn by their voices. In his hand was a sword, thin and deadly, as he looked at his daughters.

"Father! Help us!" Jestine and Grace's voices were wild, but the girls were not what her father saw.

The scene before him was created by Odette and William, working in tandem, both to conceal their presence, and to make the duke's other daughters appear to be horrific beasts. "What are you?!" he cried.

The sisters clung to each other. "Father?" Their earlier pleas now changed to confusion.

"Guards!" the duke called before swinging at Grace and Jestine.

The young women screamed and scrambled out of the way before running down the hall. The duke pursued, with Odette, William, and their entourage following behind them. Blood splattered the carpet and wall when his sword sliced into Grace's back. She clung to Jestine, who quickly abandoned her. Grace's gasp turned to a gurgle as the duke's sword plunged into her back and she stopped moving. Jestine clawed at a door handle before bursting through the door. When she tried to close it, the duke forced it open. Odette heard her scream being cut short, and it wasn't long before her father emerged, covered in blood.

Now his future would be taken from him too. Odette thought with a soft sigh.

Stepping forward, Odette spoke directly to him, allowing her true self to be seen inside the illusion she'd created. "Father? What have you done?" Odette cried, mustering whatever emotions she could to sound distressed.

"Odette?" the duke asked, confused. "I have slayed the monsters."

"Monsters?" Odette asked, trying to sound uncertain. "You have slayed my sisters."

Like a puff of smoke, the illusion vanished, and in its place was the truth. She watched as he took in the scene before him. He stumbled back, moving out of the line of sight from whatever tragedy had befallen Jestine.

Shaking his head, he pointed his sword. "They were *monsters.*"

"You are unwell," Odette said, pressuring him with emotions to make the words believable. "Grace asked me to come because she was worried something would happen to you." The next words, she choked out. "It seems I came too late."

"No." The duke shook his head. She'd never seen him so broken, and it took everything she had to keep her face straight. She needed to finish it—end it completely.

"Why, Father?" Odette asked. "They're dead at your hand. You killed your only daughters. I am all that remains."

His eyes flashed in her direction. "You are not them." Even now, he cast her out. With no other direct relatives left, he still he couldn't accept her.

"No, I'm not, and now they're dead." Odette couldn't keep the bitterness from her voice. "That is all you are capable of. Killing. You have no honor, Father, and this shame will haunt our name."

"Shame?" He was having trouble focusing; she could see he was in shock.

"I wish there was a way." Odette pressed forward. "A way to save our family name. The Wolverson honor."

"There is," he said, lifting the sword. "A sacrifice."

She was supposed to push, to say words to encourage him, but she couldn't. She stood there staring at this selfish, horrible man who loved the Wolverson name more than her. This man didn't matter, he wasn't worth her time. Yet, she didn't want him to die; she wanted him to live and suffer with the knowledge of what he'd done.

William put a hand on her arm. She felt him use her gift as she had intended to. She turned away, tears streaming down her cheeks, unchecked, as she rested her head against William's chest. Behind her, she heard the sickening sound of her father plunging his own sword into his chest.

William commanded something but Odette clung to him, overcome with grief. Her torturer was dead, her baby's murder avenged, yet she felt just as empty. Suddenly she felt William kiss the top of her head before lifting her hand. When she looked at it, he dropped gems into her palm. Rubies. Her father's blood.

"These shall make a nice necklace." And he was right—they did.

-Present-

It felt like days had passed when she felt hands on her shoulders. She was hunched in the corner, her back pressed against the wall as she tried to hide from reality. Her mind couldn't process what had happened, couldn't understand. She tried to fight the hands off; to get away from them.

"Odette?" Jareth's concerned face appeared.

She threw herself into his arms sobbing. "Forgive me." Odette begged, haunted by her father's expression. "Please, forgive me."

"I'm angry," Jareth replied, holding her close. "But I understand. Promise you won't do something like that again."

"I want to go home." Odette sobbed, unwilling to glance at the bodies in the center of the room.

Jareth held onto her as though she would disappear like smoke. She squeezed her eyes shut as she buried her face against his neck. He cradled her against him as she refused to look at what had happened.

When they left the room behind, Jareth finally spoke, "Why did he come?"

"I made him bring me. He must have followed." Odette remembered his tortured expression. "He must have figured out what I was going to do."

"I'm glad he stopped you." Jareth kissed her forehead.

Tears slid down her cheeks. "Me too."

When they reached the carriage the duke had used to get them there, Jareth helped her settle in, wrapping his abandoned cloak around her. He then joined her inside, holding her hand as she cried silently to herself. Everything she'd been managing suddenly became too much.

It was sometime later that she was able to stop the onslaught of tears. "Why can't I forgive him?"

"Who?" Jareth asked, leaning back.

"My father," Odette replied, rubbing her fingers across her damp cheeks.

"One good act does not replace a lifetime of bad ones," Jareth answered before putting his chin on her head as he tucked her against him. He let out a heavy sigh before adding, "If he were alive, I'd thank him for keeping you safe. I would not like him, but he gained my respect because of what he was willing to do."

Odette's insides twisted. "I want to leave. Why are we still here?"

"You have to activate the carriage." Jareth leaned back to point at the activation panel.

Odette leaned over and placed her hand without hesitation. When they settled at their destination, Jareth went out first. Sir Lex rushed towards them, his face showing concern mixed with relief. When she emerged, there was a general sigh among the knights.

"We were starting to worry," Sir Lex said, his gaze appraising them.

"I want to see Iris," Odette said but when she took a step her legs buckled, and Jareth had to catch her. There was a startled murmur as the knights surged towards them.

"You need to rest," Jareth said, sweeping her up into his arms. "Iris is well, thanks to you."

Odette nodded, leaning heavily into him. "Stay with me," she whispered, fearing the hollowness of an empty bed.

"As long as you need," Jareth replied, kissing her head. She fell asleep before they even reached their room.

Chapter 42

-Past-

The capital was on fire as Odette watched the chaos in the streets. She could hear a baby wailing as she felt herself wake up. It was like coming out of a fog, a haze she'd had since her son had been taken from her. Her hand touched her stomach; she'd wanted revenge, wanted to make the world suffer as she had, yet seeing such destruction, she feared they'd gone too far.

"Isn't it beautiful?" Lord Morran's hand swept in front of them.

"Now do we stop?" Odette asked, suddenly weary.

Lord Morran appeared confused. "Stop what? Do you need to rest?" He still showed such concern and consideration for her that somewhere under the darkness was her William.

"Now that the capital is won, our goal is complete, now do we stop?" Odette felt no satisfaction. She hadn't felt much of anything in a long time.

"Stop?" Her husband laughed. "This is but the beginning, my love. Soon we shall build a new world order. One that discards this classist system—one that raises up men by their merits and not their birth."

"Babies are dying," Odette whispered. "Children are hurt."

"Then I leave them in your care." He kissed the side of her head. "To care for them as you see fit."

For the first time in a long time, Odette felt like her eyes were truly open. She could no longer delude herself into thinking any part of her husband was left. Especially the one full of hope and little ambition. This man was twisted by the darkness, consumed by the need to fill the hole their unborn son had left. An emptiness she now knew could not be filled by any means.

Everything had happened so quickly, amplified by her grief and William's elaborate designs. As though many of them had already been in place. He could wield her ability to ensnare the common folk. Pushing emotions onto them that they didn't feel, even for a short time, left a lasting impression. It was no surprise the capital had fallen.

A messenger hurried up to them, out of breath. "The king is escaping,"

Fury twisted William's features. "He must die today." He mounted his horse, sparing her only a moment. "Stay safe, my love, for I shall end this tyranny."

Odette nodded, but her thoughts were elsewhere. He went off with a small party but left her many more at her command. She looked at their determined faces and knew she should save those that she could. After she mounted her white horse, Odette assessed the area. The main palace rose up in the center of the city, like a beacon.

"We should gather as many children and babies as we can. Save their mothers if we are able," Odette commanded. When they exchanged glances she added, "They will be easier to convert and raise up."

This seemed to pacify them as they began going into homes and extracting families. Most of them were without men, but she didn't stop William's forces from cutting down any men who protested. She could do nothing but watch, aware that if she showed mercy, the men may stop or go to Lord Morran.

The men split into two groups when the gathering was too large, with half of them taking those collected back to Lord Morran's camp hidden in the woods just beyond the capital. The rest would gather more crying, helpless children and their compliant kin. What else could she do if she could not stop it? Better to save those that she could.

"Stop!" A man shouted before rushing towards her. Her horse panicked, rearing up and almost unseating her.

"Lady Morran!"

Odette held onto the horse as its hooves came back to the ground. Like it had been struck by lightning, the perturbed beast shot off at a wild run. She could barely hold on as smoke filled her nostrils. She felt the heat on her face as they rushed past a burning building, ash and smoke thick in the air.

She tried to pull up on the reigns but to no avail. Then suddenly there were two figures in their path. Her horse reared nearly to the point of falling over backward, as she screamed and toppled off. Before she struck the ground, she felt strong arms around her. She heard her horse snort and stomp the ground as she glanced up into a dirty face.

The Hero of Mount Vere, Lord Chadwick, had caught her, and from his expression he'd had no idea it was her. He helped her stand, and she felt a sudden wave of pity from him in the form of pale green mixed with violet. Not fear, not concern at what she could do to him, but pity? He moved away from her like she was on fire and likely to burn him.

Yet that momentary glance of sympathy gave her pause as he moved back to the figure who was now slumped against the wall. She and William had kept their child's passing to themselves, telling lies to others who didn't know. They didn't want to give their enemies anything to use against them. So how could he know?

Her gaze narrowed on the second man, who she saw was King Enry, as Lord Chadwick helped him stand. "Take my horse." Odette didn't know where these words were coming from.

Lord Chadwick hesitated. "What did you say?"

She took her horse's reigns and held them out. "You'll never make it out on foot."

It didn't take him long to get the injured king into the saddle. Odette stood, partially shocked by her actions, but resolved more than anything. The king must live, so that someone could stop her husband. She knew now that he would never stop on his own.

"Why are you helping us?" Lord Chadwick asked after he was seated.

"I'm tired of death," Odette replied honestly. "You are the only one strong enough to stop him. Put an end to this destruction."

He studied her face a moment before nodding. Then he urged the horse forward and they were gone. Odette just stood amongst the rubble and the destruction, watching them go. Someone screamed, a baby wailed, and Odette felt something for the first time in a very long time. She felt a newfound purpose blossom within her.

-Present-

Odette sat in the garden which was shaded in the happiest of greens. The soft scent of flowering blooms wafted in the air as her daughter's excited peals of laughter only added to the perfection of the moment. One of the household cats was batting at some yarn as her daughter held onto the wayward string. When Iris tugged on the string, more of the ball would unravel, causing the cat to pounce again, starting the cycle again.

Jareth silently sat down beside her. Their daughter was too preoccupied with the playful feline to notice her favorite person had joined them. They sat silently, watching the scene in the serenity of the moment.

"Is it done?" Odette asked softly, barely a whisper of words.

Jareth nodded. "King Enry will honor your father, spreading his name as a hero." He shifted closer to her, putting his hand over hers. "Are you ready to talk?"

When they'd returned to Vallerdale Hall, Odette had slept for nearly an entire day. When she finally came out of it, she sought out her daughter. She still remembered a quiet fear that she'd changed something—that Iris wouldn't be there—but all her fears slid away with each day.

"Do you think less of me?" Odette asked, finally meeting his gaze. "That I cannot forgive him, but choose instead to have strangers honor his sacrifice?"

"No. Your father was a ruthless man who had never done a selfless thing in his life until his death." Jareth patted her hand. "You are the better person for the way you choose to have others remember him."

"And Grace?" Odette asked.

Jareth leaned back and sighed. "Your father's new will was clear. She shall become duchess whether she weds or not."

Odette interlaced her fingers with his before leaning on his shoulder. "Perhaps there is hope for the Wolverson line after all."

Jareth hesitated a moment. "Do you feel the same about the Chadwick line?" His expression was hopeful.

"Oh no, you are a completely lost cause." Odette glanced up at him, amused by his startled expression.

He laughed deeply, which caught their daughter's attention. She immediately held up the ball and cried, "Dada, kitty!"

Jareth kissed Odette's forehead as their daughter toddled over to them. She left behind the yarn as her arms stretched out towards them. When she was close enough, Jareth swept her into his lap.

"You don't think daddy is a lost cause, do you?" Jareth asked, his voice almost sweet.

Iris's face scrunched up in concentration before she let out a "Yes!" with a vigorous shake of her head. A habit she'd developed of late, indicating no with a shake of her head and then speaking an affirmative.

"I do declare that you've been outvoted." Odette rubbed her daughter's back.

Jareth kissed Iris's forehead, before cradling her against him. "She isn't wrong; when it comes to my ladies, I am always going to be beyond saving."

"That is where you are wrong." Odette kissed his cheek. "You've always been worth rescuing because no matter the choices, you'll always be a hero."

Author's Note: *A Hero Worth Saving* is the perfect mash-up of my two favorite genres: fantasy and regency. I have been a lifelong fan of Jane Austen and the regency era has always had a special place in my heart. It only took me a decade and publishing ten other books for me to realize that I could combine the two. Thus, I hope you enjoyed reading this story as much as I did writing it. If you enjoyed this book, please leave a review with your favorite retailer. Your reviews help decide which book I'll write next! Also, a special thank you to my publisher for making this an entirely enjoyable experience.

K.T. Munson is a life-long author. First published at 5 years old in the young writer's conference, she has pursued writing ever since. She was born and raised in the last frontier, the great state of Alaska. She maintains a blog creatingworldswithwords.wordpress.com that is about writing and her many fantasy, romance, and sci-fi novels.

www.ingramcontent.com/pod-product-compliance
Lightning Source LLC
Chambersburg PA
CBHW010345220726
48290CB00016B/2637